Wildlife, Wildflowers, and Wild Activities

EXPLORING SOUTHERN APPALACHIA

Written by Jennifer A. Bauer
Illustrations by Janet Brown
Additional Photography by Ken Murray and Jerry Nagel

The Overmountain Press
JOHNSON CITY, TENNESSEE

To my family, with love.

Ken Murray contributed the photographs on pages 12, 14, 18, 20, 23, 28, 48, 96, 106, 121, 123, 139, 153, 161, 168, 194.

Jerry Nagel contributed the photographs on pages 6, 46, 47, 137.

All other photographs by the author.

ISBN 1-57072-317-6

Printed in the United States of America

1 2 3 4 5 6 7 8 9 0

Contents

Acknowledgments

Living in the mountains, working with wonderful people, sharing the outdoors with a multitude of state-park visitors, and making lifelong friends are but a few of the things that have helped me experience and learn about the delicate balance of life on our planet. There are so many of you I wish to thank for all you have shared with me in our lives and excursions into the mountains, more than I could possibly list. You have encouraged me and supported me all along the way. Great memories, great friends—I bet you know who you are.

Love and thanks go to my family: Bob, Julia, Carrie, and Abigail. Their love, patience, and encouragement always kept me going, even on days when I stared blankly at a chapter and could not figure out how to approach it.

Thanks also to:

Janet Brown, quite an exceptional artist, a woman with a keen eye for detail and beauty. No matter how many words I could write, many would make little to no sense without her incredible illustrations.

Jerry Nagel and Ken Murray, both excellent photographers, with the ability to compose and see every aspect of creation through the lens of a camera. Thanks for sharing.

My first teachers in Tennessee State Parks. They opened the eyes of a young girl raised in the city. I've never been the same since.

My mentor and college teacher, John Warden, whom I will always remember for his deep love of the Southern Appalachian Mountains. His knowledge, combined with his desire to protect our environment, inspired me to walk the path I do today.

Preface

When growing up on the outskirts of a large eastern city, I did not realize that I had everything I needed in my urban environment to study and enjoy the outdoors. I was more tuned in to sidewalks, shopping centers, and an abundance of roads and highways. As a child, I found it comical watching neighbors mow their eight-foot-by-eight-foot plots of grass as they carefully pruned and fertilized a few shrubs around their homes. At the time, I did not know that those small precious areas of green all represented each person's need to have a bit of nature in his life.

Most people desire some form of interaction with the natural world; some prefer more, others less. Whatever your level of desire, and wherever you live, you will find it easy to learn about and discover the many miracles of our earth by using the activities presented in this book as a guide. My lack of understanding of the environment as a youth gives me some regret, though I am forever thankful I have managed to make up for lost time!

After leaving my early life in the city, I found my way to the Southern Appalachian Mountains. On a spring walk, I saw an overwhelming abundance of flowering plants, representing a myriad of colors and shapes. The sounds of birds, rustling leaves, and rushing water proved to be an incredible inspiration. It soon became a lifelong goal to learn as much as I could about the many forms of life that made the mountains their homes.

Yet I would often think back to those days in the city, now realizing many of these things had long existed in the background of my life, unfortunately going unnoticed. I began to recall friends and neighbors whose spirits thrived by feeding birds or watching the gray squirrels that loved the trees on our street, and how much fun I had looking for bugs in the dirt in my backyard.

Regardless of where we live, we all have a patch of dirt, a selection of plants, and wildlife within our reach. We can foster a desire in ourselves, our children, and our friends to learn more and enjoy discovering the world around us. Understanding our environment and what makes it work so well will greatly enhance our experiences with nature.

I hope this book will enlighten and inspire readers of every walk of life, living on all parts of our earth, and that they will find activities and ideas to help them, their friends, and their family delight in the discovery of the many facets of nature study. Though the book leans toward the outdoors in the Southern Appalachian Mountains, many of the activities can take place in many habitats and situations, even indoors.

Numerous books, periodicals, journals, and recordings can help you further your knowledge of what interests you. Field guides and audio recordings can help with identification of what you see and hear. In the following pages, you will find lists of additional reading to guide you to items of a particular interest. Several books not only identify an organism but also recount fascinating aspects of its behavior. The ability to identify an organism is just the beginning; nature study becomes particularly intriguing to many people when they begin to understand how an organism lives and fits into our world.

Of course, this book does not attempt to identify everything you might find in the Southern Appalachians. Therefore, I hope these words will act as a catalyst to further discovery, and spark a desire to learn more about life on planet Earth.

A Walk in the Woods

A walk in the woods in the Appalachian Mountains—at any elevation, day or night—yields a host of different environments and experiences, a delight for the lucky hiker. The communities of living things in the mountains form environments completely unique to their local habitats. Because of the abundant diversity of life they support and their fabled reputation, the Southern Appalachian Mountains attract nature lovers and naturalists of all types, who come to enjoy and study the rich beauty of these worn, ancient giants.

The Southern Appalachians hold treasures known to few places. For instance, these mountains experience the coming of spring and the emergence of the early wildflowers for over three weeks. And where else does the peak of the fall leaf color last for up to a month? These natural occurrences take place due to the changes in elevation and growing seasons throughout the mountains. The climate above the 5,500-foot elevation yields short growing seasons. Spring comes in late May and June, and the leaves on the trees start changing color in mid September to early October. Yet a 10- or 15-minute drive down the road to the 3,000-foot elevation takes you to an environment where the first signs of spring show in early April. The wildflower bloom takes place in late April and early May, and the fall color exhibits its finest about the third week in October.

No matter when you step outside in the Southern Appalachians, something different is always happening. Wildflowers peek out of the ground overnight; mushrooms emerge after a warm rain, then decay and vanish in less than a week; animal signs appear on creek banks and in the woods; and assorted birds come and go as they migrate in the fall and spring, some staying to nest, others for only a short time.

As you peer out the window on a snowy day, the solitude of the land can make you feel cold, even though the image is bright. Many things rest at this time, but life still continues. Observe closely, and you will notice the tracks of animals in the snow. Study the seedpods still hanging on the plants from the last season of growth. Look and listen for active birds and other wildlife.

With the leaves gone from the trees, winter becomes a fine time to view the shapes and curves of the high mountain ridges. Many contours obscured by vegetation during the growing season now stand out against the sky. A walk through the mountains in winter provides the opportunity to view sights hidden by the jungle-like forests of summertime.

To enjoy the mountains at any time of the year, find a trail that you like, geared to your physical comfort level. As time permits, return to this same spot and notice the changes since your previous visits. Focus not only on plant life; note as well the songs and the comings and goings of birds, look for signs of other animals and even of the positive and negative impacts of people. Animal tracks might trail beside the water, the creek may flow higher or lower, yellow flowers may cover a previously green plant, or a colorful mushroom may pop up in a formerly barren spot. Be ready for a special thrill if you walk up on an animal and startle it from its resting place. Nothing makes the heart jump more than the surprise of a few deer suddenly bounding through the woods, or the swoosh of an owl flushed from its daytime perch.

What you might expect to see in the mountains depends on the time of year you explore the forest. Every plant and animal has its own cycles and needs, depending on the season. Thus, describing the "typical" walk in the woods presents some difficulty; nothing about the forest is typical or predictable. When you head to the mountains, you should always anticipate experiencing a complex environment in action. You might imagine stepping into a movie at any point in time and becoming a part of that scene, only to step out later and return to the obligations of your world. Until you return again, that environment with all of its players will continue moving forward, providing you with changes and intrigue upon your return.

Of the hundreds of walks and hikes I have led throughout my career as a park naturalist, one of them during my second year of working left with me an inspiring memory. I had scheduled a guided hike across the tops of the highland balds of Roan Mountain on a beautiful morning in June. As the 10:00 A.M. meeting time approached, I wandered down to the designated gathering spot, hoping for a group of folks wanting to head out on a new adventure. I was pleased to find approximately 15 people waiting eagerly for me to arrive.

Across the highland balds of Roan Mountain

As we discussed what lay ahead, I spoke about the wonders of the Roan, emphasizing its uniqueness and beauty. I made inspiration my first priority whenever I led a tour. If a group or an individual did not feel renewed or inspired after visiting Roan Mountain, I would feel I should have done more, for the Roan and the Southern Appalachians surrounding it are miraculous, diverse, and inspirational mountains.

After some introductory comments, we collected our belongings and drove up to Carvers Gap, at the Tennessee/North Carolina state line. At the parking lot, everyone scurried out of their vehicles, packing their backpacks and donning their gear. I immediately noticed that most of the folks planned to carry a lot of stuff straight up the side of a steep mountain. No one possessed fewer than three field guides, and one fellow had a pack full of books! Others carried large cameras and binoculars around their necks simultaneously.

I had never encountered a group with a personality like the one that day. They moved along quietly, and rarely did anyone even smile or grin. I became a little disconcerted; nothing I said or shared seemed to change the solemn mood of our trip. We would stop along the way and talk about some of the amazing attributes of the Roan, yet I always received the same, seemingly uninterested, non-communicative expressions.

Finally, the day reached a point where I felt ready to panic, or maybe just cry. I had put every ounce of energy I had into my presentation, only hoping my charges would feel and experience the mountain in a positive way, at least a little bit. I thought, *Oh, Jennifer, you have failed miserably,* a sentiment I truly felt with all my heart.

Before long, we reached the top of our climb. A gentle breeze caused the thick grass of the balds to wave openly to the sky above. The warmth of the sun made me want to drop into the grass, which felt as soft as a featherbed. There we stood, each person looking at the view without expression, saying nothing.

Then something totally unexpected happened. A gentleman in the group suddenly began removing all of the trappings that loaded him down. Off came the camera, binoculars, backpack, and water bottle. He stood for a moment, not speaking a word, then he turned to me and said, "If it's the last thing I do, I'm going to roll down this mountain!" And off he went, rolling through the lush, soft grass of Round Bald, laughing with the spirit of a child.

For a brief moment, I stood completely dumbfounded, watching and laughing with him as he rolled away. The remainder of the group gazed in amazement, still expressionless. One person said, "Look at him, a grown man! I can't believe it!" Everyone else nodded their heads in disbelief; yet on closer inspection, I could see a few subtle smiles on their faces.

Instinct took over, and I also hit the ground, rolling down the side of the mountain and catching up rather quickly. His actions so moved me, I didn't notice at first that one by one, each person dropped to the ground and began rolling down the mountain in the thick grass. Laughter and happiness unlike anything I had ever experienced filled the side of Round Bald.

I learned a great lesson then, one that has stayed with me and has served as a profound inspiration during those times when I've felt a little low. I have traveled extensively through our beautiful nation and overseas but feel the Roan possesses the most profound natural beauty of all.

The Southern Appalachians hold the spirit of the earth, a spirit that can give us strength and renew us at all times. Here, a walk in the woods holds the most meaning and opportunity for personal growth, a place where you can experience nature in its finest.

Creating Journals and Recording Memories

Not everyone likes to write. The mere mention or suggestion of the idea sends chills down many a spine. Yet despite it all, I would like to suggest a few ways to record, write, etch or draw, and preserve your memories and feelings. Practicing writing techniques can only result in making you a better and more self-assured writer.

Once you work your way past the fear, you will discover that writing can become personally fulfilling. Unless you plan to publish your work, you don't need to write carefully. Just consider your activities and journal entries as words and illustrations recorded for you and you alone. Above all, the process of writing and journaling will keep you in touch with your innermost self. It gives you a way to relieve stress while allowing you to focus and reflect on the world around you.

As you engage in the activities here, your journal will prove extremely helpful. You can use it to record what you perceive before, during, and after a particular activity, in addition to first-time discoveries. When you return to your journal later, your words will bring positive experiences back to life. Your records will also act as a source of inspiration at times when you need an extra pick-me-up.

Keeping a journal can be a valid and rewarding pastime. When you find things in the mountains that you cannot identify, when the first frogs call in the spring, or when the first warbler sings in the forest, always take a moment to record the event. Over the years you will find it fascinating to go back and reflect on your

The wood frog, an early winter/late spring caller

findings. As time passes, your data may also become valuable if natural populations and events change.

For instance, in late winter in the mountains, the wood frog always calls and breeds before the end of February. Year after year, the frogs go to reliable temporary pools of water found throughout the area. Yet during the winter of 2000, these much needed breeding areas remained dry, with little rain falling to replenish them. As a result, by March 6, only one egg mass could be found as the temporary pools all stayed bone dry. A record of this type of information can give biologists good data to help them evaluate the state of our natural populations. If, in the future, the wood frog no longer inhabits this area, it might be possible to track its decline and hopefully understand what factors have affected it.

You can begin a journal in a number of ways. A composition-style, spiral-bound notebook is easy to carry and pull out at a moment's notice when something exciting and unexpected jumps into your life. Or you could carry a sketchpad and draw your findings, adding words to further elaborate. Keep a pencil handy, rather than a pen, because if your paper becomes damp, ink just will not cooperate. Colored pencils can add a little extra touch to your entries.

If you wish to encourage a young child who has not yet mastered the written word, a sketching journal can provide the inspiration needed to get started. Children love to draw, and you will want to nurture their uninhibited ability to express themselves in this fashion. Also, young people keenly observe everything around them. After twenty years of leading children through the woods as a park naturalist, I am still amazed by the enormity of what they observe. They will easily notice mushrooms the size of a pinhead, or the remains of animal tracks that have been nearly washed or trampled away. We all can draw energy from a child's thrill of discovery. Their contagious enthusiasm may inspire us to look a little harder and enjoy our experiences even more.

To study life up close, try sketching something unusual or intriguing, which will provide an opportunity to look for the details that make this thing unique. You don't have to be an artist to keep a journal of drawings. Your journal is your personal record and something you do not have to publicly display, so feel free to relax and enjoy expressing yourself.

What you write or draw in your journal is totally up to you, but I might offer a few suggestions to help you get started. If you find yourself on a hike or engaging in an activity in this book, or if something unexpected happens to you, take a moment to record your thoughts and feelings. After the hike, you might write, "Walked the trail to the top of the mountain today. There was an enormous amount of bird song and evidence of many deer as seen by their tracks. Clouded up, the air was cool but pleasant. The biggest surprise was the beautiful hawk that soared above me for at least 10 minutes." You could also add a sketch of the hawk or an etching of any memorable part of your day.

ACTIVITY Guided Writing

Writing in verse is a popular way to record observations, feelings, and experiences. If you have never tried it before, you may find that writing poetry comes to you naturally. Guided writing helps to show how to focus and use colorful adjectives to describe something to another person. Your goal is to create an image for your readers, a visualization to aid them in becoming a part of your experience.

I have enjoyed using the following example of guided writing with groups of all ages. Though not complicated, it produces vivid works in words.

Line Number	How Many Words	What to Write
1	1 to 2 words	What are you writing about?
2	3 words	Where is it?
3	4 to 5 words	What is it doing?
4	3 words	What are you doing?
5	1 to 2 words	How does it make you feel?

Students visiting outdoor recreation areas on field trips have written some of my favorites poems. The following examples will give you an idea of what your imagination can do:

#1 Storm clouds
Cresting the mountaintop
Floating quietly through the sky
Watching from below
Exploding within

#2 Peepers
By the pond
Singing to the sky
Sitting, listening, watching
Free

Recording and keeping a journal is a personal and individual activity. Use the ideas in this book to help you, but always remember that your interests and inspirations fuel the creative process. Experiment with methods of writing that work for you, and keep in mind that you write to preserve your own special memories and events.

ACTIVITY Observation Skills

Enormous amounts of information bombard our senses. In order to focus on what presently seems meaningful to us, we often filter out apparently less important details.

This activity will help you hone your observation skills. By closely watching a given object, you can tune yourself in to things you may not normally notice. The purpose is to completely discover all you can about one "thing"; therefore, what you choose is totally up to you. You might pick something seen daily or something a little more unique.

Remember not to destroy any living thing as you search for appropriate items. Suggestions for nature discovery include fallen leaves, pinecones, rocks, bark found on the ground, or small sections of blown-down limbs or sticks. Gather enough objects for the number of people participating in the exercise. You will find an ample supply of fallen items in the forest and field that will work well. Avoid anything potentially poisonous or dangerous in any way! If you are not sure, just leave it alone.

Bring everything you have gathered to your group, whether in an outdoor or indoor setting. Either hand out or let each person pick an item. When everyone has something, have them closely study their object for five minutes. Pass out magnifiers or hand lenses if you have them. Encourage folks to look at every little detail, imagine what it might do, where it might live, and what its life might be like. Check out the colors and subtle changes in shades, shapes, corners, and textures. Notice any odor or any unusual characteristics.

After five minutes of observation, spend ten minutes writing about the object. Use descriptive words that would help a reader visualize what the writer sees and feels. Try to avoid saying the same thing over and over again using different words. When you go back and read what you have written, make sure you have described the object just as you saw it.

The ten-minute time limit will aid in learning to get to the point while writing and will help you focus on the important aspects of the subject. If you still haven't gotten to the good part after ten minutes of writing, you may need to concentrate more on individual peculiarities instead of a general description. Go back and look at your words; try to remove the unnecessary ones and clarify any confusing passages.

All writers, new and old, can benefit from sharing their work and hearing what others have written. If you do this exercise alone, read your entries to a family member or a friend. If working with a group, participants can read their entries to each other. If some feel uncomfortable and would prefer not to read, encourage them, though not forcefully. The personal satisfaction gained by sharing their thoughts and ideas makes the effort worthwhile.

ACTIVITY Hike and Write

Find an outdoor area where you would enjoy casually walking and exploring. Plan ample time—you don't want to rush or watch the clock. Try to take care of any chores or obligations so they don't inhibit you from fully immersing yourself in the outdoor experience. Disregard all other concerns and remind yourself that this personal time belongs to you alone.

If you have trouble tuning in to the world around you, try one of the sense-awakening activities outlined in the next chapter. Sit, listen, and absorb the sounds and smells of life. Many find it difficult to slow down their thoughts enough to develop an awareness of the inner workings of the environment. Consciously make this slowed-down state of awareness your goal, and you will feel even more fulfilled after your walk.

As you hike, with journal and pencil in hand, stop and record everything

This filmy angelica hosts a number of visiting insects

that strikes you: new sounds, odors, or visual experiences. Pause and look around. Notice the tiny details of plants and insects. Observe one particular living thing and discover what it does or where it goes.

One day while working in the garden, I saw a fly land on a large stump beside me. A veritable maze of insect borings, the stump held an entire world unto itself, a community of activity. To my wonderment, the tiny fly carried a piece of a leaf at least three times larger than itself. In a split second it landed and scurried into a hole in the stump, dragging the leaf right in with it, folding it like a canoe in order to pass through the opening. As I have just told you about my experience with the fly, you can write about similar experiences in your journal.

If you do decide to start a journal, keep in mind that it doesn't have to be a chore. You don't have to write every time you go for a walk in the woods, though each time you go, you may find something memorable. But you don't want to burden yourself with the process, so make sure to keep the journal for fun, as a way to record feelings and experiences you will enjoy reading about later.

ACTIVITY Creating a Story

To begin writing a story, choose a subject that inspires you. A newly blooming wildflower, the coming of a winter snow, the grandeur of a towering oak, or something as small as a spider may impress you. Try to pick something relatively specific so your subject isn't too broad to handle. If you get something started you just can't finish, you might get frustrated and never complete your work.

For this activity, you will write a somewhat reflective story and look through time at the subject matter—its past, present, and future. As you begin composing, consider the entire history of the topic you have chosen. If you need to organize your ideas, create an outline, which will help you stay on track and avoid jumping in and out of unrelated thoughts.

Begin by describing your subject's past: what it looked like, what it did, where it was, and what type of existence it had before you discovered it. Next consider the present: what you see now, why it exists, its purpose, and why it is special to you. Finally, project the future of your subject. What do you think will ultimately happen to it? Will it return again, or pass on, leaving its offspring to continue its existence?

Depending on the subject, your story can relate many fascinating ideas and thoughts. Don't limit yourself to the suggestions above; use them as a guide, but elaborate wherever your thoughts take you.

This time spent writing will provide you with the opportunity to open up your mind to the incredible changes that occur within just one organism in our environment over the course of time.

Further Reading

The Best Nature Writing of Joseph Wood Krutch by Joseph Wood Krutch
The Heart of Burroughs' Journals, edited by Clara Barrus
A Sand County Almanac by Aldo Leopold
Thoreau by Joseph Wood Krutch
Walden's Pond by Henry David Thoreau
The Wilderness World of John Muir, edited by Edwin Way Teale
The Yosemite by John Muir

Reawaken Your Senses

Standing quietly, deep within a mountain forest, can lead to eye-opening experiences. Beyond the silence of the moment, an overwhelming amount of life will emerge as you listen and observe things around you. Plants, animals, insects, fungi, and other creatures all make this habitat their home, and they interact in intricate ways. Awareness of so many happenings sometimes necessitates a specially trained ear and heart.

In a world where many unpleasant sounds, smells, and sensory experiences surround us, we often turn off our senses to block out unwanted stimuli. Traffic sounds, car exhaust, noises associated with congested areas, and mechanical sounds, just to name a few, typically are not considered pleasing. We all have our own list of sensory stimuli—within our homes, at work, at the store, or outside—that we would live happier without. Stop and consider for a moment the sounds and odors you encounter and tune out on a regular basis, possibly because you find them unpleasant. If you did not block them out, these negative inputs would probably leave you on edge.

Sometimes I recall some of the sensory experiences I dealt with in my youth. As they come back to life in my memory, I often wonder how I put up with those constant unpleasant sounds, odors, and the feelings they produced. For example, when I was about twelve years old, city planners chose the road I lived on—the widest one available—for the community transit bus route. Prior to that time, I had not appreciated the peacefulness of life without those gigantic vehicles. During the day, a bus would pass our house every twenty minutes; at night, every hour. Every time one came up the road, I would hear its loud, roaring motor and, if outdoors, smell the strong exhaust. Our house would shake from top to bottom, and after the bus passed, all the pictures on the wall had shifted. Eventually, I stopped hearing them, smelling them, or even noticing the vibrations of the house.

Unfortunately, when blocking out the unpleasant, we often begin to miss the pleasing aspects of life. The positive stimuli to our senses are also blocked out, often unknowingly, through the conditioning of our everyday surroundings. The subtle effect on our perceptual abilities frequently goes unnoticed. Even when we enter the realm of the great outdoors, we sometimes miss its special ways or messages. In returning to our mother earth, we need to slow down, relax, and take the time to reawaken our senses to the softness and beauty of our natural world.

Some of the activities that follow are designed to stimulate senses dulled by the harshness of everyday life. The first two focus on touch, and the third on sight. The chapter culminates by bringing all of our senses back into play. Use common sense at all times, ensuring that you do not use any poisonous plants or other potentially harmful natural objects, and make safety your first consideration.

These activities, designed to aid children and adults in awakening their senses, will help you to slow down, observe, appreciate, and once again relish the subtle parts of life. By learning to use all of your senses and enhance your awareness through nature study, you can become a better learner, listener, and observer in all of your life experiences.

ACTIVITY One Special Leaf

Which Sense	*Touch*
Ideal Location	*a. Have your group find a quiet, soft spot in the forest* *b. Leaves can be collected and brought indoors*
Preparation	*Select a variety of leaves from trees and shrubs. Have one leaf for each person participating.*

This activity works best with three to fifteen people plus one person who acts as a leader. The higher the number of participants, the more challenging the activity.

Gather everyone together and sit in a comfortable position, preferably in a circle. If you are in the woods, clear a space in the center so the leaves you have picked up won't mix with the rest of the forest floor. Always remember, though, to return the woods to their natural condition before you depart.

Ask everyone to close their eyes—you can use the honor system, or blindfolds if you wish—and then give each person in the circle one leaf. While they have their eyes closed, encourage them to trace every vein, outlining the edges with their fingers. Have them use their sense of touch to become so acquainted with their leaf that when all the leaves are taken back and mixed up in the center of the circle, they will be able to find their "special leaf" amidst the leaves in the pile.

Don't worry about keeping a record of who has which leaf. If everyone *feels* as though they have found the correct leaf, then the activity was a success. The important aspect of this activity is that everyone has taken the time to notice and touch something they had previously passed by without a second thought.

ACTIVITY Out of Sight!

Which Sense	*Touch*
Ideal Location	*Anywhere!*
Preparation	*Collect nonliving objects from the forest floor, from fields, or any outdoor setting. Place each object in its own brown paper bag and fold down the top.*

Mystery shrouds this exciting activity; the anticipation will mount as everyone wonders what hidden object they must touch! Two or more people can participate, with one person preparing and presenting the activity.

First, collect nonliving things with various textures and shapes from the forest floor. Do not use anything that might be poisonous or could injure someone. A pinecone, a small rock, a leaf, a stick, a piece of bark, or even a piece of crumpled up paper (a good catalyst for a discussion on pollution and littering) are a few good examples. You can find all kinds of interesting things lying on the forest floor or in open areas. Place each object in separate paper lunch bags and fold down the tops.

This activity will guide you in using your sense of touch to become better acquainted with the world around you. Each person will take a turn reaching into a bag, feeling the object, and then describing it. After the initial description, the rest of the group tries to guess what the object is.

In this game, it will be more important to accurately *describe* what is being felt, so that everyone else can identify it without seeing or touching it. Young people will be tempted to reach in and say, "That's a pinecone!" They get so thrilled that they have correctly identified the object, they temporarily forget that they are not to name it, so be sure your group understands the directions before you begin.

Before beginning the activity with younger players, share descriptive words they might use. It is easy to get stuck and use the same words—such as *rough, sharp, smooth,* and *hairy*—over and over again. Don't be surprised if someone feels a rock and says, "It feels like a rock." If the group needs help, encourage them to imagine describing the object to someone who cannot see. If a person had never seen an oak leaf, it would mean nothing to him to hear, "It's an oak leaf." Only a vivid description would work to relate the nature of the object. Therefore, all the advance explanation you can offer will move the activity along much easier.

So why does such a simple activity sound so complicated? Mainly because we depend so much on our sense of sight that we automatically convert what we touch into a visual image, relaying it to our peers by name. It takes a little practice, but once you get the hang of it, you'll find yourself noticing the many fine and intricate details of our natural world.

ACTIVITY Recall

Which Sense	*Sight (with emphasis on noticing the details of nature and sharpening your abilities to observe)*
Ideal Location	*Good for a little indoor mind exercise*

Preparation	*Take a large piece of paper or poster board and draw a cartoonish picture of a woodland, river, or open field scene. Make it as fun and silly as you like, and include details that are not too complex to remember. For example, you can draw a tree, an owl on a limb, three eyes on the owl, a swing from a branch with a spider wearing tennis shoes, two or three rain clouds, six drops of water coming from the cloud, and so on.*

Recall requires two or more people, with one person preparing and presenting the activity. The presenter starts with a drawing as suggested above and then composes ten to twenty questions relating to the picture. Using our example drawing, you might ask:

How many raindrops are coming out of the clouds?
What is on the spider's feet?
How many legs does the spider have?
What is sitting in the tree?
How many eyes does the owl have?

Let your imagination run wild as you draw the picture. Preparing it is half the fun!

Gather the group and tell them they are about to test their observation skills. Explain to them that you are going to let them look at a picture for one minute, then you will remove it and ask them to answer some questions. Emphasize that they need to look closely at all of the details of the drawing.

Often, as you ask the questions, you will see lots of puzzled looks. They might have noticed the rain but hadn't considered counting the drops. When you ask how many eyes the owl had, many will answer *two*, as we often assume things without really looking.

You could have a second, different sketch prepared to give

everyone another opportunity to observe a little more deeply. Almost every time I have presented this activity, the second attempt produces much better results. Those involved suddenly realize that they do not always look closely at things nor observe all that there is to see. For many, this activity can be an eye-opener.

When you have finished presenting Recall, discuss the meaning of the activity and its importance to each individual. Give the participants the first opportunity to comment on what they noticed about their observation skills. Points to mention might include:

> Did you do better on the first or second drawing? Why?
> Do we take things for granted to the extent of not really seeing them?
> In observing life around us, do you feel that you see all there is to see?
> Do you feel you might miss intriguing things when on an outdoor trek?

If the opportunity arises after completing this activity, head to an outdoor setting and take a walk in the woods, through a park, or even a meadow. Give everyone a small pad of paper and a pencil, and encourage them to record everything they notice. After your walk, sit down as a group one last time and have everyone share their observations. Participants will notice that this activity has helped them sharpen their skills as they more fully observe the world around them.

ACTIVITY A Sniff-and-Feel Hike

Which Sense	*Smell, Touch*
Ideal Location	*Outdoors*
Preparation	*Find a good location*

In our daily lives we often rush about, making deadlines or needing to get somewhere at the correct time. With such demanding schedules, we do not always have the time to absorb everything around us. A Sniff-and-Feel Hike will help you find new ways to experience the odors and textures of the outdoors and the woods. Slowing down to a crawl, participants will investigate every little life-form growing beneath their feet or towering above their heads. This activity works well for one or for many.

The title tells you what you will do on the walk: smell and touch. Use caution, however, so you don't touch poisonous plants or stick your nose into a hornet's nest! A hand lens will help you see the minute details of the world around you. Take the time to gently feel the small hairs on a leaf or sniff the luscious odor of the bark of a wild cherry. Get down on your hands and knees and feel the soft texture of the soil; smell its rich, earthy tones.

As you discover all these details, take time to reflect on how the new odors and feelings affect you. If you present the activity to a group, ask the participants if they have found an odor or a texture they had not previously encountered. Though we see leaves fluttering on trees every day, we might not have realized that a forest of soft, tiny hairs covers some of them. Be sure to notice the odd and distinct odors that come from particular plants growing on the forest floor.

Don't let these skills fade away; rather, use your new abilities on a daily basis. Pay close attention to nature's odors and textures, and they will enhance your daily experiences as a part of life's creation.

ACTIVITY Trust Hikes

Which Sense	*Smell, Touch, and Hearing*
Ideal Location	*Outdoors (a combination of field and forest works nicely)*
Preparation	*Blindfolds*

By turning off your sense of sight, you may find it easier to open up your remaining senses and experience the wonders of our world, magnified to an exceptional degree. This activity requires at least two people, though it works just as well for groups.

First, organize participants in pairs. For each twosome, one person will close his eyes or put on a blindfold, and the second person will lead the blind one. The blindfolded person will have the opportunity to heighten his senses other than sight. The leaders must ensure the safety of their partners as they make new discoveries.

As a leader, you can have your partner touch the bark of a tree from the ground up, feel the coolness of the water and the texture of the bottom silt in a creek, smell the blooming of a rose, or listen to the sounds of a coming storm. Many of the things you will notice while blindfolded will seem extraordinarily vivid, as you find yourself tuning in to previously unnoticed aspects of the life around you.

Remember, sighted partners must protect their charges. They need to tell them where to stop, duck, and step, protecting them from hazards. Leaders should keep their eyes open for poisonous plants or anything that might inflict pain or injury. If you don't know what something is or if it is safe, stay away from it. In addition, this is a perfect way to teach young people the importance of the ability to depend on others; after all, this is a trust hike!

After one partner has had a turn behind the blindfold, change positions so everyone can experience opening up their senses to the world. Have the members of the group discuss how they felt when they led their partners, and how they felt when they wore the blindfold. You may ask which they liked better, and why. Did they trust their partners? Did they feel safe?

ACTIVITY Fly with the Wind

Which Sense	*All*
Ideal Location	*Indoors or out*
Preparation	*A copy of "A Windstorm in the Forest" by John Muir, written 1894, and recordings of nature sounds (preferably wind and rain)*

In December 1874, along a tributary of the Yuba River, John Muir rode the tops of the highest trees of the Sierra Nevada, recording his experiences in "A Windstorm in the Forest." This passage appears in various publications, including *The Mountains of California* by John Muir, first published in 1894.

Though designed for a group, this activity invites individual exploration as well. You will not climb to the tops of trees to sway in the strong winds of a storm, but you will attempt to re-create that experience in a safer mode.

As the group leader, you should try to find a recording of sounds from nature. Many retail establishments, including department stores and bookstores, carry CDs and tapes of nature sounds, sometimes easily found on racks attributed to that subject only. Ideally, you want a recording with the sounds of wind and rain in the forest.

First, you will read "A Windstorm in the Forest" to the group, while you play the nature sounds in the background to help re-create the described scene. Muir's story tells of a time when he climbed to the top of a tree to fully experience the sounds, feelings, smells, and sensations of a strong storm in the Sierra Nevada. His perspective shows an entirely new way to experience what we often consider the more violent and frightening parts of the natural world.

You might also like to share a few thoughts about John Muir, his historical importance in the development of our country, and his conservation ethic. Called "The Father of our National Park System" among other honorable titles, Muir inspired President Theodore Roosevelt's many conservation programs, in addition to the creation of Yosemite National Park. Muir ventured throughout the wilderness, writing about his experiences for all to enjoy and appreciate. With others, he formed the Sierra Club in 1892 to "make the mountains glad." Many books, articles, and Web sites discuss his writing and his personal life, and can help you to relate as much information as you would like to enhance this activity.

After introducing Muir and reading his story, break up into smaller groups and begin brainstorming ideas on how to dramatize the events of "A Windstorm in the Forest." To get everyone in the proper mood, ask them to sit quietly and visualize as you play the sounds of rain and wind in the forest. Take the time to help participants get into the moment, to feel as though woods surround them as a storm batters the land.

Everyone will now decide what characters they will need and who will portray them to act out a similar situation. Some may become trees, plants, wildlife, the wind itself, rain, thunder, and whatever else they might consider important in their re-creation. Emphasize the need for the actors to immerse themselves in the experience and try to become one with what they portray.

When they have had time to design their re-enactment, each group will stage their drama, set to the sounds of nature. The different perspectives presented will enlighten all the participants as they share the drama of the natural world.

"In every walk with nature, one receives far more than he seeks."
John Muir
(1838-1914)

Further Reading

A selection of the many books by John Muir:

My First Summer in the Sierra
The Mountains of California (which includes "A Windstorm in the Forest")
Our National Parks
A Thousand-Mile Walk to the Gulf
Travels in Alaska
The Wilderness World of John Muir
The Yosemite

Additional reading:

The Life and Letters of John Muir by William Frederic Bade
A Sense of Wonder by Rachel Carson
www.sierraclub.org

Looking for the Little Things

Gazing across a landscape, you can see many shades of color, character, and texture. Stepping through the woods, you can find many small yet significant things beneath your feet. But you might overlook them because of their minute size, even though they are just as special and colorful as their larger counterparts. Viewed as a whole, all of those little things paint the picture we see—a blending and gathering of life's creations.

DECAYING LOGS—SUBTLE COMMUNITIES

A fallen tree or log provides an excellent opportunity to see many of the smaller parts of nature's realm. No decaying log is the same as another, so prepare for an exciting adventure. Take along your sketchbook to record your findings while exploring the details seen in these communities that thrive from the process of decay, places as significant in their own right as our individual towns and cities.

When you get into the woods, look along the ground until you locate a fallen tree or large branch. What grows on the surface of the log? If you look closely, you might discover patches of flat, blue-green plants spreading across the exterior. Some may have protrusions growing out of them, but they will all take on a characteristic blue-green color. Known as *lichen*, this unusual flora is composed of not one, but two types of plants—one a fungus, the other an alga. In order for a lichen to thrive, it needs clean, unpolluted air. With this requirement fulfilled, they will grow in abundance.

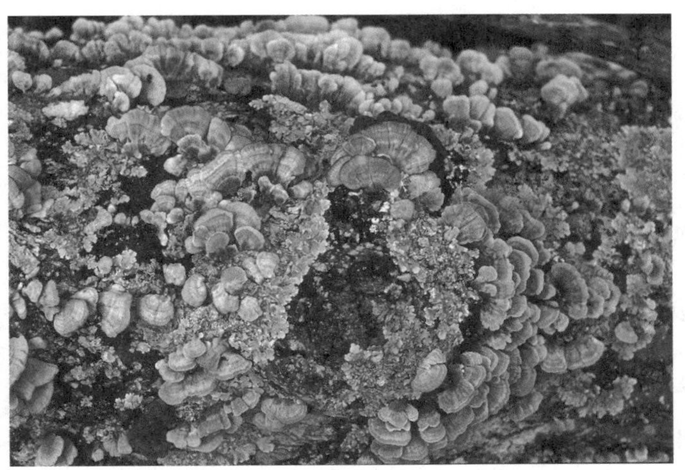

Mushrooms of all colors, shapes, and sizes might also be found growing on the log. Mosses, growing long and compact, may spread in a sea of deep green across the surface, accompanied by seedlings of trees, shrubs, and herbs that have found the log a perfect habitat to germinate and begin their new life.

An amazing number of insect species can live within the log. A field guide to insects would help you identify what you see, but your sketchbook will save you the burden of carrying a library out into the field. When you return from your trek, look at the sketches you made of the life on the log. If you want to learn more about what you found, refer to a guide or two to focus on the special characteristics of your discoveries.

The next time you step over a fallen log, remember that it represents more than just a chunk of wood lying on the ground; the life it hosts makes up a special part of the forest. In the constant cycle of life, nature gives back to the earth all the energy gathered during the lifetime of the log.

ACTIVITY Create an Environment

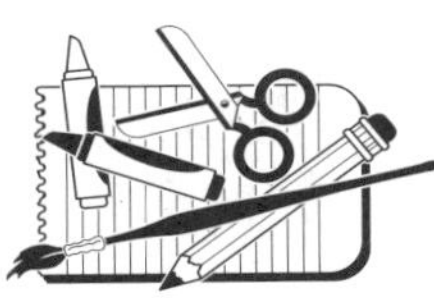

- *Inner cardboard roll from wrapping paper or paper towels—the wider the diameter of the roll, the better. If you have a carpet shop nearby, the discarded inner core of a carpet roll works well. Most carpet shops will cut off sections for you if they are finished with it. Though sturdy, they will require something stronger than a pair of scissors if you decide to cut holes in your "log."*
- *Box large enough to use as a shadow box. The "log" should fit in this box when it is turned on its side, with room to spare around the edges.*
- *Poster or acrylic paint and brushes*

- *Poster board in natural colors*
- *Pipe cleaners*
- *Low-fire, nontoxic clay that can be safely baked in your home oven*
- *White sewing thread*
- *Felt—shades of green*
- *Craft glue (which will hold clay, paper, pipe cleaners)*
- *Patterns for insects, plants, backdrops, etc. (see page 25)*
- *Field guide to insects (several available for all ages)*

Before beginning, explore the outdoors and observe decaying logs and trees in their natural habitat. Carry along your journal, and carefully record observations of what you see. Your research will help you decide how you would like to populate your log.

Ample traceable drawings to prepare your entire habitat are provided on the next page. Use a copy machine to enlarge or reduce the images to match the size of your project. To further enhance your living log, you can discover additional ideas online, in books, and from your observations and journals.

Step 1: Preparing the log and the shadow box

Your cardboard roll can be used in one continuous piece, or you can make it even more interesting by cutting holes or cutting one side from end to end, so you may open the log and look inside. After all, many log dwellers work beneath the bark.

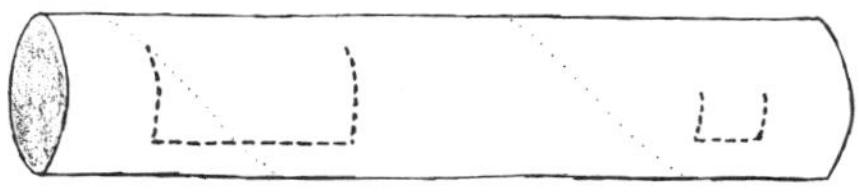

Using poster or acrylic paint, take a wide brush and paint the entire log brown. You can make it look realistic by using different shades of brown to almost black. After it dries, you can add dark brown or black lines to give the log depth.

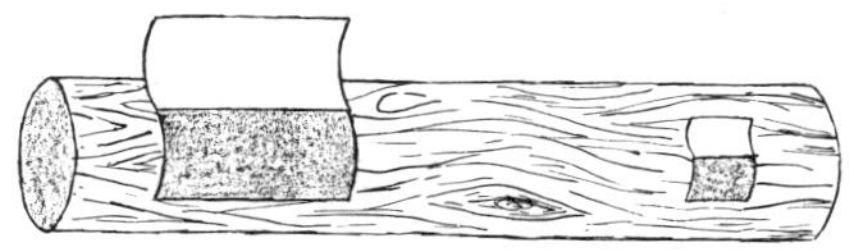

The log will be glued into the shadow box when completed, so paint the shadow box beforehand. Place the long edges of the box parallel to the floor. Use

natural paint shades to add color to the exterior (outside of box). Inside the box, paint the ground area (long edge) green and brown. The backdrop (box bottom) should be white to off-white until you complete Step 2. Then you can decide if you want to paint a detailed scene or use poster board forms for a 3-D effect.

Step 2: Making the inhabitants of the log

While your paint job dries, start making the insects, fungi, mosses, homes, and larvae that might live within your log. Following are some ideas on how to get started.

Use Fimo or another low-fire clay to shape mushrooms, insects, oblong insect larvae, and more. Use illustrations on the previous page for ideas, and then check out some of the great books available on insects, mushrooms, plants, and all the creatures in our natural world for more ideas. Fimo clay is fun to work with, because you can bake it after you have made your models. Each pack of clay, which is available in most craft stores, includes the instructions for baking the finished pieces.

Use pipe cleaners to create dragonflies, butterflies, long worms, insect bodies and legs, and absolutely anything you can imagine, by twisting and shaping the pipe cleaner. Your pipe-cleaner critters can easily be shaped and reshaped until you get them the way you want them. Green ferns and small plants growing on and around the log can also be easily formed using pipe cleaners. Their ability to bend will make it easier for you to attach them under, on, and around your log.

Cut natural shapes, such as trees, ferns, and clouds, out of the poster board to decorate the back wall of the shadow box. To get a 3-D effect, cut three to six successively smaller, but matching, shapes. Glue down the largest first, the second largest centered on top of it, and so on, until the smallest is on top. You will create a form that seems to grow out of your scene. If you prefer, you can cut your fern leaves out of poster board, rather than using the pipe cleaners, or you can do both.

Use the green felt to cut out small patches of moss to glue on the log, or use the 3-D approach with your felt to make your moss stand up higher and add texture to the finished piece. If you have cut your log so you can peek inside, remember that moss grows primarily on the outside, where the sunlight can reach it. Moss will not thrive inside the darkness of the log.

Use your thread to make small spider webs inside and on the log. Short pieces of thread can be cut and glued into the log when you get to Step 3. By crossing your threads, you can make a realistic web. You might even add a small fly that has been caught for a spider's dinner. Don't forget the spider, too.

Step 3: Putting it all together

Now you need to finish the backdrop of your box. If you are going to paint in trees, bushes, clouds, sun, flowers, or critters, you will need to do it before gluing the log in place. In addition, the 3-D shapes you've created need to be glued in. Once the log is in the shadow box, you will have difficulty working around it to reach the background.

Before gluing in the log, take some time to arrange and rearrange all of the parts. Do you have a hole in the log? Decide which insect might be crawling out of the hole. Does your log open on one side? If so, what is going to live inside, and what will live outside?

If you plan to add one or more spider webs, consider their placement now. You can add dimension to the log by attaching your threads on a curve, causing them to droop a little and stand out from the log.

Think about the plants and decide their placement. Should you attach the ferns near the bottom in the back and fold them up around the side of the log? Or would you prefer them all over the bottom of the shadow box? Decide where to place your moss and if you'd like to have a small insect crawling on it. With so many ways to put your habitat together, you may wind up changing it many times before finding satisfaction with the final result.

When you have an arrangement you like, take your craft glue and attach everything that goes inside the log. Next, glue anything that needs to fasten to the back of the log. While these parts dry, make sure everything is attached to the background before proceeding. After everything dries, glue the log in place in the shadow box. Add additional critters around and on the log to fill out the scene.

Save the spider webs until last, as their delicateness makes them harder to place. The end of each little thread will need a small dab of glue to hold it down. As you add each thread, work on crisscrossing your pattern to give a more realistic effect.

With everything in place, you will have created a beautiful replica of one of nature's most active and intriguing environments.

Mushroom Madness

If you're looking for an adventure in color and shape, you'll like studying mushrooms. I have yet to find a group of organisms as intriguing and full of surprises as the fungi. They come and go with the seasons and the rains, ensuring continued change on favorite trails.

Fungi come in a myriad of shapes, ranging from the commonly illustrated

brown mushroom, to those resembling the coral found in the oceans. Fungi wear colors ranging wide like their shapes—some have shades of camouflaging browns, while some are as bright red as a flashing stoplight.

Fungi hold highly important roles in our environment, acting primarily as decomposers, because they lack chlorophyll. Some parasitic fungi will kill living plants and animals, while others form mutually beneficial relationships between the fungus and the plant.

The body of the fungus mostly lives and spreads beneath the surface of the ground. When you look at an emerging mushroom, you do not see the entire plant, but merely its fruit. Gathering a mushroom is much like picking an apple off a tree. When you remove the apple, you have not injured the tree in any way.

The fruit of the fungus waits below the ground for the right conditions to arrive. Its tiny, compacted cells form a bud, which will swell and grow when the proper amount of moisture arrives. The cells fill with water, and the mushroom breaks through the ground into view.

Generally, picking and gathering mushrooms is not recommended. Observing their beauty and uniqueness of form in their habitat and leaving them for others to enjoy can prove just as satisfying. Those who collect mushrooms usually do so for the purpose of eating them; however, a great majority of mushrooms in the natural environment contain toxins of one form or the other. Some are deadly, while others can make you very, very ill. Eating wild mushrooms should be left to the experts.

A typical mushroom consists of the cap, gills, stipe (or stalk), and in some species, the annulus, which looks much like a fibrous veil around the edge of the cap. The annulus begins as a ring around the stalk, which tears away as the mushroom grows. Remnants of the veil may surround the stem or hang on the stalk. Aesthetically speaking, it will give the mushroom an attractive and airy appearance.

Within the gills, on the underside of the cap, lie rows and rows of spores. The reproductive spores come in many colors; this color aids in the primary identification of the fungus. Scientific keys written to identify and group species of fungi begin by asking for the spore color. The Spore Print Activity on page 31 will aid you in learning how to gather such information.

Numerous species of mushrooms grow in the Appalachian Mountains, so it helps to place them into similar groups. A review of the different groups and a few of the predominant characteristics of each follows.

The *agarics* represent the typical mushroom we tend to visualize when thinking about fungi. These fleshy mushrooms have gills and may or may not have stalks. They range in color from pure white to brown, orange, green, or red. Some are very tiny and hard to spot beneath the leaf litter, while others stand several inches above the forest floor.

Chanterelles do not have the obvious gills, but they have wrinkles or soft ridges that contain the spores. They always possess a stalk. Their caps often curve so the ridges turn out and do not point down to the ground. The cap often develops the look of a trumpet or small swimming pool. This unusual form creates a mini environment teeming with microscopic life within the small area of the cap.

Boletes tend to grow larger, and they have distinctive, spongelike pores instead of gills on the underside of the cap. The old-man-of-the-woods, a bolete that looks as though it has lived for a long time, has a broad, dry cap covered in blackish-brown scales. It does not rot quickly and will often remain into the fall and become covered in a green fungus.

Polypores also have pores and may or may not have a stalk. They are described as woody, not because they grow on wood—which they do—but because they are not as soft and fleshy as other mushrooms. The commonly seen bracket fungus, sometimes called the artist's fungus, is a good example of a polypore.

Once you see a *tooth fungus,* you will not forget it. The teeth fungi are aptly named, as the gills resemble spine-like teeth hanging down from the cap. These mushrooms can be fleshy and tougher in texture than typical ones, and will have a stalk.

Puffballs, which contain the reproductive spores inside their outer covering, look like tiny balls. Once they mature and dry, they do seem to "puff," ejecting smokelike clouds of spores. Other familiar puffballs are earthstars and bird's nests, both of which resemble their respective names.

The *jelly fungi* also suit their name, as they have the look and texture of jelly. With colors ranging from yellow to black, they usually grow on wood.

Coral fungi look much like the coral found in the oceans. Their fingerlike projections reach to the sky as they grow out of the earth. Some grow quite thin, while others are thicker and flat, like paddles.

Stinkhorns possess an interesting but unpleasant odor. Their chambered tops and stalks can usually be seen with a good crop of flies in residence.

False morels and *true morels* look similar to each other, but they differ in their edibility. Highly sought after by the mushroom lover, the true morel is considered a delicacy. Potentially toxic, the false morel should be identified using a field guide and not eaten.

Cup fungi look like shallow cups or discs with little to no stalk present. The spores form on the inside of the cup and sometimes grow in clusters.

Earthtongues come in many shapes; the most common look like little tongues reaching skyward from the earth. Dead-man's-fingers, an earthtongue with a colorful and descriptive name, is probably one of my favorites seen on mountain trails.

Browse through a field guide before you start your activities with fungi. Familiarize yourself with pictures of the different shapes and forms you might encounter, and then delve into the world of fungi beginning with the following activities.

Spore Prints

- *Black construction paper*
- *Small knife*
- *Clear, plastic cup, big enough to cover the mushroom cap*
- *Mushrooms from the grocery store*

Spore prints are fun to observe and can also be the basis of an attractive craft project. The mystery comes from not knowing what color of spores you will find.

First, find a place where you can leave your project sitting overnight. Then, take a piece of black paper large enough to accommodate the entire cap of the mushroom, leaving a border around the edges. Cut the stalk close to the cap of the mushroom, trying not to leave too much stalk attached. Set the cap on the paper, with the gills pointing down and the cap facing up.

Cover the cap with a plastic cup to keep it from drying out and to ensure the spores do not blow away. When you check your print the next morning, you will find that the spores have dropped out onto the paper in thin, colorful lines.

To set the spores so they will not wipe off, spray them with an artist's fixative or aerosol hair spray. Spray in a light, sweeping motion, keeping the can several inches away from the paper. Allow the fixative to dry sufficiently and then you won't have to worry about smearing your print.

You have many artistic options for your spore prints. As you stare at their beautiful shapes and forms, your imagination will allow you to see many unique designs within the print. They can become the base for a creative drawing, using the print as the center of an abstract design or the body of an animal. Or you may choose to simply frame the untouched spore print and display it in an area of your home or office.

You can also repeat this activity in the field by collecting wild mushrooms to produce additional spore colors, taking the opportunity to observe the variety of spore color found in nature. I recommend this approach only if you are with an expert who can reliably distinguish the poisonous from the nonpoisonous specimens. Remember to wash your hands after handling wild mushrooms. Mycologists, scientists who study fungi, begin the process of identifying fungi by finding out the color of the spores.

Collect several kinds mushrooms so you will have a greater chance of finding different colors of spores. Keep them cool and dry until you return home, so they will not begin to rot or become soft. If you allow them to sit a long time, you will not be as happy with your results.

Remember, when you gather a mushroom, you are not killing the plant. Therefore, this type of activity would not permanently destroy the group of fungi you are collecting.

Keep the principles of conservation in mind on this, and any, outdoor excursion. Do not cut a basket full of mushrooms, and then make only three or four spore prints. If you come across several mushrooms of the same species growing together, take only one and leave the rest. Those left will ensure survival of that particular species by allowing it to complete its reproductive cycle and release its spores into the environment.

CAMOUFLAGE IN NATURE: THE BENEFITS OF ELUSIVENESS

The living things in the forest blend together in an amazing way. As a whole, a woodland scene appears as a mass of color and shape, yet if you break down the mass into its smaller components, you will find a wealth of insects, birds, animals, and plants, all blending so well that it sometimes takes a sharp eye to pick them out.

If Mother Nature were to do the human race a favor, brighter and different colors would make up the environment, jumping out at us and exclaiming the presence of all the living things. Being able to easily see the many life-forms around us would enhance our viewing pleasure but probably wouldn't help the natural scheme of things very much. Camouflage, an important survival mechanism, allows an organism to blend in with its background environment.

Survival in our natural world can be a bit complex at times. As each day or night unfolds, animals search for food while trying not to become food for something else at the same time. Nature guarantees nothing, and sometimes, for creatures living in a natural environment, meals do not come at all. If they are going to eat, they have to find their own food. No one is back in the den, cooking breakfast with ingredients purchased at the local grocery store. Thus, it is important that they do not make a spectacle of themselves. If they are too obvious, some other hungry critter will likely come out of nowhere and make them his lunch!

In the Southern Appalachians, the environment is primarily composed of greens, browns, and variations on those hues. The plants and animals living there also take on those colors, and some possess the ability to alter their colors with the seasons. The shade of an animal's fur will change to match the landscape, a bird's feathers will molt, and plants will bloom in vivid color and then fade into the background.

When it comes time to reproduce—a short period of time in the calendar year—many plants and animals become a little more flamboyant in order to stand out in the crowd. Animals attempt to attract mates, and plants boast bright, showy flowers to attract pollinating insects. This quickly becomes the choice time for people to get out and observe nature in all of its grandeur. Wildflower hikes, bird walks, and all types of nature observation treks are especially popular when there is a better chance of seeing something special.

During the rest of the year, life is not as obvious when you walk through the woods, but it is just as special. I often remember the comment of a friend who was visiting the mountains for the first time. He lived in a large city and had few experiences outside of that environment. I drove him to the top of Roan Mountain in July, when lush vegetation blanketed the area. Thrilled to share this special place with a good friend, I hoped that he, too, would love the mountains as I do. After driving for a short time, I turned to him and asked his impression of what he saw. "Sure is green," he responded.

The following game, designed to sharpen the eye and imagination, will help you see beyond all of that overwhelming green so common in the summer months and make it easier to spot the finer things outdoors. You will be searching for small variations in color that closely mimic the subtle changes of nature.

ACTIVITY A Camouflage Scavenger Hunt

- *Pipe cleaners in natural colors and bright colors*

This activity, similar to an Easter egg hunt, will demonstrate the amazing variety of color in the natural environment. Two people should be involved, but the more the merrier! Shape the pipe cleaners into little animals or birds that you can tie onto tree limbs or perch on rocks, much in the same spots you might expect to find a real animal or plant.

At least one person will hide the pipe cleaners along a given stretch of trail or field. When hiding the natural-colored pipe cleaners, try to find spots that blend with the color of the pipe cleaners to illustrate the concept of camouflage. Use the opposite approach when hiding the brightly colored pipe cleaners, realizing that they represent those plants and animals involved in reproduction, thus making themselves more obvious for a short period of time.

When the trail is stocked with pipe-cleaner creatures, the rest of the group may go along the same path and see if they can find where all the creatures are sitting. As the members of the group become conditioned to what to look for, it will become a little easier. Visual patterns often develop, making some colors easier to pick out. Once the group picks out what is obvious to them, they can try focusing on the shades and tones that are more difficult to see. After everyone arrives at the end of the trail, they can gather to see what each person has found.

Now that your eyes are trained to find the pipe-cleaner creatures, it will become easier to find the many living things that blend in naturally outdoors. Take a second walk and look for all the varying shades of green, brown, yellow, and blue that you may not have noticed previously.

For a twist on this activity, prepare an indoor setting at home or in the classroom. Use the same concept of picking colors that will blend well with the inside decor, with other colors standing out like a sore thumb.

MICROHABITATS

ACTIVITY An Exploration in Miniature

- *Pad of paper and a pencil for each team*

This activity will explore tiny worlds that sometimes seem insignificant. You will look closely at individual areas that can be passed over in just one step! An activity for any number, it works exceptionally well with small teams of two to five.

Give each team a pencil and pad of paper and send them out on a journey to explore a particular microhabitat. They may go to the bank beside a creek, a flat area in a field, or a rocky spot in the woods. Any area will work fine, just remem-

A mound of moss covered in spore capsules

ber the purpose—to become thoroughly acquainted with the habitat assigned to each individual or team.

Consider the world of one small insect, which might spend its entire day on one leaf. The leaf miner—so small that you can barely see him with the unaided eye—is a good example of this concept. It's not hard to walk down a trail and step on the leaf miner inside of his leaf without giving a second thought. If you see a green leaf with many light green lines squiggling all over the surface, you could be seeing the path of the leaf miner. The leaf looks as though it might have a disease or has had paint scrolled across the surface. What you actually see are the tunnels of an insect eating his way between the top and bottom layers of a healthy green leaf. Slowly but surely, he continues his trek through this one leaf, which no doubt is a great part of his world.

In this activity, you will look closely at just one small area within a vast, spreading world. Mark off approximately one square yard of ground for the microhabitat you and your team will explore. Notice what lives there and the environmental conditions. Possibilities include homes, nests, colors, wet and dry areas, plants that are dying back, new growth, seeds in the ground, animal tracks, bones, and even signs of people. In other words, look closely at everything in your designated area. Be cautious of any poisonous plants or animals. If conducting this activity with children, an adult should inspect each microhabitat and its surrounding area for any such hazards before beginning.

Each team should appoint a secretary, who will take notes and record the team's observations. If working alone, carry along your journal. As you explore your area, list absolutely everything there, even down to the holes in the leaves and the bark chips from the tree above. As you observe, try not to destroy anything, and make it a point to leave the area exactly as you found it.

Bring the groups back together after everyone finishes their observations, and then have each secretary read what his team has found. Then, as a large group, discuss what the discoveries mean to the ways of our natural world. Why are there holes in the leaf? What made the bark fall to the ground? Do insects live under the bark? What made that hole in the ground?

You will find that each and every thing listed by each team can open up the door to a whole new world beneath your feet. When the discussion ends, draw a picture or write a narrative in your journal of the most outstanding elements of the microhabitat studied.

On your busier days, when life seems a little too hectic, let this experience slow you down a little and remember the tinier things in nature.

ENJOYING WINTER'S DELIGHTS

One morning, I awoke to falling snow. Overnight, five lovely white inches of softness had delicately carpeted everything outside my bedroom window. As I pushed my eyes open, I noticed a bright, almost blue cast to the day, accompanied by the constant chirping of birds at the feeder near the door.

I wandered over to check out the activity and was amazed by a total free-for-all. Juncos, chickadees, titmice, white-throated sparrows, goldfinches, and pine siskins all competed feverishly for the meaty, black sunflower seeds. A hungry sparrow suddenly harassed a goldfinch, resulting in a short scuffle that ended when the sparrow won the perch.

My daughter, Julia, looked out and said, "Look, Mom, that bird is kicking up the snow; it looks like it's moon walking."

There on the porch, a plump, white-throated sparrow used its feet to dig into the snow, looking for buried seeds. With each little dig, the bird would scoot backward, leaving a short trail. Its little dance continued all over the porch, and one bird after the other soon joined in. Their efforts were not in vain, for before long, the white snow soon became speckled in black sunflower seeds.

The flurry of activity continued all day, as the snow fell without a break. Each bird gave its best to get the share of nutrition and energy needed to carry it through another cold night. Watching them reminded me of how different, yet alive, life is in the wintertime. The coldness that sends us indoors to build a fire and peek out through the blinds is a time when wildlife continues working for food and shelter.

We often get the impression that the coming of fall, the first frosts, and then winter is a time when life almost ceases. As the frost falls overnight, we systematically see the autumn wildflowers turn white, then brown, before they ultimately die. Our gardens and crops are cut down, and the ground is prepared for next year's planting. Animals begin to store food for the approaching winter, and many hibernate until the days become longer in early spring. To many of us, winter takes on the appearance of a cold, lifeless season.

Yet, on closer inspection, life is still on the move outside our heated homes. Survival becomes an important part of the day-to-day activities of wildlife, contrary to the impression of lifelessness we sometimes feel due to the extreme cold and stillness. Let us adopt a different perception by looking deeply into the sparkling covering of white that grows during a heavy snow. An intricate beauty emerges within each individual flake of snow as it falls gently from the sky.

Snow Crystals

The anticipation of a coming snowfall certainly can be a time of great excitement. As falling snow systematically blankets the surrounding landscape, a feeling of warmth and insulation seems to emanate from the life around us. Snowflakes and crystals act as amazing examples of the myriad of shapes in the natural environment.

As a teenager, Wilson "Snowflake" Bentley (1865-1931) developed an interest in snow crystals. In January 1885, after two years of painstaking trial and error, he succeeded in photographing a snowflake through his microscope. Though Bentley did not gain the confidence of those around him at first, over time he was recognized for what he had achieved. During his life, he took pictures of over 5,000 snowflakes, proving that no two snow crystals are exactly the same. Many years later, he became famous for his discovery, and meteorologists now believe that there are one trillion, trillion, trillion different types of snowflakes.

All snow crystals have six sides and are separated into seven groups: needles, columns, plates, capped columns, spatial dendrites, irregular crystals, and stellar. By the time a snowflake gets to earth, however, it probably will not have all six sides. Scientists estimate that less than 25% of the time, a six-sided snowflake will make it, as it must travel through other snowflakes, wind, and water, which all will alter its shape.

Water vapor, ice crystals, and dust are the first three ingredients needed to create a snowflake. When water vapor freezes on a microscopic piece of dust, ice crystals form. As cold-water droplets and ice crystals come together in a very cold cloud, snow begins to form. The temperature in the cloud determines the shape of the snowflake, while the size of an ice crystal depends on the amount of moisture in the cloud. The more moisture present, the larger the crystal. A snowflake results from many ice crystals sticking together. Its shape and size will more than likely change before it reaches its final destination on Earth, as it will pass through other clouds with different temperatures and moisture levels. Occasionally, snow composed primarily of single ice crystals will fall.

ACTIVITY Snowflake Viewing

For a quick look:

- *Smooth black fabric or black construction paper*
- *Hand lens or magnifying glass*

Prepare for the next snowfall, and keep your fabric or construction paper in the freezer. When the snow falls, take your materials out of the freezer and go outside so you can catch some snowflakes on your black background. Don't leave the paper or fabric outside for an extended period of time, for before long, you will have too many snowflakes. By using your hand lens, see if you can identify different shapes of ice crystals present. The snow will melt quickly, so be ready to check them out.

To keep a permanent record:

- *Aerosol hair spray*
- *Piece of glass*

Keep the glass and hair spray in the freezer until the next snowfall. Remove them from the freezer when the snow begins to fall. Spray the glass, take it outside, and let a few snowflakes fall on it. When you have several snowflakes on the glass, bring it inside and thaw at room temperature for about 15 minutes. You will have a collection of snowflakes preserved for present and future observation.

ACTIVITY Snow and Water

- *Clear plastic soda bottle*
- *Ruler*
- *Smudge-proof marker*

Try this easy experiment to find out just how much water melting snow generates. Cut off the top of a clear-plastic soda bottle and wash it out. After drying, take a ruler and a smudge-proof marker and mark each one-inch increment from the base of the container to the top. When it starts to snow, set your bottle outside in a place where it won't tip over.

Periodically check the depth of the falling snow. When you have collected several inches of snow, bring the bottle inside and allow the snow to melt. Record in your journal the depth of the snow in the bottle, and then the depth of the water after it melts.

BEGINNINGS: SIGNS OF A COMING SEASON

ACTIVITY Popping Up!

- *Paper, pencil, and clipboard*

With spring well under way, when the wildflowers show their full bloom, the ferns have unfolded their fronds, and seedlings grow rapidly by the day, we easily forget that only a few months earlier, these flourishing plants began a new life as the tiny offspring of their predecessors.

On a warm spring day, nothing is more exciting than going on a search through the fields and forests, looking for the faces of our green friends poking up through the ground. With a group, alone, or with your family, devote a little time on a pretty day to an outdoor trek to search for the signs that reassure us life is once again renewing itself.

The bloom of a Canada mayflower peeks out from between the leaves.

To make the journey a bit challenging, see who has the sharpest eye and can find the most "little" signs of spring. Bring along a pencil and paper with the name of each person in the group listed across the top. Draw columns down the page and have someone keep track of anything discovered by placing it under the name of the person who found it.

Children especially enjoy this type of exploration, as they love to find something first and will look extra hard for new discoveries.

Everyone should carry a sketchpad, so they can draw the special things they have found, as well as jot down what these things are doing. You can give your drawings comical characteristics and make them seem almost human.

A mushroom just pushing its way through the ground sometimes keeps a roof over its head, composed of twigs, leaves, and soil, which looks much like a curved hat. The tiny uncurling frond of a new fern seems to reach out its hand to those who pass. As a new leaf unfolds at the end of a tree branch, you can almost see a dancer spinning in motion. Remember, the spectacle of spring occurs but once a year—don't let it pass you by!

On This Date

- *Your journal*
- *Writing/drawing utensils*
- *Paper, preferably legal size or larger*

This project can extend through weeks, months, and even years, if you so desire. Begin by recording the current date on the top of a page in your journal and head outdoors. Find a relaxing place to sit back for a while and absorb all that happens around you.

You can start at any time of the year, for nature is always changing and emerging. Springtime is ideal, though, as great numbers of changes are happening quickly. Spring will provide you with much to see as life regenerates after the cold, quiet time of winter. Listen for the sounds, sights, and fresh new odors of the season.

Record what inspires and impresses you; make note of the first birds and dragonflies you see. Look around and notice trees in flower as well as those that already have all of their summer leaves. If you can't identify what you see, sketch it instead, or create an elaborate drawing in colored pencil or watercolor.

Use these same approaches for everything you observe, be it wildflowers, butterflies, or weather changes. Every opportunity you get throughout the year, note the changes that occur, always making a point to date your entry.

Don't feel you need to sit down for an extended period and observe. Of course, after a hectic day, a long visit to the outdoors can relieve some of the tension we accumulate as we go about our busy lives, but life does not always provide us with as much time as we would prefer. Train yourself to always be aware, whether you are walking to your car, running into the grocery store, or working in a job situation where you can be near an open window or the outdoors.

If you keep adding entries over the course of a year, you will find the second year just as interesting, but in a different way. As spring approaches, notice all the "firsts" you recorded the year before. Continue dating your pages and note when they occur the second year; they may be the same or very different. Over time, the information you have written in your journal will become increasingly interesting to review. Your observations may also become important if the time comes when natural populations change in your area.

As an example, for five consecutive years you may have noted hearing and seeing large numbers of spring peepers breeding in exactly the same vernal pool. If, at some future time, they slowly decrease in number or disappear from that location altogether, you will have documented that they did reproduce there. Your documentation may raise many questions as to what changes might have occurred to eliminate their population.

Create a poster to hang in your home, classroom, or business, to turn your journaling into a visual project to share with others. Choose something you have observed—either once, or many times—as the subject of your poster. Title it "On This Date," and insert the month and day. Then follow it with a drawing of the subject and words that describe where you saw it and what it was doing each year. The following example might help you get started:

On This Date, February 22

In 1998 the wood frogs were calling from the temporary spring pools near the Doe River.

In 1999 eight inches of snow covered the ground, and the wood frogs were not heard.
In 2000 the wood frogs had finished calling and had laid three masses of eggs.
In 2001 only one mass of eggs could be found in the same location.
In 2002 wood frogs were again calling in deafening numbers.

Decide how much information you want to include. Create and design the layout of the poster to your liking, letting the space you want to allot to each entry determine its size.

Further Reading

Claws, Coats and Camouflage: The Ways Animals Fit into their World by Michael J. Doolittle and Susan E. Goodman
Insects Through the Seasons by Gilbert Waldbauer
Life on a Little-Known Planet by Howard Ensign Evans and Arnold Clapman
Mushrooms and Other Non-Flowering Plants by Floyd Stephen Shuttleworth and Herbert Spencer Zim
Mushrooms of North America by Orson K. Mill, Jr., and E. P. Dutton
National Audubon Society Field Guide to North American Insects and Spiders by Lorus J. Milne and Susan Rayfield
National Audubon Society Field Guide to North American Mushrooms by Gary A. Lincoff and Gary H. Lincoff
Peterson First Guide to Insects of North America by Christopher Leahy and Richard E. White
Snow Crystals by W. A. Bentley and W. J. Humphreys
Snowflake Designs by Marty Noble
The Snowflake Man: A Biography of Wilson A. Bentley by Duncan C. Blanchard
Stokes Nature Guide to Observing Insect Lives by Donald Stokes
What are Camouflage and Mimicry? by Bobbie Kalman and John Crossingham

A World of Water

The Appalachian Mountains hold a maze of waterways. Beginning as springs and seeps at the highest areas, they meet and join other branches of water and culminate at the lower elevations as vibrant creeks and streams.

Mountain wetlands, abundant prior to the settling of the Appalachians, have become a rare sight. Glacial in origin, they require up to 10,000 years to form naturally. These spongy, unique areas provide important breeding grounds for a host of organisms that must remain moist most of the time in order to survive and reproduce.

The Southern Appalachians provide a home to more species of salamanders than anywhere else in the world, and nowhere are they more plentiful. Those who study them often find their way to the area for a closer look at their habitats.

A good number of frogs populate the region, though lower elevations have a greater number of species than the mountains. In the mountains, you can find green frogs, bullfrogs, gray tree frogs, spring peepers, chorus frogs, and wood frogs, to name a few. Their soothing vocalizations fill the air during breeding season and rainy spells.

Amphibians absorb moisture and oxygen through nearly 100% of their body surface, which exposes them to both the good and the bad parts of their surroundings. They have an extreme sensitivity to pollutants, making them unique biological indicators. Deformities and declining populations of these organisms are often early signs of their environment's exposure to some type of undesirable outside influence.

AN AMPHIBIAN FORAY

Observing frogs and salamanders is gratifying and extremely interesting. Their presence is not always obvious, so when you find or hear one, it can be quite exciting! To ensure a positive experience for you and the amphibians, monitor them by ear or eye and avoid handling them.

As you participate in the activities below, take special precautions if you choose to touch a salamander or frog. Do not spray yourself with any type of bug repellent, and make sure your hands and collection bag or dish are clean and free from chemicals.

If you find yourself turning over rocks to look for salamanders, use care so you don't crush them when you set the rock back in place. Replace everything in its original position and carefully return the salamander or frog to its home if you pick it up to observe it.

ACTIVITY A Peeper Party

- *Flashlight*

My favorite sounds of spring include the mysterious, high-pitched chorus of "peeps" seeming to arise miraculously from deep within the grass during warm rain showers. This happy little song that croons us to sleep by the wetland's edge and keeps us company on rainy summer evenings comes from the male spring peeper, a tiny tree frog.

Spring peepers call primarily to attract mates, and the loudest displays usually happen in the spring, when mating occurs. Though nocturnal, they often call during light rains or in cloudy weather. When calling in great numbers, they can often be deafening.

Usually no more than an inch long, and camouflaged in gray to brown coloring, with a darker X on the back, the peeper is sometimes hard to spot. Its round toe pads, one of the unique attributes of the tree frog, act as miniature suction cups and aid in climbing and hanging onto tiny substrates, such as a blade of grass.

If you hope to get a look at this creature, you'll need a great deal of patience and a keen eye to pick them out of their surroundings. However, it is worth the effort, for when you spot one of these vocal frogs, you will be amazed and delighted by its tiny size and wonder how something that small could make so much sound!

Vernal pools—marshy areas during late winter and early spring that usually dry up in the summertime—are ideal spots to search for peepers. They will

A spring peeper hidden in vegetation

congregate on rainy nights in temporary wetlands to find mates and lay their eggs. When looking for spring peepers, pretend you are a cautious hunter silently stalking your prey; you will have to approach them slowly and quietly. You need only a flashlight and some waterproof boots.

To start your search for this elusive tree frog, stand quietly near a wet area where you hear peepers calling. Close your eyes and concentrate on just one voice in the crowd, preferably one close to you. Look directly at the area where the voice you have chosen comes from and take gentle steps in that direction. Now stop. Is he still singing? If he isn't, stand silently and he should start up in a moment. (If the frog hears you, he will stop his call until you are still again.) Once the frog continues his call, take a few more quiet steps in his direction, repeating the process until you can see his perch. More than likely he will be down in the vegetation, so you will have to look closely. Shine your flashlight toward the spot you have tuned your ears to, and as a reward you will probably get a great look at a frog we frequently hear but seldom see!

You can search for other species of frogs in the same manner. Listen quietly for the unique calls of frogs and toads on wet evenings, and you may find species other than the peeper by approaching them slowly and gently.

ACTIVITY Salamander Hideouts

- *Flashlight or headlamp*
- *Field guide to amphibians*

Salamanders need to stay wet—they could die if they dry out. Damp, humid, or rainy nights provide the ideal conditions to look for salamanders, because the cover of darkness protects them from the heat of the day as they hunt for food.

Red salamander

During the daylight, choose an area to explore and become familiar with any tripping hazards along your path of travel. Notice rocks, logs, and such, which may not seem too troublesome when you can see well. In the dark, however, with only the aid of a flashlight, these innocent objects might prove a little more dangerous. Find areas with water, rocks, logs, and spots that would offer good cover and protection for amphibians.

Reviewing a field guide or book describing the many species of salamanders living in the Southern Appalachians will make a salamander hunt all the more rewarding. With luck on your side, you might run across the northern dusky, the Appalachian two-lined, or the yonahlossee salamanders.

At night, travel with a companion or with a group, for wandering around alone in the dark is not recommended.

When you observe a salamander, make note of its habits and actions. Notice how it walks, the design of its body, the number of toes, the shape of its tail, and its coloration patterns. Keep records of how many you find and their differences. Knowledge of their names is not necessary; instead, note the variances seen, and group them into what appear to be similar species.

You can also search for salamanders in the daytime by peeking under rocks, in the damp leaf litter, and beneath logs. If you raise a rock to reveal a hiding salamander, carefully replace it so as not to crush the soft-bodied animal. To ensure their survival, do not pick them up; observe them with your eyes only.

MOUNTAIN WETLANDS: A NATURAL SPONGE

When we think of wetlands, often the image of huge expanses of land, such as the Florida Everglades, comes to mind. We might envision a large marshy river bottom, teeming with migratory waterfowl, that spreads for miles. In the Southern Appalachians, wetlands do exist, usually in small remnant parcels of land, tucked away in a cove or hollow. Mountain wetlands are generally no larger

A mountain wetland

than an acre because the clearing of the land and the building of homes have decreased the amount of land historically covered by water.

Three characteristics determine if an area is a wetland: water, soil, and the plant species present. Needless to say, water must be present for an ecosystem to receive a wetland classification. The water has varying amounts of dissolved oxygen present at different times, which establishes the characteristics of the soil and the plant species that can survive in this type of environment.

Many factors, including rain, wind, temperature, seasons, and movement, affect the amount of dissolved oxygen present in any body of water. If you compare a wetland to a nearby creek, they both receive approximately the same exposure to the elements, and the most pronounced difference between the two is the rate or speed the water moves.

In a creek, river, or stream, oxygen from the atmosphere is introduced into the water as it splashes over rocks and flows down the course of the waterway. Since quickly moving water comes in contact with the air for a longer period of time, it will contain more dissolved oxygen.

In a wetland, water does not move rapidly, if at all, resulting in a low amount of oxygen in the water. The lack of oxygen causes chemical reactions that change the soil color, usually to gray-brown, and sometimes greenish. Wetland soils often have rusty-looking specks and streaks throughout, created during dry periods when air can temporarily get into the soil.

Because certain plants will thrive in no other environment, you can determine if a habitat is a wetland, even if you visit it during a dry spell, by knowing which plants are classified as wetland species.

Wetlands are necessary for the balance of our environment. They filter pollutants, excessive nutrients, and silt from the water, preventing them from running rapidly into our waterways. By absorbing excess water during floods, wetlands minimize or eliminate damage and erosion to surrounding lands and creeks. Wetlands, as the first step in many food chains, provide food and shelter for numerous plant and animal species throughout the year.

There are two classifications of mountain wetlands: the bog, fed by precipitation, and the fen, fed year-round by drainage and groundwater. Both habitats are commonly found in the Northeastern United States, the Great Lakes region, the Rocky Mountains, and Canada.

A typical bog in the Appalachian Mountains would be characterized as an area where peat has accumulated faster than it can decompose. Sphagnum moss is the dominant living plant, but the acidic water creates conditions that do not support a large variety of plants and animals. Deer, black bear, beaver, bobcat, snowshoe hare, otter, and mink are associated with this habitat. In addition, many bird species nest, feed, and breed in the bog environment. Specific species of salamanders, frogs, turtles, and plants can survive only in a bog or fen.

Because the acidic conditions of the bog are not present in a fen, it has a larger variety of plant and animal life than a bog. It is possible that the fen represents an early bog, in which peat has not yet accumulated to form the deep, acidic sphagnum. Grasses and sedges are common, along with willows, wetland herbs, trees, and shrubs that require a wet environment. Many forms of wildlife use the fen for feeding, nesting, breeding, and refuge.

Destruction of upland groundwater sources can prove fatal to a fen. Draining pressures from 1950 to 1970 caused fens to decline in acreage approximately eight percent nationwide. With so few mountain wetlands still existing and a 10,000-year time frame needed for them to form naturally, it is crucial to identify and protect these remaining areas.

ACTIVITY Create an Environment

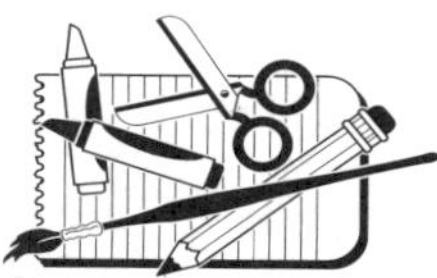

- *Crayons with a wide range of colors matching the suggested shades in the chart below*
- *Copies of the blank wetland soil chart*
- *Approximately 1 cup of soil from a dry site (no standing water during the growing season)*
- *Approximately 1 cup of soil samples from a wet site*

This activity can be done individually or in groups. Give a copy of the chart below to each person or group. Have them find matching colors in the crayon box and fill in the corresponding blocks. This important step will teach everyone to look at the variations in the shades. For the examples requiring added gray, a soft, light shading of gray on top of the base color will suffice; pressing down on the crayon will cover up the underlying color.

Wet Soils			. . . to . . .				Dry Soils
Black	Gray	Sea Green & Gray	Forest Green & Gray	Brown & Gray	Tan	Peach	Goldenrod

Prepare observation sheets similar to the one below. Use a separate sheet for each soil sample, and give each person or group a copy.

Soil Sample #______	
1. Which color on the chart matches this sample?	
2. Do you see any areas of rusty-looking streaks or spots?	
3. Does this sample match the profile of a wet or dry soil?	

Without identifying the soil type at the beginning, let each person carefully observe and compare the two soil samples and try to match them with the colors in the chart. Then they will complete the observation sheet to determine which soil is from the wet area and which is from the dry.

ACTIVITY Filtering Fun

- *2 coffee filters per person or group*
- *Pepper*
- *Empty cup, bowl, or small container*
- *Rubber band*
- *Water*

Now that we have determined the characteristics of a wetland soil, let's demonstrate how the filtering process works. This important wetland function helps to keep pollutants and excessive nutrients from pouring into surrounding creeks, streams, and rivers, resulting in cleaner, purer water.

Place a coffee filter in the container, using the rubber band to hold the filter around the rim and keep it from falling in. Sprinkle a teaspoon of pepper in the filter and then fill it with water (no more than the container will hold).

Watch the water drip through the filter and then record what you have observed by using the following suggested questions.

1. What does the filter represent in this activity?
2. What does the pepper represent?
3. What happened to the water?
4. What happened to the pepper?
5. If the pepper were a pollutant (for instance, road salt or excess fertilizer), would it have been a good or bad situation for it to be rushing into the waterways surrounding the wetland?

Repeat the activity by cutting small holes in the bottom of the filter. Once again, answer the questions above, in addition to the following, and compare the results of both experiments.

1. What do wetlands do to protect our major waterways from inundation by excess nutrients and pollutants?
2. Write your conclusion comparing the results of both experiments. Tell what happened in each and whether the first or second experiment demonstrated the filtering aspects of a wetland.

ACTIVITY Soak It Up!

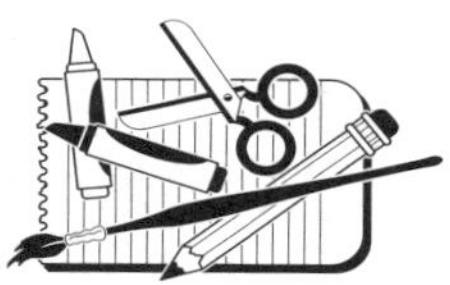

- *Water*
- *Several sponges (at least 6)*
- *A watch with a second hand*
- *Empty cup, bowl, or small container*
- *Cookie sheet or jellyroll pan with approximately a 1" edge*
- *A container to set the pan in at an angle to catch the water*

During heavy rains, which produce much runoff, water rushes downhill into lower-lying areas and rapidly reaches the streams. This activity will demonstrate how wetlands act like sponges and absorb excess water before it can fill creeks and rivers to dangerous levels, preventing floods. Be sure to use the same pouring container and the same amount of water for all three experiments.

Experiment #1: A wetland in a slow, steady rain

Place the pan in a water-catching container at an angle of 15 to 25 degrees, imitating a small slope. Line the bottom edge of the pan with dry sponges. If they keep falling forward off the pan, lower the angle of the pan.

When everything is in place and stable, pour the water *slowly* onto the top of the pan, recording the time you started pouring. Observe what happens as the water runs down.

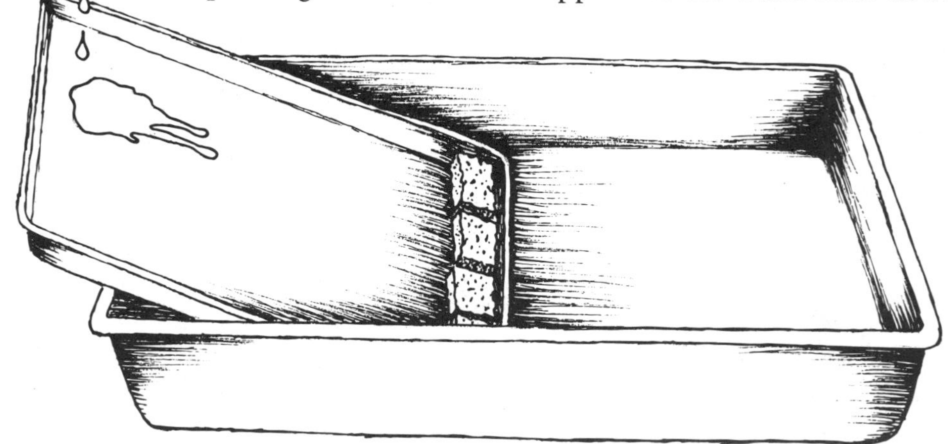

Continue pouring until the sponges have absorbed their maximum amount of liquid and the water is running into the container. Record the stop time. Before moving on to Number 2, answer the following questions.

1. How did the sponges function in this experiment?
2. How long did it take for the water to fill up the sponges and flow into the container? (Subtract your start time from stop time.)

Experiment #2: A wetland in a hard rain, often producing fast runoff

Pour the water out of the container, dry the pan, and replace the wet sponges with dry ones. Set up the activity in the same fashion as before, and try to get the pan at the same angle. This time, when you pour the water, let it flow at a quicker pace, but not so fast that it knocks the sponges out of the pan. Once again, record the time you start pouring and the time that the sponges can no longer hold water and begin overflowing into the pan.

In addition to answering the questions above as they relate to this second experiment, compare your results by addressing two additional questions:

3. Did the sponges absorb water quicker the first time or the second?
4. Did the sponges help to slow the water down the first time? The second?

Experiment #3—Absence of a wetland in a slow, steady rain

Pour the water out of the container and replace the pan at the same angle as in the first two experiments, this time without sponges. The pan will represent a non-wetland soil, which does not absorb much water and often reacts to heavy rain by allowing it to pour over its surface, directly into creeks and rivers.

Repeat the same procedure as the previous experiments, recording the start time and the number of seconds passed when the water leaves the pan and begins filling the container. Compare your results to the first two experiments by answering the questions below:

1. How many seconds did it take for the water to pass over the pan and begin filling the container?
2. Did the sponges in experiments 1 and 2 help to slow down or speed up the water flow?
3. How does a wetland act in controlling the speed, flow, and amount of water fed into our waterways?

ACTIVITY Wet Feet

- *Two wetland plants that grow in saturated soil*
- *Two plants that grow in non-saturated soil*
- *Two flowerpots*
- *Potting soil*
- *Small container deep enough to hold water and accommodate two plants*
- *Tray with 1" – 2" sides to hold water and pots*

Understanding adaptation is important when studying plants, animals, and other inhabitants of our environment. One of the first steps to identifying the many species present in mountains is to discover who, or what, likes to live where. Some organisms can survive only in specific habitats, while others may have more versatility.

In this activity you will try to determine if all plants can grow in a wetland habitat or if only certain ones, with special requirements, will survive there. Choose two plants (both can be the same species) that float in water and two that grow in soil, preferring drier feet (for instance, geraniums). Look for the them at a local garden center that sells plants for water gardens as well as flowering annuals and perennials.

Fill the small container with water deep enough for the root structure of the wetland plant. Place a free-floating plant in this container, along with one usually planted in soil.

Place the two remaining plants—you should have a wet and a dry example—in each of the flowerpots filled with potting soil, and set the pots in the tray. Saturate the soil until the water runs out the bottom of the pots. When the soil dries out during the experiment, water the two plants from the top only.

Record in your journal or on a pad of paper exactly what you have done thus far. Prepare a page for the two floating plants and a page for the plants placed in soil. Check the plants daily and record what you observe in each situation. Note the appearance of each plant, if it is thriving or dying, and any other notable changes. Is there a variation between the plants in soil and the plants in water?

Take a cross section of a stem on each plant and record the differences. You will see holes and channels in the stalks of the wetland plants but not in those adapted to growing in soil. The channels help conduct water and air into the entire structure of the plant. The wetland plants, more than likely, will survive in excessive water, and the plants that prefer to be a little drier will not. The non-wetland plants have, in a sense, drowned, as they cannot get air through their root and stem systems.

For a plant to survive in a wetland environment, it needs to have special adaptations that enable it to exist in water for most or all of the time. As you learn which plants thrive in wetlands, it will become easier to identify wetland areas during field trips and outdoor observations.

ACTIVITY Visit a Wetland

The ideal way to experience a wetland would be to find one and check it out in person. Some wetlands take in huge expanses of land, while others cover less than half an acre. You may find unnoticed spots along roadsides, along edges of streams, or near ponds, all of which fit the classification of a wetland.

Keep your eyes and ears open for the telltale signs of a wetland: standing areas of water, cattails towering high or the presence of various other wetland plant species, and the vocalizations of frogs. Notice after a rain whether or not certain spots do not drain adequately. Be observant of wildlife that may visit. If good cover is available, a wide variety of birds may find their way to these special wet spots.

The active wetland environment is exciting to watch. After locating an area you would like to observe, visit it on a regular basis. Make notes of what you see in this changing, unique environment, and identify or sketch your findings, including numbers and types of plants, frogs, and birds. Notice the presence of dragonflies, damselflies, and other aquatic insects teeming about. Be alert for signs of litter or pollution, and consider making a project out of protecting and cleaning up the area, if necessary.

Organizations and schools in many communities are often interested in helping protect wetlands near their homes. In addition, you may live in a community with environmental organizations devoted to watching wildlife. Take advantage of these opportunities to learn and share with others who hold similar interests.

THROUGH THE MICROSCOPE

While exploring rivers and ponds, even without the aid of magnification beyond that of a hand lens, you can observe many creatures who make their homes in still and moving waters. Amazingly, there is still more to discover, as much of the life teeming in our waters is so small that we could never see it without a microscope.

The hay infusion study below, designed to help grow and find microscopic organisms that live in any given water sample, will provide the opportunity to grow and view some unusual fauna, much like an aquarium but without its obvious, eye-catching inhabitants.

ACTIVITY

Hay Infusion Study

- *Large glass jar or a similar container, possibly a fishbowl.*
- *Microscope*
- *Handful of hay*
- *Few grains of charcoal*
- *Small piece of screen or thin netting*

Take a glass jar or fishbowl to a pond or creek with a good standing pool, and line the bottom of the jar with approximately two to three inches of debris such as decaying plant matter from the bottom of the pond. By sampling from the lower reaches of the pond, where most organisms find plenty of food and protection, you will have much more success in this study. Fill the jar with murky water from the bottom of the pond, then pour a little out so the level is a few inches from the top of the container.

Bring the container indoors and set it in a spot where it will remain undisturbed but where it will get some indirect sunlight; try to avoid direct sunlight. Place just enough hay to cover the surface of the water in the jar. The nutrients in the hay will enable the organisms in the sample to breed and flourish. Because the odor may become a little strong as the hay and debris begin to decay, add a few grains of charcoal to the water to help deodorize your environment in a jar. Add a piece of screen or thin netting over the top of the jar.

After the infusion sits overnight, the murky water will have a chance to settle

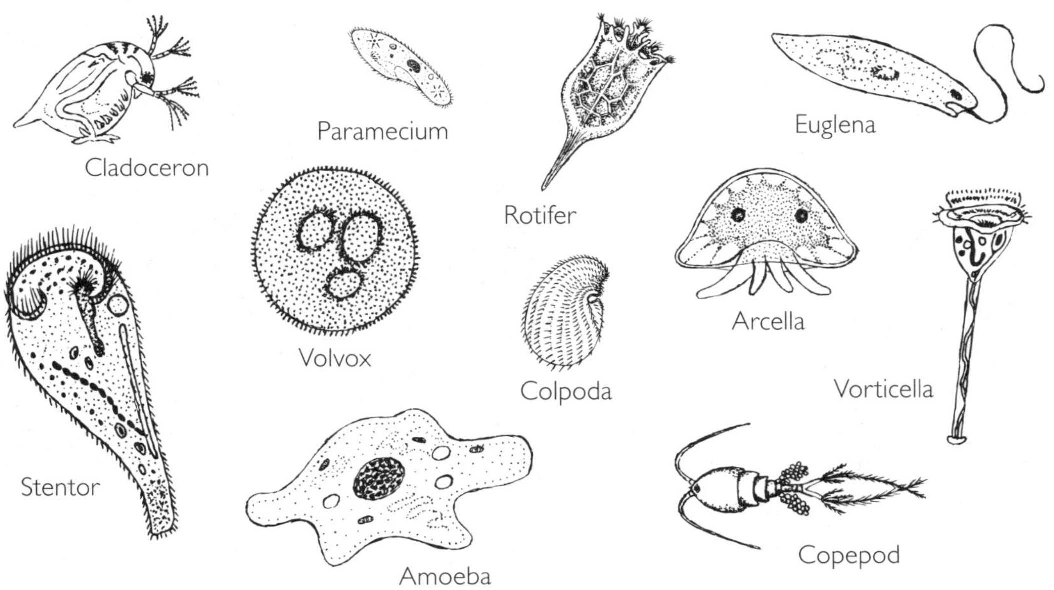

and you can see the larger creatures climbing up on stems or swimming to the top. Look for the nymphs of mayflies, dragonflies, damselflies, and small water bugs, or possibly a caddis fly casing gathered from the bottom debris. Within a few days you will have a population of microscopic and minute creatures thriving within your jar of water.

From the moment the water settles you will want to pull out your journal or find a notebook to keep records of what you find. Also make note of how many individuals you see of each organism. Include with your entries the date and time you observed something new living in your environment.

After three or four days, take an eyedropper and put a couple of drops of the water (preferably from the bottom of the jar) on a glass microscope slide with a cover slip on top. By scanning the slide under the microscope, you will discover a whole new unseen world just bubbling with life. A field guide to pond life or freshwater biology invaluably aids in the identification of the life found in the water. If you have no access to a microscope, contact the science department at a university or high school and inquire into the possibility of using one of theirs.

Remember to keep recording what you see, sampling the hay infusion study every day, if possible. You will likely find something new each time you look into this amazing yet often unnoticed world. Through discovering new and previously unseen life, a deeper appreciation and understanding of the world of nature often develops. When finished, don't forget to return the water and its inhabitants to the spot where you found them!

AN AQUATIC EXPEDITION

The mystery and comfort of water stays with us. Sitting on a rock by a creek on a warm summer day can be a most rewarding and spiritually uplifting experience. The sound of the water crashing against the rocks, seemingly rolling itself up in a ball, only to unwind again, is a sensual experience unlike any other.

Creeks, rivers, and streams flow out of almost every mountain hollow. Working hand in hand with the principles of gravity, water continually runs downstream from the highest peaks, ultimately finding its way to larger lakes and rivers. Often traveling a course that would challenge a person attempting it on foot, it drops off high cliffs, forming cascades and waterfalls. The water twists and turns, hopping and sliding over obstacles as it pushes rocks, limbs, and other debris.

We commonly enjoy energetic waterways for their beauty and the attributes immediately obvious to us, such as fishing or wading on a hot summer day. Watching a river as it courses along can be relaxing, almost hypnotizing, as your mind focuses on the surface, the most obvious part, which overwhelms your senses and keeps you from seeing the life below.

But below the water's surface exists a community of life and survival not always obvious to the casual viewer. In this world, larvae cling to rocks, crayfish lie in wait for their unknowing prey to stumble by, and life-forms move here and there, often at the mercy of the currents.

Above and below the surface of the water, a miraculous system exists in a complex environment in constant motion. Small, single-celled plants, algae, planktons, bacteria, and fungi begin the food chain. Insect larvae, nymphs, crustaceans, salamanders, and fish feed on these smaller creatures. Land-dwelling mammals also depend on the water system, coming there to drink and to hunt food such as fish or crayfish. Under the water you will find many species with varied breathing mechanisms, eating habits, and methods of moving. Some immature insects look almost like the adult they will turn into; others look entirely different.

The presence or absence of particular insects can tell a lot about water quality. Certain species cannot survive in water that is polluted or low in oxygen. The presence of these indicator species will tell you that the water is clean.

The next activities include some easy and inexpensive techniques to explore the unique water world. Before moving into the activities, take a moment to learn a little about some species that you might encounter on a creek walk or pond exploration. Since there are thousands of species of aquatic insects, the charts on pages 60–65 focus on those most typically found, noting their more obvious or interesting characteristics. To help you identify what you see in the field, compare your observations with drawings of each immature and adult form. Also notice whether or not the immature form of the insect looks like the adult form. But before you read on, learn the meanings of a few words and concepts on the charts.

Predator—An animal that hunts and eats other animals (predaceous).

Herbivore—An animal that eats plants (herbivorous).

Omnivore—An animal that eats plants or animals (omnivorous).

Filter feeder—An omnivore that strains pieces of food in the water through structures in and around its mouth, or by creating a structure that will catch the food. For instance, the black fly larva has a structure called a fan that traps the food, which in turn is cleaned off into its mouth. The caddis fly spins a net, which catches the food; it then consumes the net and all.

Scavenger—Eats dead and decaying things.

Breathing—Insects do not have lungs. A network of small tubes carries oxygen through their bodies. The oxygen enters their bodies through openings on the body surface, but aquatic insects would flood their body if they breathed through these openings. Instead they have developed several different methods of obtaining oxygen:

Breathing tubes extend from the insect's body to the surface of the water, where they take in oxygen from the air.

Air bubbles, which can be seen as a shiny area on the underside of the insect's abdomen or trailing behind the insect, are carried under water.

Gills, a special structure on the insect's body, can absorb dissolved oxygen in the water.

Oxygen is sometimes absorbed across the surface of the insect's body.

A *spiracle*—a breathing orifice or specialized external opening—leads to the insect's tracheal tubes.

INSECTS THAT DEVELOP FROM LARVA do not look anything like the adult insect and u dergo complete metamorphosis, changing their appearance. They develop from eggs laid by		
Immature / Adult Name	**Food of Larva**	**Home of Larva**
Caddis fly (stick bait) / Caddis fly	Most—Scavenger & filter feeder	Case made of twigs, leaves, sand, or small pebbles; a few species do not build cases.
Water penny / Beetle	Algae on rocks—herbivore	Cold, moving water
Diving beetle larva (represents 40% of aquatic beetle larva) / Water tiger	Predaceous—mouthparts puncture prey and suck out fluids	Still freshwater
Cranefly larva / Cranefly (looks like a large mosquitoe!)	Omnivore	Stream & pond bottoms
Blackfly larva (almost 3500 flies begin as aquatic larva) / Blackfly	Omnivore by filter feeding	On rocks in fast-moving sections of creeks
Whirligig larva / Whirligig beetle	Predator or scavenger	Still water

ult in or near the water. While in the larval stage, they live and feed underwater. The adult form the insect does not always live in the water but may stay near the water to eat and mate.

eathing	Movement Observed	ID of Nymph
rough body surface	Pulls head into case!	6 hooked legs on upper $\frac{1}{3}$ of body
lls on underside of body hind 3rd set of legs	Moves slowly, grazing underneath rocks	Round, flat, and streamlined—protects it from being washed away—looks like a raised bump from the side
rough body surface	Diving	Strong jaws, body $\frac{1}{4}$" to 3", narrow abdomen, 3 pairs of legs
iracles, or breathing holes end of abdomen—through mosphere	Buries head in 1st body segment	Body thick and long—caterpillar-like
rough body surface	Anchors to rocks with small hooks at end of abdomen. Silk helps to attach larva and pull itself back in if knocked off.	Black head; opposite end wider
r from atmosphere	Congregate in groups, on surface of the water, spinning around each other like bumper cars.	Carries air bubble so it can remain underwater. Has two pairs of eyes—one set looks up to see surface prey; other looks down to see prey

INSECTS THAT DEVELOP FROM A NYMPH IN WATER AND LEAVE WATER AS ADULT
The nymph somewhat resembles the adult more than the larva does, and you can more eas
predict what the adult will look like by looking at a nymph. Notice in the drawings that they ha

Immature / Adult Name	Food of Nymph	Home of Nymph
Mayfly nymph / Mayfly	Algae on rocks; some scavengers	Fresh, running water; ponds and lakes. Under rocks, burrowing in the silt, or swimmin
Damselfly nymph / Damselfly	Predator	Around pond plants; along stream edges
Dragonfly nymph / Dragonfly	Predator	Around pond plants; along stream edges
Stonefly nymph / Stonefly	Predator or herbivore	Streams with cool, fast water—needs high oxygen level

beginnings of small wings, called wing pads, and fully developed legs. They grow into adults ough a process called incomplete metamorphosis. They also develop from eggs laid in or near water.

eathing	Movement Observed	ID of Nymph
s—waved to create current ncrease amount of dis- ved oxygen	Lies flat against rocks, crawls in cracks	Usually 3 long tails; look for gills alongside of abdomen
eaflike gills at end of abdomen		No gills alongside abdomen
s in internal body chamber	Pumps water into abdominal chamber, then forces it out, propelling it forward	Stout body, grasping jaw, large eyes
rough surface of skin or gills der legs	Lies flat against rocks, crawls in cracks—active throughout winter	2 leaflike tails; no gills down side of abdomen; 2 sets of wingpads

INSECTS THAT REMAIN IN THE WATER AS ADULTS		
Immature & Adult Name	**Food of Nymph**	**Home of Nymph**
Water strider	Predator	Surface of ponds or still wat
Water scorpion	Predator	Under surface of still water
Backswimmer	Predator	Ponds or still water
Giant water bug	Predator—adult injects enzymes that dissolve internal body parts of prey, which they suck out.	Ponds or still water
Water Boatman	Omnivore or scavenger	Ponds or still water

eathing	Movement Observed	ID of Nymph
m atmosphere through racles	Moves on water surface; feet have a waxlike, water-repellent surface area.	Lives on water's surface; long legs like a spider
athing tube that barely ends above water surface	Little movement—hangs below water surface	Appears as stick beneath the water; long and slender
m atmosphere; carries air bble from water's surface	Swims on back	Oblong; light color above, dark beneath to avoid predators
eathing tubes extending to ter's surface from backside	Up to 3" long	Offspring pale yellow a few hours after birth, then begins to darken
m atmosphere—carries air bble from water's surface	Swimming hairs that help legs act as paddles	Long, oarlike legs, with long hairs

Insect Trivia

- Mayfly adults exist only to mate and then die, living just a few hours. They do not even eat, as they have no moving mouthparts.
- Whirligig beetles have two pairs of eyes—one pair above the water, and one pair below.
- An adult whirligig beetle, moving at a speed of three feet per second, can propel itself 1,000 times its own body length across the water's surface.
- Water striders sense the vibrations of the water through their feet to find their prey.
- Stonefly nymphs can change into adults any time of the year, even in winter.
- Dragonflies have been around since the Carboniferous Period 300 million years ago. Dragonflies today have a maximum wingspan of four inches; those of the Carboniferous Period had wingspans of three feet.
- Adult dragonflies can fly through the air in sudden bursts of speed up to 75 miles per hour.
- Giant water bugs can eat frogs and other prey several times their own size after injecting digestive enzymes into the bodies of their victims. Their bite to a human toe is painful but not deadly.

ACTIVITY A Water Ramble

To discover firsthand who and what lives beneath the currents, you need to personally become a part of the water. Find shallow areas to explore where the water moves slowly and you can see nearly every rock on the bottom. Please do not venture out in fast-moving water much past your ankles to mid-calf, and stay away from flooded rivers or streams. For added safety, wear life vests when exploring waterways.

Wade into a creek or stream slowly, trying to make as few waves and ripples as possible. The more you disturb the water, the less you will be able to see. To observe more, stop frequently and scan the area around you. Your movement works against the constant motion of the water, so you will have to try to stand as still as possible.

Ankle-deep water provides a much better view of the bottom of the creek, where small organisms can be gently touched and then returned to their homes.

It is important to handle aquatic organisms carefully, if at all, and make sure they remain wet.

Crayfish will sit in little holes and under rocks and wait for dinner to come by. Small snails may hang on to the larger rocks, and water striders may dart across the surface of the water. Check the bottoms of rocks for small larvae hanging on. Refer to the information prior to this activity for a more in-depth look at all of the fascinating creatures you might discover in the water.

ACTIVITY What Lies Beneath

- *Tube-shaped, waterproof object*
- *Piece of clear cellophane*
- *Rubber band*

When walking by a creek or pond, you can easily see what happens on its surface: the rippling waters of the creek, water striders skimming along the top, and the occasional splash of a fish. But what goes on underneath? For a fun way to zoom in on the deeper realms, you can make an underwater scope. You'll feel just like the captain of a submarine as you peer through your scope in search of hidden life in the waters below.

To make an underwater scope, find a waterproof, tube-shaped object. A can works well, but don't get one with sharp edges. Another good choice would be some type of plastic pipe with a diameter of three to five inches, available at a hardware or home-improvement store. The longer the tube, the better, as the length will enable you to look deeper below the surface of the water.

Remove the top and bottom (if present) of your object so your tube remains open at both ends. Stretch a piece of clear cellophane over one end and secure it tightly with a rubber band so the tube does not fill up with water. When you place it under water, the cellophane will make the images you observe much sharper and clearer.

Take the completed scope to a pond, creek, or stream. Kneel down on the bank or lie on your stomach, and put the scope in the water, taking care not to fall in. When observing near water, it is always a good idea to have a companion with you to share in the excitement and also to hold your feet!

Incredible new worlds will reveal themselves as you have the opportunity to see many living things scurrying to and fro beneath the water. Take your scope with you on an ankle-deep water ramble, so you can also explore the life in the center of the creek.

Further Reading

Amphibians and Reptiles of the Carolinas and Virginia by Bernard S. Martof

Antony Van Leeuwenhoek and His Little Animals by Clifford Dobell

Explore the World Using Protozoa by Roger O. Anderson and Marvin Druger, eds.

Free Living Freshwater Protozoa: A Color Guide by David J. Patterson

Guide to Microlife by Kenneth G. Raines and Bruce J. Russell

A Guide to the Study of Fresh-Water Biology by James G. Needham

The National Audubon Society Field Guide to North American Reptiles and Amphibians

Peterson Field Guide Series: Reptiles and Amphibians of Eastern and Central North America by Roger Connant and Joseph T. Collins

Pond Life by George K. Reid

Using the Microscope: A Guide for Naturalists by Eric V. Grave

Getting Acquainted with Plants

Boasting many diverse habitats at varying elevations, the Southern Appalachian Mountains provide a multitude of ecosystems for different plant species to survive, making it the premier region of the United States for the study of botany and plant ecology. Learning the habitat requirements for each plant species can help you begin your study of plants.

Soil types change from ridge to valley, providing nourishment for different kinds of plants. Some plants that grow at lower elevations could not possibly survive in the highlands. Certain species prefer dry ridges, while others will grow only in or near creeks, where it is wet. Many of the endangered plants of the Southern Appalachians live on isolated mountain peaks because the higher ranges are generally not close enough to each other to allow seed or pollen to pass between them.

Your understanding and ability to identify plants and their uses, as well as your knowledge of their place in our environment will grow with experience and exposure. Learning the habitat needs of plant species will enhance your enjoyment and understanding of what grows around you. It could take a lifetime to know all of the plants, or even 75% of the plants growing in the mountains, but your appreciation and interest may kindle a fancy that will keep you searching for more information. If you find that you enjoy learning about plants, you might end up studying botany as a profession or spending time in the field with fellow naturalists and botanists.

The greener portions of our earth have an amazing ability to adapt and survive in changing environmental conditions. Notice these aspects of plants in addition to how people and other creatures depend on and use them. Strive to enjoy and appreciate the beauty and uniqueness of our mountain flora. Take the time to view them as a whole, noticing similarities and differences. Observe the colors, shapes, and variance of blooms.

Do not approach the activities in this chapter fearing that you need to know more plant names. Your knowledge and botanical vocabulary will grow with interest and time, enhancing your ability to relate experiences and share plant finds. Remember, prior to naming and classifying plants, people were intrigued by the individual characteristics of our native flora.

In order for a species to thrive, it needs to reproduce. Each plant has its own special seeds that differ in appearance, in the times they mature, and in how they travel, or disperse, across the landscape. Since plants do not move about as animals do, they must use their seeds to enable their offspring to relocate. Some plants will colonize an area by spreading along the ground, while others will drop seeds directly onto the ground below the parent plant. Other seeds can travel incredible distances by blowing with the wind, attaching to the fur of animals, or being eaten by animals and dropped in their scat.

A relatively heavy seed, such as a bean or a kernel of corn, drops to the ground in the vicinity of the plant that produced it. A sticky seed, such as one from a rhododendron, readily hangs on to a passing animal, which will carry it on its body to a new home. Other seeds have spines, hooks, and various barbs, resulting in a similar method of dispersal.

Exploring the plant life emerging on the top of Roan Mountain

Of course, all of this moving around has to come to an end if the plant is to produce more of its kind. The seed eventually works its way into the soil, and each spring a miracle occurs beneath our feet as the seed awakens from a winter's rest. One by one, tiny dots of green poke forth from the ground, beginning a new season of growth, reproduction, and color.

Yet before this new life becomes obvious to us, a lot has already happened beneath the earth's surface. The seed has cracked open, sending its roots into the ground to anchor the plant and begin providing fresh nourishment and water. Prior to this time, the seed survived on food stored within its seed coat. The warming soil, moisture from the spring rains and melting snow, and the lengthening days all act as signals to the dormant seeds. Conditions become favorable for successful growth, enabling the multitude of seeds produced the previous fall to begin the development process.

Rooting Around

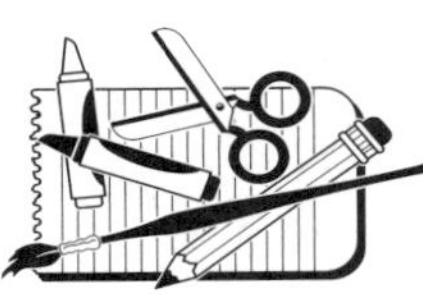

- *A glass*
- *Piece of blotting paper or thick paper towel*
- *Water*
- *Seeds (a regular garden bean seed works very well, as it is large and easy to view)*

Roots are amazing and fascinating to observe. The beautiful plants we see above the ground could not exist without a good, strong root structure. This activity will help you view what you usually cannot see as the roots of a new plant dig their way into the soil.

Cut your blotting paper to a size that will lay flush against the inside curve of the glass. Fill the glass with water and let it sit just long enough for the paper to become saturated. Then pour out the remaining water, leaving a little in the bottom to keep the paper damp. Slide your seeds down between the paper and the glass so you can watch what happens to them from the outside of the glass. This placement will provide a safe spot for the seed to grow undisturbed.

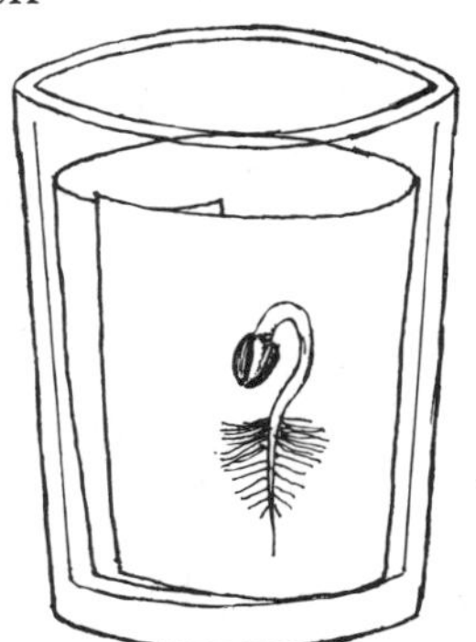

Keeping a record of the next week's accomplishments will be exciting, for every day the seeds will slowly change as you observe their germination right before your eyes. Each day, take a few minutes to record and sketch your observations in your notebook or journal:

- Record the date and time you "planted" the seeds.

- Record the date and time you first noticed the seeds cracked open. Each day, take a small ruler and measure how much longer the roots and stem have grown.
- Notice the smaller, fibrous roots that begin to branch out. What do they remind you of? Do they resemble other things you have seen before?
- Do the roots grow up or down? If they started by growing up, what did they do as they grew longer?

After the roots outgrow their temporary home, find a permanent location to plant the seeds where you can watch them grow to maturity and produce even more seeds for next year. As each plant becomes larger and larger, remember how it began and imagine the size and intricacy of the roots now growing below the ground, sustaining its life.

ACTIVITY Amazing Travelers: Seed Dispersal

- *An old sock*
- *A roll of masking tape, or Velcro*

This activity takes a closer look at seeds that attach to moving objects. The moving object is usually an animal or a person, but anything passing by is fair game. Barbs, hooks, and protrusions help the seeds hang on.

A seed that matured on one side of a mountain's ridge may attach to the coat of a fox and end up several miles away before it falls off and returns to the ground. More than likely, if you have walked through a field or through the woods, you have found seeds attached to your clothing.

This activity involves the use of "seed catchers" to help gather even more seeds on an outdoor walk. To equip yourself for seed collection, you may put one or two old socks on over your shoes, or you could wrap your shoes in masking tape with the sticky side out, or you could attach strips of Velcro to the bottoms of or around your shoes. When you get wrapped up and ready to go, take a walk through an area rich in a variety of plants that are going to seed.

When you feel relatively prickly and seed coated, find a place to sit down and check out the assorted seeds you have collected. Notice the protrusions on the seeds that help them to attach to passing creatures. This is a great time to pull out your journal and sketch what you observe.

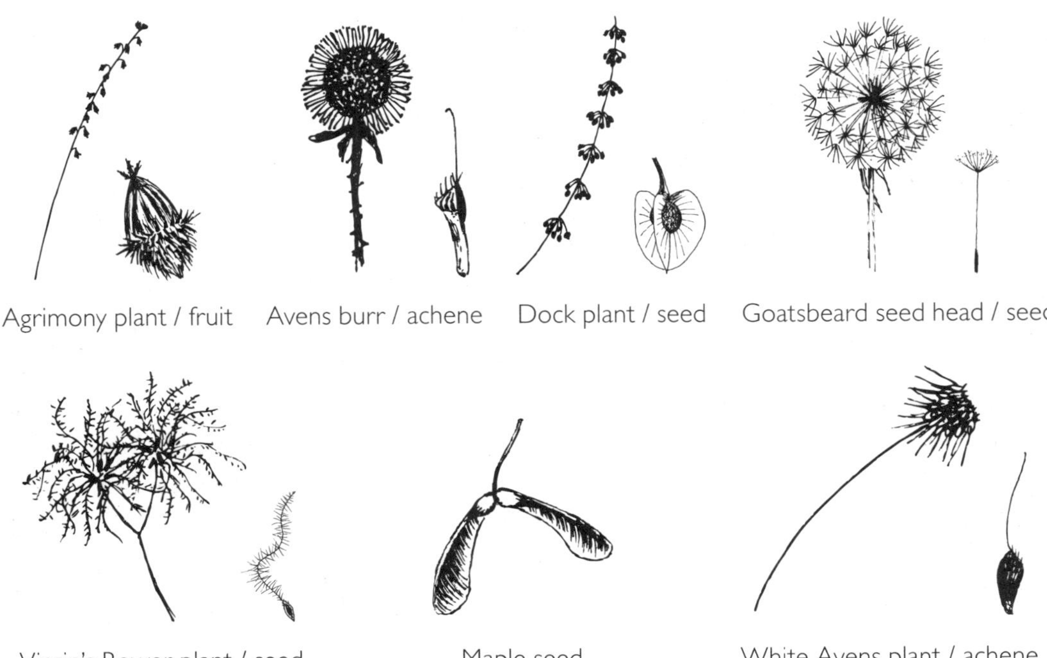

Agrimony plant / fruit   Avens burr / achene   Dock plant / seed   Goatsbeard seed head / seed

Virgin's Bower plant / seed   Maple seed   White Avens plant / achene

As you notice plants germinating in the spring, remember that the seed each plant grows from may have ventured many a mile to get to its new location and take root. Whether it attached itself to something, blew in the wind, or passed through a critter's digestive tract, the process of seed dispersal is indisputably remarkable.

NATURE'S COLOR SHOW: TEACHING WILDFLOWERS TO ALL AGES

One of my favorite quotes comes from Ralph Waldo Emerson, who wrote in one of his poems, "The Earth laughs in flowers." Such appropriate and colorful words certainly describe the emergence of the many wildflowers that bloom from spring to fall.

With the approach of spring each year comes the thrill of seeing life renewed. Even when the snow still covers the ground, green shoots begin to reach toward the sun. With this emergence comes nature's promise that another beautiful season of color and change is about to begin.

Early in the season, the young wildflowers need the warmth of the sunlight to begin growing. By the time the trees have leafed out, these woodland beauties have completed their blooming cycle and are setting seed to assure the continuance of their kind. Fortunately, this cycle does not mark the end of the season for Appalachian wildflowers. Around 3,000 feet in elevation, spring arrives in late March and early April; yet the spring and summer cycle will not begin on the 6,000-foot mountains until late May and June. Throughout spring, summer, and fall, different wildflowers come into bloom at all elevations, enabling their study throughout the growing season.

The large-flowered trillium blooms early in the season, usually in the forest or on the forest edges. It would be extremely unusual to find one in flower in the middle of June. Many types of wildflowers grow only on top of the highest mountains, over 5,000 feet, in open bald situations where no trees grow. These plants would never be seen at the lower elevations or growing deep within the forest. As you discover the particular needs of individual plants, it will become easier to identify them in their environment.

The activities that follow will enhance your ability to observe both the obvious and subtle details of wildflowers. This knowledge will make it easier to identify the different species and inspire an interest in learning more about the unique attributes of plants.

ACTIVITY Beginning with Pictures

Prepare a selection of slides, photographs, or digital images that provide a good example of the different colors and shapes of wildflowers. Include a variety of plants that come into bloom throughout the seasons. You might also consider contacting a local park, forester, or wildlife agency, all of which usually have personnel available to present programs on these subjects. Your local library is another possible source for wildflower images.

If you use slides or PowerPoint, set the projector on automatic so your images will change at the same interval. Set an atmosphere by explaining to the viewers that they are about to "take a walk in the woods" from their seats. Encourage them to sit back, relax, and watch carefully.

Following the presentation, ask the viewers to write specifically about what they have observed. What catches the eye of one person may not even be noticed by another.

Discuss with the group their different observations; repeat portions of the slide show, searching for especially interesting points to revisit after the discussion. Share a little information about the wildflowers, but not so much that the subject becomes overwhelming.

ACTIVITY Build a Flower

- *Paper (preferably colored)*
- *Scissors*

In preparation, cut out flower petal sets that represent at least three distinctly different types of wildflowers. A wildflower identification guide can help you choose shapes.

Divide everyone into small groups, based on the number of participants. Each team is to re-create flowers that accurately represent each variety's true shape, with the correct number of petals. After the team agrees on its final product, have each group compare their results to pictures that will show them the right answer.

Use this activity to start a discussion on the shapes of flowers. It is also fun to compare everyone's newly created flower and note the variety of shapes.

ACTIVITY Matching Shapes

- *Paper (preferably colored)*
- *Scissors*

This activity is designed to teach your eye to recognize differences in shape. Begin by cutting out the completed basic shapes of our Appalachian wildflowers as shown on the next page, then give each person participating a set of these shapes. Show him or her a picture or slide of a wildflower and ask each person to respond by holding up the correct shape. If you are using this activity to teach a group (a class, scouts, enrichment, etc.) or are sharing with your children, you will be able to easily monitor their ability to distinguish between the shapes of wildflowers. If working with more than one person, try presenting this activity either as a competition, by dividing into teams, or as a cooperative project.

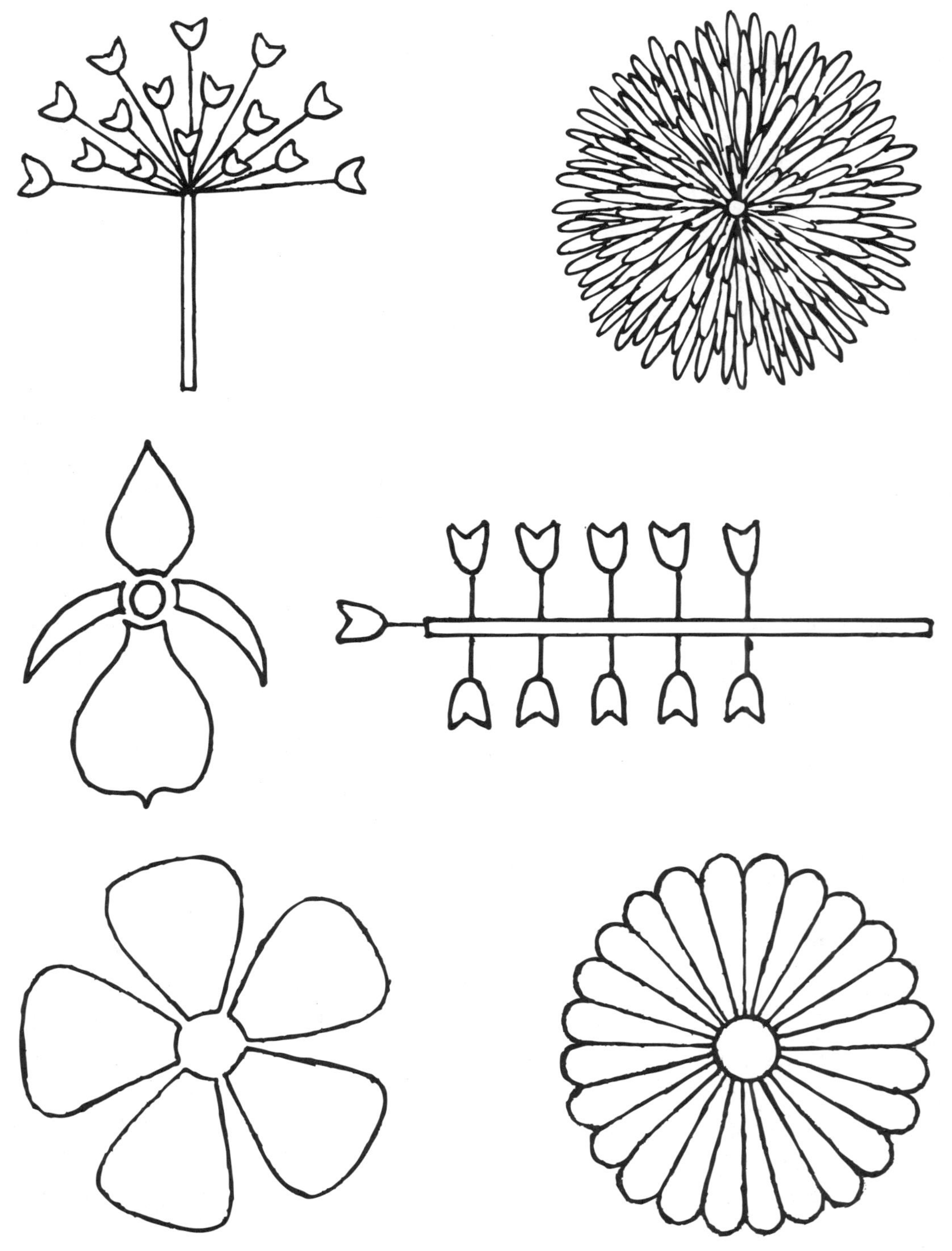

A second approach to Matching Shapes is to head out into the woods and fields with flower shapes in hand. It enthralls young people to find something new. Discovering for the first time that flowers have distinctively different shapes creates a real sense of excitement. The simple paper cutouts become more meaningful when you compare them to a living thing.

ACTIVITY Hands-On Flowers

- *Colored pipe cleaners*

This creative art project lends itself well to children, but all ages will enjoy the imaginative activity. Participants create their own flowers from colored pipe cleaners, paying special attention to the shapes of flowers that you have discussed.

Nature's Runways: Using Colors and Patterns to Attract Pollinators

Did you ever wonder why flowers possess so many beautiful colors, patterns, spots, stripes, and vivid centers? Try to imagine yourself as a bee or pollinating insect, looking for a flower. Nature's addition of eye-catching petals, or runways—like the painted trillium shown on the left—aids the insect in its search for a landing pad in a massive field of plant life, enabling pollination to take place.

ACTIVITY Landing Pad Observations

This fun activity teaches how to observe the intricate details of a flower. Browse through a selection of books, slides, or photographs for examples of flowers with especially eye-catching runways or color patterns. Some flowers, such as rhododendrons and orchids, have one petal that is different from all the rest; the odd petal might have spots or stripes, while the others are plain. Other flowers, such as a lily, have spots on the insides of each petal all around the center of the flower.

After becoming familiar with these differences, follow up with an outdoor field trip to look for runways in the natural world. You will never look at a flower the same way. The next time you notice a bee or an insect on a flower, you will most likely think about the pattern that attracted it to the flower in the first place!

Using Field Guides

The field guide is a remarkable tool to help identify a particular organism. A guide can baffle and confuse you if you are not familiar with its arrangement, but after a little practice, your favorite field guide will become your constant companion.

Many field guides are available on the market. Some are keyed by color, some by shape, some by taxonomic group. If you present these activities to a group or a class, have several different guides available for everyone to see, and spend some time explaining how to use them. Each book will have an explanation in the front to help you.

Some wildflower books divide flowers into groups depending on their color, and some divide them according to the number of petals and related structures. Most beginners prefer guides that start with the flower color, as they generally notice color first. Many wonderful books for beginners offer great practice without being as overwhelming as the more comprehensive guides. However, beginner's guides may not describe as many species as their more complex counterparts; thus, you may try to identify something that is not in the book at all. Keep this in mind as you read these guides so you don't become confused searching for something that is not there.

The following activities will help you get started using a field guide. The more you read and practice in the field, the more comfortable you will become with it.

ACTIVITY What's in a Name?

- *Wildflowers or their images in field guides, or photographs*

Remembering names of wildflowers can be quite exasperating and sometimes discouraging to the beginning wildflower enthusiast. Learning the names of what you observe is rewarding and fulfilling, but as you begin studying wildflowers, try not to put too much emphasis on names. You don't want the process to be a frustrating. If you focus on the purpose, beauty, and appreciation of the wildflowers of your region, the names will come in time.

Where do taxonomic names come from? Many are dedicated to the person who discovered the plant, like the *Abies fraseri*, or Fraser fir, discovered by John Fraser, or the *Lilium grayi*, or Gray's Lily, discovered by Asa Gray. Others denote appearance, like the trillium (3 leaves, 3 petals, 3 sepals), cinquefoil (5 leaves), three-birds orchid (3 birdlike flowers on each stem), and lady's slipper (looks like a slipper or shoe). Some refer to their uses, such as liverwort (cures ailments of the liver) or toothwort (good for toothache)

Ultimately, a name given to a person, place, or thing is a communication tool. When you refer to something or someone by name, those engaged in the conversation visualize the same entity. As you learn the names of the wildflowers, you can more easily communicate your observations with friends and family. You may also choose to record in your journal what you see.

The names of our Appalachian wildflowers were all given to the plants at some time in the past by botanists and biologists. This activity gives you the opportunity to name plants as though you are the discoverer honored with naming a new find!

Choose flowers while on a hike, or use slides, photographs, and field guides. For each plant, pretend you have found it for the first time. Ask each participant to give it a name and explain their choice. Keep track of the correct names of the flowers to compare notes at the end of the session, or share some of the new names while you are still looking at the plant.

Participants often will choose plant names comparable to the names in use today. The similarities and differences will be fun to share and help you look even closer at the flowers you are naming.

ACTIVITY Practicing with Field Guides

- *Field guides*
- *Photographs, slides, or pictures of wildflowers*
- *Flower shapes on page 76*

The following exercises are easy to administer in an indoor setting. When working with individuals, present the ideas without including the team concept.

I. Divide the group into teams. Give each team one of the flower shapes used in the Matching Shapes activity on page 75. Using the field guide, each team is to find two flowers that match the shape given to them. Have them write down the common and taxonomic name and an interesting fact about the wildflowers they have chosen.

II. Find a few easily reproducible wildflower photographs and make copies for each team. Try to find an example of each flower shape or color, depending on whether your guide is keyed to shape or color. Give each team one or more pictures and ask them to identify the flowers by using the field guide.

III. As the group becomes more confident in using their field guides, plan a more competitive game that will require some fast thinking. Prepare a selection of slides or photographs of wildflowers, or choose pictures from magazines. Showing one flower at a time, ask the teams to work together quickly, but accurately, to be first to identify the wildflower. Remind them that their goal is to find the correct answer, not merely be first.

Preservation/Appreciation/Conservation

When you teach about wildflowers, emphasize aesthetics, conservation ethics involved in nature study, and the need for preservation. A large number of wildflowers are illegally gathered annually for various reasons, and many are now in danger due to over-collecting. The great white trillium, for example, is a once-widespread mountain wildflower whose numbers have significantly decreased due to collection.

A plant will flower and subsequently set seed to reproduce. If picked too early, a flower's reproductive cycle comes to an abrupt stop. You can help preserve wildflower populations by observing them with your eyes and leaving them alone to complete their purpose.

TREE TALK

Appalachian forests hold many varieties of trees, grouped into different forest types. The most common distinction seen between forests is whether they are comprised of deciduous or evergreen trees. Deciduous trees lose their leaves in the wintertime, creating intricate and interesting silhouettes against the backdrop of the sky. Evergreen forests exist at many elevations, with different species gracing various ridges and hollows. Evergreen trees keep their green cast and hold the bulk of their needles all year. As they grow and flourish from season to season, they provide shelter and food to the inhabitants who live in, around, and beneath their cover.

In the early 1990s, a strong hurricane system made it into the Southern Appalachians. As its impending advent was forecast, few residents realized the power the winds of such a storm could produce and how it would affect the strong trees of the mountains. On the morning of its expected arrival, folks were readying for a typical day, as if they had no concept of what would soon take place.

Around 7:00 A.M. that morning, I stood out on the high porch of my house, which sat surrounded on all four sides by towering hemlocks, pines, and a few interspersed hardwoods. To view the treetops, you had to turn your head straight up to the sky, risking a bit of a crick in your neck. The wind was gentle then, and I marveled at the seemingly orchestrated swaying of the trees. They softly bent as the wind blew, ensuring me that they would not snap like toothpicks when put under stress.

As I watched, the show began to change quickly and dramatically. The wind increased, lashing the trees from left to right with great speed and force. I could hear the storm rushing and roaring through the valleys and over the ridges as it moved into the area in a fury.

At such times it becomes evident that what has taken so many years to create can easily be destroyed. Similar scenes often occur in the wintertime, when heavy, wet snows weigh down limbs and branches until they finally give in to a strength greater than their own. Not only has the climate made survival hard on the trees of the mountains, so have the folks who have settled around them.

Different species of trees have served us well through time. We harvest some of them for lumber to build houses, and we burn logs for warmth. Some trees provide remedies and medicines, and we can extract colors from others to dye fabrics. Trees are important to us economically and aesthetically, yet, at times, people have overused and abused them. Prior to the constant clear-cuts of the 1800s and early 1900s, the southeastern forests boasted many trees well over 100 years old. As people continually cleared the land for pasture and agriculture, the magnificent towering giants began to disappear.

In addition, disease sometimes wiped out entire populations of a particular species. The American chestnut blight, probably one of the most well-known diseases, pushed a common species nearly to extinction. I frequently reflect on how fortunate I have been in getting to know individuals who lived during the days the American chestnut flourished in Appalachian forests. Many have told me remarkable tales of trying to walk through the woods in the autumn when the chestnuts had fallen in incredible numbers. A relaxing hike would sometimes become a lesson in agility, as folks tried not to fall in a sea of round, hard-shelled nuts rolling beneath their feet.

Whenever I hear the phrase "if trees could talk," the thought sets my mind wandering. For before their final fall, trees begin their lives as tiny seedlings, sometimes surviving predators and disease. As the world goes on around them, they stand firmly rooted in one spot, frequently growing for hundreds of years. Unlike an animal, they cannot run or search for water or nourishment; they begin, live, and end in a place where they must face whatever happens, good or bad.

Today, stands of virgin timber are rare, but on occasion you can find a stump or a log incorporated into a building, or possibly a cross section preserved in a museum. Old photographs sometimes show groups of people holding hands around exceptionally large trees, which helps us visualize just how large these trees once were before so many were logged.

A true example of combined strength and fragility, a tree, as with all living things, is subject to the negative and positive changes of our earth. Yet it offers us a feeling of stability, a place we can return to and depend on. A favorite tree that we have visited time and again, feeling comfort beneath its branches and shade, may give us fond memories.

As an interesting component of our ecosystem, trees have rightly earned the credit of being protectors, providers of shelter, food producers, and air enhancers. No one can deny the value and importance of a living thing that can do all of the following:

- Trees produce oxygen while using up carbon dioxide.
- Trees clean the air by trapping dust, pollen, and ash. The foliage acts as a filter to clean smog and small particles from the air.
- Trees can absorb and deflect sound waves, thereby reducing noise levels.
- A tree's decomposing leaves and needles give nutrients back to the earth.
- A tree's roots help hold the soil in place, preventing erosion. The roots and can-

opy lessen flooding problems by allowing water to percolate into the ground and not run off the surface of the soil. Slowing runoff also helps to replenish groundwater supplies and keep harmful pollutants from rushing into our waterways.

- Trees can reduce home heating and cooling costs by acting as a windbreak, providing shade in summer, and insulating your home if properly placed in your yard.
- A tree's beauty and aesthetics add to property values and promote positive attitudes by enhancing recreational settings for hiking, relaxing, or playing.
- Trees act as a home to many wild things, providing us contact with nature.

ACTIVITY Celebrating Birthdays

- *An increment borer, if available, or a cross section of a tree*

While it is satisfying to learn a tree's name, it's even more exciting to discover its importance and its contributions. Each season, every tree species strives to produce a crop of seeds or cones. Of utmost importance, reproduction ensures the survival of a species. Seeds also provide a nourishing food source that helps the forest wildlife endure the cold winter months ahead.

Discovering how many birthdays a tree has experienced can be quite an eye-opener. It can instill a great appreciation in you when you realize just how much time has passed as each tree grows to its present state. Just imagine the number of seasons a particular tree has lived through as it stands firmly in place, surviving a wide variety of conditions.

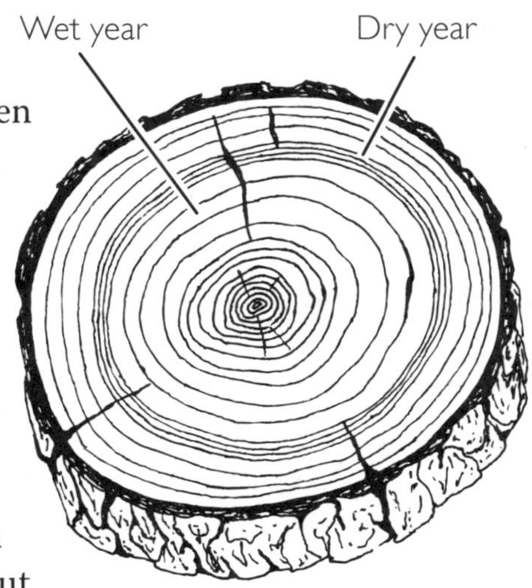

To determine the approximate age of a tree, take a core sample using an instrument called an increment borer, which enables you to count the tree's rings without hurting the tree. Drill the borer into the tree and extract a piece of wood the size of a drinking straw. Of course, increment borers are not generally available in everyone's home, so a stump or a cross section of a tree will give you a different way to visualize a tree's history.

You can discern a wealth of information about the life of a tree and the climate in which it grew by looking at the tree rings. As you look at the cross section, you will see a series of rings, one encircling the other, starting in the center. Get your eyes ready to focus, so you can begin at the exact center, and count the number of rings across the surface of the tree stump. Each ring represents one year or season of growth. The distance between the rings also provides additional information. A big space between two rings signifies a wetter, more productive growing season, while rings lying close together indicate dryer years not hospitable to growth.

The giant Sequoias of our western states are said to have the capability to live up to 5,000 years! The American Museum of Natural History in New York has on exhibit a Sequoia measuring 16½ feet in diameter. Its tree rings date it as 1,341 years old, just a "child" when it died.

An Honorable Gathering

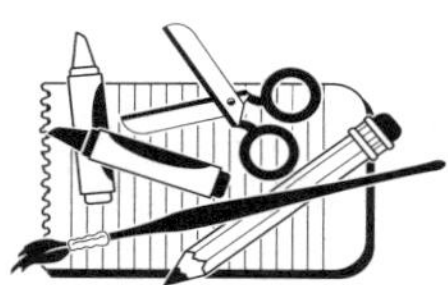

- *Picnic lunches*
- *Small pieces of paper (approximately 3" x 5")*
- *Pencils*
- *Container to hold slips of folded paper*

Host a birthday party for your favorite tree! Maybe there is one in your front yard, in the woods near your home, or possibly at school. Wherever it may be, find that special tree where personal memories have grown—a tree you would like to honor.

Invite your friends and plan a picnic lunch and tree roast. (No, you're not going to cook the tree!) Before you gather around the tree for the celebration, preplan the roast by writing down some story ideas on pieces of paper and placing them in a container. Everyone can draw an idea out of the container and create their own rendition of the tree's life thus far. Some ideas include:

- Tell the story of this tree's birthday.
- What was it like growing up in America?
- Did the tree ever live out here alone? If so, what was life like?
- Describe some of the hardships the tree might have faced (bad weather, insects, human activity, animals, birds).
- Describe positive things that might have happened around the tree.

As the official tree roast begins, each person will lead into his story by saying, "If this tree could talk. . . ." For instance, in starting the story of the tree's birthday, one might begin by saying, "If this tree could talk, it would be able to tell us about the day in which it first sprouted in this very spot!" If you pick "growing up in America" for a subject, you might start off with, "If this tree could talk, if would have many stories to tell about how things have changed here over the years."

Use these examples to get you started, but add your own fun and creative ideas to the mix. As the roast progresses, a beautiful picture of the possible life of just one tree on our huge planet will be painted by the imaginations of you and your friends. After the storytelling, have everyone join hands, circle around the tree, and thank it for being there and making your life and our world a better place!

ACTIVITY The Trees in My World: Mapping

- *A compass*
- *Several sheets of legal size paper (8½ x 14)*
- *A clipboard*
- *Pencil*

As a follow-up to your favorite tree's birthday party, continue by discovering all of the trees that make up a part of your own world. Choose a familiar area that is part of your daily life. You might pick your own yard, your schoolyard, or a favorite place in your neighborhood.

Begin by walking and thinking about the area you have chosen. Mapping a huge forest would be a little complicated, so try to find a spot with several trees, but not too many! As you wander around your "world," notice the following:

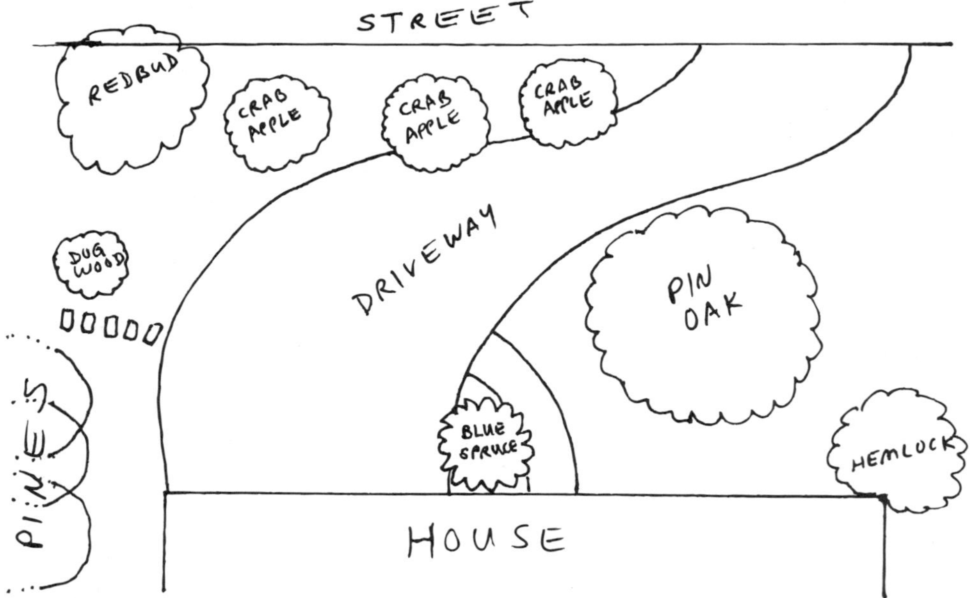

- How many trees are here?
- Where are they growing in relation to each other (spacing)?
- How big are they?
- Do they look like the same kind of tree, or are different species present?
- Is there obvious wildlife present?
- Have people altered the landscape around the trees (with playground equipment, birdhouses, bathhouses, mowed grass, a house or building, etc.)?

Now get your clipboard, paper, and pencil to begin mapping the area that makes up your world of trees. The edges of the paper will reflect the boundaries of the area you have chosen. First, make a light "X" on the paper at each spot where a tree grows. After all of the "X's" are marked, look at your paper again and make sure the spacing is relatively accurate and that you have left room to include everything.

Erase each "X," one at a time, and replace it with a number. The separate notes you make on each tree will correspond with the number on your map. On a second sheet of paper, create columns across the top with the following headings:

Column 1—Tree Number

Column 2—Deciduous or Evergreen?

Column 3—Opposite or Alternate Branches?

Column 4—Bark Texture
Column 5—Seeds Present? (If so, sketch their appearance.)
Column 6—Leaf Shape

Now start with the first tree number and fill in your columns. After you have answered all the questions for each tree, you will have what you need to identify the trees in your world.

Libraries and bookstores have many books available to help you identify your trees. A few are suggested at the end of this chapter.

ACTIVITY Toothpick Silhouettes

- *Construction paper or poster board*
- *Toothpicks*
- *Craft glue*

No two trees are identical in shape or silhouette, giving each a unique character. Trees of the same species will have a similar growth pattern, but their skyward branching always lends each its own personality.

Winter is the ideal time to conduct this activity, when all the leaves have fallen from the trees, making their silhouettes more noticeable and pronounced. Begin by taking the time to observe many trees in your area, noticing whether the branches all point to the sky, or if some turn back to the ground. Is the tree tall and slender, or round as a marshmallow? Does the tree have so many tiny branches that it seems thick and dense, or are there spaces between branches, giving it an airy effect? These and many other questions will come to mind as you look at different species of trees.

After taking adequate time to look around, take your toothpicks and begin arranging them on the paper and re-create the silhouette of the tree that appeals to you the most. You may break or cut your toothpicks to make shorter branches. When you have laid the toothpicks out in a pattern that you like, glue them to the paper. Be sure to allow plenty of drying time before trying to move it around.

When you have finished your first tree, don't stop there! When time allows, continue making new "toothpick" drawings of different shapes that you are observing in the world around you.

ACTIVITY Quite a Roof!

- *A LARGE ball of string*
- *Yardstick*

On a hot summer's day, the shade of a large tree is a welcome sight. The place where the shade meets the sunshine marks the edge of the tree's canopy. The branches of the tree spread out, shading the ground, creating a semi-shelter that protects what is under it from the elements, keeping you a little drier in the rain and cooler in the heat of the sun.

Because the ground is drier beneath the shady area, the roots of the tree must extend, at least, to the edge of the canopy to gather water. With the absence of sunlight beneath the shade of the tree, it is unlikely that many plants will germinate and grow there. As a result, the tree is left with an area that will nourish it and it alone.

To determine how far the canopy of the tree spreads on either side of the trunk, get a partner and a large ball of string. One person will hold the string up against the base of the trunk, next to the ground. The second will walk out to the edge of the shade and cut the string at that point. Take a yardstick and measure the length of the string. If you multiply measurement by two, you will know the diameter of ground space shaded by the tree you are measuring.

This impressive number gives us yet another sense of the importance of trees in our environment. Above the shade, the canopy of the tree, hosts many forms of wildlife, providing them nourishment and shelter. The "roofs" created by the trees in our forests and neighborhoods are needed by large and small wildlife to provide good habitat and a healthy environment.

ACTIVITY Opposites and Alternates—A Game of Tag

- *A field guide to trees*

This two-team game is fun while also requiring a bit of thought during the play. Before beginning, everyone should

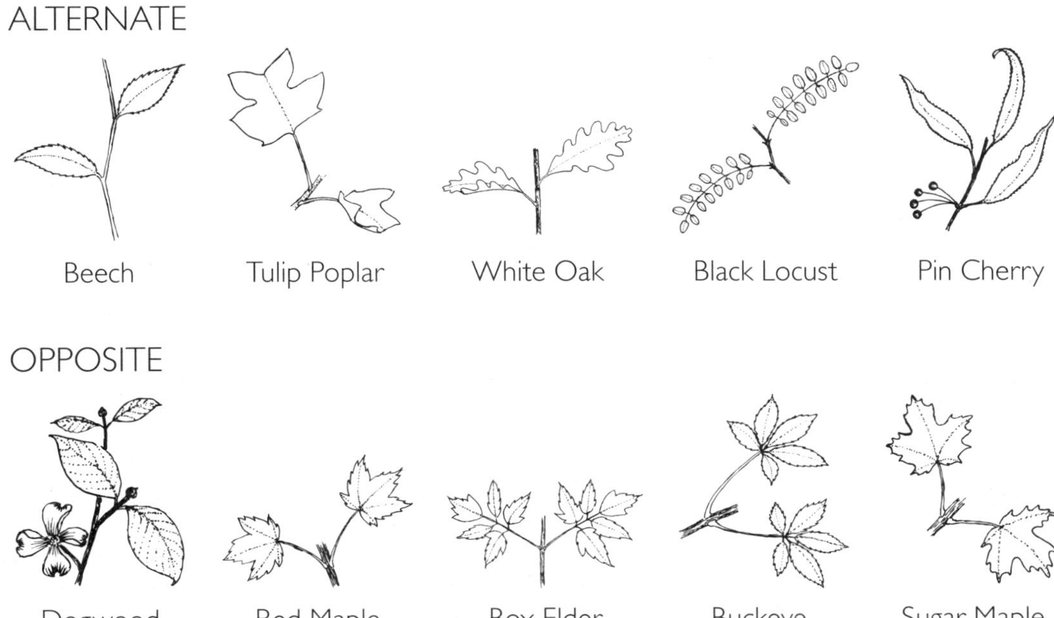

be familiar with the branching patterns of trees, so they will be able to recognize the difference in opposite and alternate branching. Notice how some trees have opposite branches and leaves, while others alternate. Recognizing this difference is the first step in learning to distinguish the different types of trees. Learning some of the names of trees while preparing for the game will add to the meaning of the activity.

To play, the group should divide into two equal teams. Team 1 will be the "opposite" team, and Team 2 will be the "alternate" team. One person, who is not on a team, will be the leader. The leader will call out either "opposite" or "alternate" as the play begins. If the opposite team is called, they must run from the alternate team and are safe only when they tag a tree with opposite leaves. Every member of the opposite team who is tagged before reaching a safe place has to join the alternate team. When the players reach a safe spot, the first play is over and both teams reassemble.

The process is repeated again, with the leader calling "opposite" or "alternate." If they say "alternate," the play is the same except the alternate team is not safe until they tag a tree with alternate leaves. In this case, everyone tagged by the opposites before reaching their safety zone must join the other team.

The game continues until either the opposites or the alternates have captured all the other team members. When the first game is over, reassemble the teams and change their team numbers, so that the "opposites" will become the "alternates," and vice versa.

ACTIVITY Tree Scents

- *Small bowls*
- *A variety of fresh tree leaves*

Earlier today I wandered home from a trip to the store. Upon stepping out of my car to grab the mail, I found myself overwhelmed by a strong yet warm, earthy odor. It had been rainy and thunderstorms were rumbling around, creating a mixed scent of rain and decaying leaves. I scooped up a small handful of leaves from the forest floor, enjoying the odors produced by the different species blended together.

Let us separate all of these mixed scents with this "sense-ational" activity aimed toward our sense of smell. We can bring home the wonderful scents of the earth by gathering a selection of fresh leaves.

Crush each leaf and put it in a separate bowl and then cover it with very warm water. The addition of water enhances the odor, and in some species, will really send off a strong scent; others might be a little subtler. Number each bowl and keep a record of what went in each one so you can compare results at the end.

Give each person participating a pencil and piece of paper and ask them to number it from one all the way up to the number of leaves used. Then tell them to go to each bowl, close their eyes, and sniff the fragrance generated by the crushed leaves and the water. Next to the corresponding number, ask them to write down what it smells like, as descriptively as possible, and name the tree if they wish.

Once everyone has had a chance to check out all the scents, gather together in a group and share notes. Finish up by letting everyone know what was in each bowl and encourage them to notice more openly the scents that are all around us in our southern forests.

Enrichment Activities

To learn more about the trees in your world, try these old artsy ideas!

Leaf Rubbings

Lay a piece of paper on top of your leaf. Hold it steady and rub a crayon over the paper. You will create a beautiful image of the leaf, complete with veins and marvelous textures. Add a little variety to your drawing by experimenting with different colors of paper and crayon.

Leaf Shadows

Lay your leaf on top of a piece of white paper. Brush thin layers of paint from the edge of the leaf, outward onto the paper, stopping your brush about one inch from the leaf. Allow the leaf to stay on the paper until the paint dries. When you lift it up, you will have created a white shape with a colorful border. Try different colors of paper and paint for new effects.

Leaf Stencils

Trace leaf shapes onto poster board. Cut out the leaves to create a stencil. Use this stencil to design T-shirts and sweatshirts with fabric paint, or stencil onto paper images of your favorite leaves. As you paint inside the stencil, take care not to get too much paint on your brush or sponge. It will ooze under the stencil and ruin the edges of your leaf image. Dab the paint on across the inside of the stencil, and you will be pleased with your results.

UP HIGH OR DOWN BELOW: FOREST ECOLOGY

Up High: High Elevation Balds and Canadian Forests

Not much can compare to the thrill of visiting the higher elevations of the Southern Appalachian Mountains. The enormous change in habitat and climate is striking after leaving the forests below 4,500 feet.

Reminiscent of Canadian forests, the higher elevations, ranging from 4,500 feet to a little over 6,500 feet, offer such a specialized habitat that plants and animals can survive there only if they have adapted to the short growing sea-

The spruce/fir forest meets the edge of the grass balds on Roan Mountain

son and the harsh, cold winters. Covered in evergreen red spruce and Fraser fir trees, these mountains produce lush, cool forests that provide homes to a variety of unique plants and animals. The forest floor may be blanketed with clover-like wood sorrel, ferns, and a host of herbs that can survive in no other environment.

Open, grassy areas called "balds," found in select areas of the Southern Appalachians, represent an ecosystem in need of continued study. Though the origins of the highest balds are unknown, theories abound. Intrigued by the balds, biologists and scientists have explored and written about them since the early frontier days of our nation. Native American legends have attempted to explain the mysteries of these natural features.

Devoid of many trees, these areas tend to remain open, offering spectacular views. The warmth and sunshine atop the balds provide a habitat for rare plant species, some so unusual that they have been found sparingly and in very specific locations. In addition, certain wildlife species can generally be found only near the tops of these mountains. The northern flying squirrel, the saw-whet owl, various birds, and many other unique creatures prefer this climate over that of the lower elevations.

To add firsthand knowledge of this endangered environment, and to make the following activities more meaningful, plan a trip to a mountain above 4,500 feet. If a trip is not possible, read about and study the biology of these special areas.

ACTIVITY A Bald in a Bowl

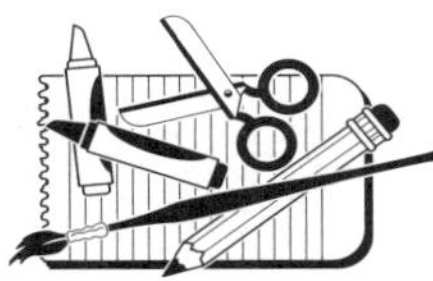

- *Small bowl for each bald*
- *Potting soil*
- *Grass seed (creeping red fescue is a good choice)*
- *Toothpicks*
- *Construction paper*
- *Scissors*
- *Glue*

Prior to this activity, either take a field trip to a bald, study about them on the Internet, or read books on their ecology. If you present this activity to a group, encourage everyone to engage in research, including names and pictures of organisms that might live in a bald environment.

Before beginning the craft project, share all of the gathered information with everyone involved. Fill each bowl with potting soil, rounding off the top to look like the top of a rolling mountain. Saturate the soil, but do not leave water standing in the bottom. Then take the grass seed and press it gently into the soil, trying to cover it completely. Creeping red fescue produces a longer blade than many other grasses and will better replicate the appearance of grasses on a true bald.

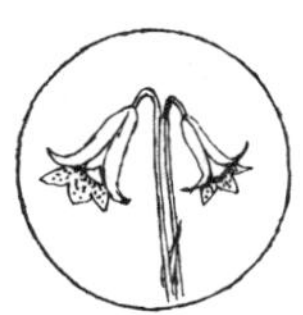

Gray's Lily

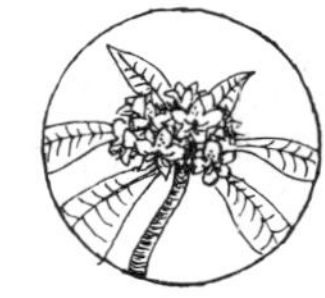

Catawba Rhododendron

Michaux's Saxifrage

Filmy Angelica

Lowbush Blueberry Roan Mountain Goldenrod

Next, refer to your reading and research, and choose three plant species that you feel are important to the bald environment. Common plants found on many balds include the rare Gray's lily, St. John's wort, filmy angelica (an intriguing plant that "intoxicates" insects), lowbush and highbush blueberry, Catawba rhododendron, green alder, wineleaf cinquefoil, hawthorn, numerous fern and grass species, and many more. Draw and color each plant you choose, or you can use illustrations from magazines. Cut them out when finished, and glue them to the toothpick, allowing adequate drying time. Place them in the bald and then set it in a window that receives the morning sun. It will take over a week for the grass seed to germinate, so be patient! When it does, you will have created a miniature bald that you can enjoy in your home.

ACTIVITY Scent Jar

- *Jar with a lid (decorative or otherwise)*
- *Dried needles from a Fraser fir tree*

This wintertime project is ideal for bringing home the warm memories of trips to the forests of the high mountains. After a summer rain, as the heat of the sun strikes the forest floor, rich odors of fir seem to wrap around you. The soft and pleasing smell is enjoyed and treasured by many.

The Tree Scents activity on page 90 involves crushing leaves to release their various scents. A prominent tree scent comes from the Fraser fir. Once a dominant species in the high-elevation forests, the fir is now giving way to the red spruce. Though an insect infestation has eliminated many of the mature fir trees, young seedlings remain, ready to reclaim their spot.

Grown commercially as Christmas trees, Fraser firs are readily found during the holiday season. Fir is also used for roping and wreaths, so you should be able to find something to work with for this project. If you have a fir for your holiday tree, save several branches—or the entire tree if you wish—and lay them out to dry thoroughly. Allow adequate airflow so they do not get moldy or damp. A wreath or section of roping will produce the same results.

After several weeks, when your branches dry completely, fill your jar with dried needles. Any size jar will work, depending on how and where you plan to

The Fraser fir produces a vibrant scent perfect for a scent jar.

use it. Before you place the lid on top, take a good deep breath of the fine odor. Prepare more than one scent jar if you wish, and place them around the house. Then when you want to remind yourself of the great experiences and scents of the Canadian forests, simply remove the lid and you will be greeted by the delectable aroma of the Fraser fir tree.

Down Below: Forests of Lower Elevations

The forests below 4,500 feet offer a distinctively different environment in contrast to those found in higher elevations. Spring comes to the lowlands a few weeks earlier, while fall arrives later.

The longer growing season and warmer temperatures create lusher vegetation and more species of trees, herbs, and shrubs. The low-elevation forests are comprised of a wide range of hardwood trees, including oak, maple, hickory, beech, birch, dogwood, cherry, linden, and deciduous magnolia, to name but a few. Evergreens such as white pine and eastern hemlock also grow here.

Water bubbles out of the ground from springs and seeps, and small creeks and branches find their way down to the rivers below. Low areas become small wetlands, and these temporary fens provide superb breeding areas for amphibians.

Many wildlife species thrive below 4,500 feet, where the habitat offers appropriate food sources, plenty of water, and numerous forms of shelter and cover. The bobcat, black bear, and white-tailed deer are all common. Smaller mammals such as raccoons, groundhogs, and opossums are regularly seen; even tinier mammals, such as shrews and mice, abound.

The complexity of the low-elevation forest provides diverse avenues for exploration and discovery. This section focuses on plant-oriented projects.

ACTIVITY Sunlight Painting

- *Colored construction paper*
- *Leaves or flowers*

This simple but delightful activity for folks of all ages can produce pleasing results. Begin by collecting leaves, flowers, or parts of plants whose shapes interest you. Choose from common plants, and take only what you need, leaving plenty behind to produce seed and propagate. If possible, gather from your personal garden, where you know what you are growing and can guarantee its survival.

Arrange the leaves on a piece of dark-colored construction paper. Lay your paper in the sunlight, and do not touch the project. After five to ten minutes, carefully raise one of the leaves and see if the paper has faded where it was not covered. If you like the contrast between the dark under the leaf and the exposed paper around the edges, then take it out of the sun and remove all of the leaves. For a stronger contrast, leave it for a few more minutes and check again.

If you wish, cut out the images, leaving a border of light against the darker print. Create note cards, personalized paper, framed pictures, or decorations with your sun paintings.

ACTIVITY Natural Brushes

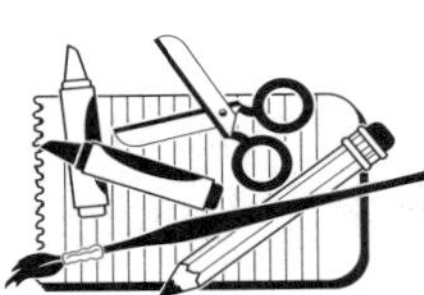

- *Paint*
- *Paper*
- *Branches from evergreen trees with needles*
- *Sticks and twigs with the ends feathered open*
- *Plants with interesting flowers and seed heads*
- *Ferns*
- *Grass blades*
- *Feathers*
- *Anything else that strikes your fancy!*

Painting with paintbrushes from the store allows you to create an image controlled by the well-shaped tips of brushes produced in quantity. The brushes used in this activity will enable you to create natural paintings.

Plan an exploratory trip outdoors to search for the items listed above. As in the previous activity, collect cautiously and wisely. When you have all your "brushes," dip them into the paint and experiment with the shapes and patterns offered by nature.

Plant Keys: How Botanists Identify Flora

Taxonomic keys help identify a plant or animal by giving a series of questions or choices that lead to a known organism's identity. Each answer sends you on to another set of choices until you reach the correct identification. As an example:

A – Leaves are opposite – Go to B
A – Leaves are alternate – Go to C

Advanced keys can be hard to use, as they ask questions about highly specific anatomical parts of an organism and require a deep understanding of the biology of the organism you are trying to identify. Some keys fill three or more books! The following activity will expose you to taxonomic keys, to make you aware of their existence and provide you with the opportunity to learn how to use one.

ACTIVITY Learning to Read Keys

To teach the basics of how a key works and to understand the process, I suggest designing two practice keys, one to identify items common to your everyday surroundings, and another planned around an outdoor environment or plants in your house or classroom. First pick a few simple objects and write down their characteristics, similar to the chart below, which uses stuffed animals for subjects. Then use those characteristics to create a key like the one that follows on the next page. Look at keys provided in field guides for further guidance.

Pass out copies of the keys to members of the group, and place the three critters where everyone can easily examine them. Then explain how the keys work, and tell them to imagine they have never seen these strange animals before. Walk the group through the identification of one of the critters, and then let the participants use the key to figure out the identity of the other two.

Unknown Critter #1	Unknown Critter #2	Unknown Critter #3
Small, approximately 6" high	Very tall, 22" high	Tiny, 2" high
Solid, light brown color	Brown with white spots	Bright red
Four appendages	Four appendages	Four appendages, including two wings
Small, round ears	Tall, pointy ears	No obvious ears
Black nose	Pinkish nose	No nose, holes present
Brown eyes	Yellow eyes	Dark eyes

A. Height under 12" – go to B
A. Height over 12" – go to C
B. Color, light brown – go to D
B. Color, bright red – go to E
C. Brown with white spots – Go to E
C. Green with some speckling – Go to E
D. Brown eyes – Teddy Bear
D. Hazel eyes – Go to E
E. Two appendages, two wings – Stuffed Bird
E. Four appendages – Go to F
F. Tall, pointy ears – Giraffe
F. No ears – Go to G

You may create keys using a multitude of objects, plants, or fictitious creatures designed by yourself or your group. After completing this activity, the concept of a scientific key will be much clearer.

Traditional Uses of Plants

Many different plants, trees, and shrubs grow across our continent, not to mention those found on the entire Earth. Plants are fascinating, with each species finding its ideal habitat in which to thrive.

Through the years, people of various cultures and ethnicities have been sustained by plant life, not just for food, but also for medicine and remedies, natural colors and dyes, flavors and herbs, and for perfumes and scents. Our Southern Appalachian ancestors could not run to the store to fill a prescription or buy clothes, so they turned to plants. The Native Americans realized they would have to provide for the survival of the species they used, but members of other cultures often collected to the point of destroying a healthy population.

Crimson bee balm, or horsemint, has been used as a medicinal plant for generations.

For the most part, families in the Appalachians attempted to preserve plant species by gathering only what they needed, but plant collecting for herbal and medicinal purposes soon became a booming business. People would gather the high-demand plants in staggering numbers, then sell to individuals who resold them to companies outside of the area. Most collectors realized the value of these species and selectively chose only the parts of the plants needed. They always ensured that plenty of seeds and rootstock remained to guarantee that over-collecting would not destroy the plants.

With little cost involved, the herb business flourished for several generations. In those days, the plant life seemed so plentiful that no one could imagine the disappearance of a species. But some collectors, who could see only the dollar sign, literally wiped out the mountainsides gathering herbs, and the species they depended on for their livelihood became harder to find.

In the mid-twentieth century, the U.S. Forest Service began buying much of the mountain land. Gathering wild plants is now illegal on all public lands unless the collector has obtained a permit from the managing agency. Most nurseries and garden centers sell wild plants propagated by native growers, enabling us to leave the natural populations alone and give them a chance to regenerate and grow. But we will probably never again find them growing in their historical abundance, covering the mountainsides as far as the eye can see.

Many folks today are becoming increasingly interested in understanding and practicing the old ways of doing things. It is easy to buy ready-to-use items from a store, but maybe not as personally satisfying. After all, collecting and preparing plants involves a considerable amount of work. But we often forget that many ready-to-use commodities began as products derived solely from plants. Thus, many people desire to learn how these plants were once used, and to return to the early ways of survival.

The roots, leaves, stems, flowers, and even seeds of some groups of plants have been used over the centuries to produce liquid remedies, salves, ointments, and the like in efforts to heal illnesses and discomforts. The gentle colors seen in the garments, coverlets, and fabrics of our ancestors were derived from plant extracts. Many of the flavors used to season meals came from the leaves of plants.

Books, guides, workshops, and video and audio recordings can aid in your study of traditional plant usage. Within the Southern Appalachian Mountain area, folk schools, state and federal parks, and universities offer courses about native plants. Remember that many plants are poisonous. You should be cautious as to what you touch, and never ingest anything unless you are working with an expert who can insure that what you are doing is safe.

ACTIVITY A Natural Dyeing Experiment

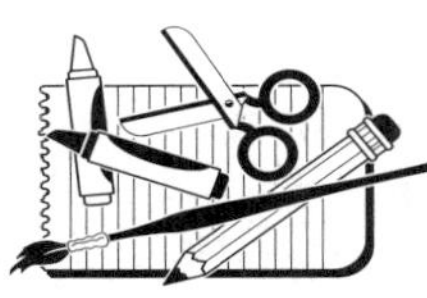

- *Tin pail, enamel pot, or iron pot that you do not—and will not—cook in. Your dye pot can be used for dyeing only!*
- *Onion skins from a two-pound bag of yellow onions*
- *Cheesecloth*
- *Half-gallon glass jar*
- *Natural colored wool skeins*
- *Wooden spoon*
- *Firewood, kindling, matches, and fire circle*

Though most natural colors historically came from native plants, the dyeing process in this experiment uses a product you can purchase in the grocery store if you don't grow them in a home garden. Of course, onions primarily provide a food product, but you can use their skins to create a natural colored dye.

Several days prior to the time you plan to dye your thread, remove the onion skins from the onions and tie them up in a piece of cheesecloth. Put them in a glass jar and cover with hot water. While the onions sit for a few days, the color will begin to emerge from the skins.

Wind your wool into skeins that are tied loosely to prevent tangling but will allow the color to reach all of the threads. Gently submerge the skeins in a bucket of room-temperature water, but do not stir. Overworking your wool will destroy its texture, and the fibers will begin to felt together. Presoak for at least 24 hours to ensure that the color will be absorbed through your skeins.

Traditionally, dyeing would have been done outside over a fire, as it takes several hours to heat and extract the color. Since you are using natural products, you could dye in the house on your stove, but if a fire ring is available in a safe location outdoors, you may choose to approach this activity the old-fashioned way.

Prepare a grating, a hanging apparatus, or an arrangement of cinder blocks to elevate your pot so it does not sit directly in the fire. Fill your pot half full of water, and pour in the onion skins, still wrapped in cheesecloth, along with the water they have been soaking in. Gently add your presoaked wool, pushing the skeins down carefully with a wooden spoon. Add water if necessary during the process to keep the threads submerged. Suspend the pot over the fire pit, and start your fire. Once the liquid begins to simmer, try to maintain the heat but do not let it boil.

As the mixture gets hot, the wool will absorb color from the onion-skin dye bath. Periodically check the shade of your wool; if you want it darker, leave it in longer. When you have achieved the desired result, carefully remove the skeins from the bath and hang them outside to drip dry and cool off. Remember, they are hot, so don't grab them with your hands!

When you bring your finished product into the house, wash it by hand with a mild soap, such as Ivory, in a sink filled with room-temperature water. Some color will wash out into the sink but the amount will decrease with subsequent rinsing.

Submerged in pots over an open fire, skeins of wool absorb the colors produced by the added plant material.

Books on natural dyeing often recommend the use of *mordents*—harsh chemicals, such as aluminum or chrome—to help the color stick to the wool. Some colors from plants, such as onion skins, stick well to the fiber without the use of a mordant; other plants must be mordanted, or the color will wash out and continue to bleed. Many natural products, such as ashes or parts of plants like sumac and galls, were once commonly used to mordant wool.

I prefer to experiment using pots as mordants. A tin pail will release some tin into the dye bath, a brass pot releases the brass, and cast iron releases iron. Placing samples of the same plant in these three pots will yield three different shades of color and may alter the texture of the fiber.

If you would like to learn more about natural dyes, several publications and Web sites offer information about the different species of plants and the expected colors produced.

Further Reading

The Art and Craft of Natural Dyeing: Traditional Recipes for Modern Use by J. N. Liles

The Audubon Society Field Guide to North American Trees: Eastern Region by Elbert L. Little

A Dyer's Garden by Rita Buchanan

A Field Guide to Wildflowers: Northeastern and North-Central North America (Peterson Field Guides) by Margaret McKenney and Roger Tory Peterson

Great Smoky Mountains Wildflowers: When and Where to Find Them by Carlos C. Campbell, William F. Hutson, and Aaron J. Sharp

Magic and Medicine of Plants, Reader's Digest Books

Manual of the Trees of North America, Volumes I and II, by Charles Sprague Sargent

National Audubon Society Field Guide to North American Wildflowers: Eastern Region by John W. Thieret

Newcomb's Wildflower Guide by Lawrence Newcomb

Textile Art from Southern Appalachia: The Quiet Work of Women by Kathleen Curtis Wilson

The Tree Identification Book by George W. D. Symonds

Wildflowers of Tennessee by Jack Carman

Wildflowers of the Eastern United States by Wilbur H. and Marion B. Duncan

Life on the Wing

Another beautiful spring day, and there I sat at the computer, listening to the *whrrrrrr* of its fan. It was much easier to stare out the window and wish I could wander outside for a while, but that certainly wouldn't get any work done. Though I had the day off from my job, I had bills to pay and chores to do, and "playing" did not show up on my list of viable options. So I continued to plunk away at the keyboard, attempting to accomplish the task at hand.

I would always work with the window wide open so I could hear the sounds of the woods around me. I tended to subconsciously listen for the arrival of several spring warblers, which reliably stopped off in the trees every season. About 20 minutes into my project, I finally took notice. In the back of my mind, I thought I heard an unusual sound nearby, but I brushed it off and typed on.

Unable to ignore it for long, I grabbed my binoculars and stepped out onto the third-story back porch of my house. I listened intently and, a moment later, knew exactly which way to look. At eye level in the woods beyond me sat a flock of wild turkeys, near the tops of the hemlocks, obviously roosting there the night before. The cues of the morning were getting them started for the day.

As if playing a game of hide-and-seek, one would rise up from its perch, making it more visible, and then would lower itself down, nearly vanishing against the darkness of the tree trunk. A fanciful little rhythm of turkeys, popping up and down on the branches of the trees, played itself out for almost fifteen minutes before they began their descent to the ground for the day's activities.

We remember inspirational moments like these—when an adventure unfolds right in front of our eyes. We anticipate having the opportunity to experience the natural world and its wildlife.

BIRDING NEAR HOME, FIELD, AND FOREST

Birding is a fulfilling pastime that you can enjoy anytime and anywhere. You don't have to travel long distances or hike into the forests to observe native wild birds; you can easily see them from the window of your home or work.

Some species stay in certain parts of our country only during certain months, but the Southern Appalachian Mountains provide an exciting place to observe birds year-round as they feed, set territories, or build nests. Birders anxiously wait for the migratory seasons as the birds fly north in the spring, looking for suitable breeding areas, and south in the fall, trying to find food and escape the harshness of winter. Many northern species venture into the area in the wintertime, filling the trees with color and song.

Listening to a chorus of bird songs from the edge of a field can be a little overwhelming and confusing at first. Each bird species has its own distinct song or call, and a seasoned birder can recognize vocalizations without seeing the bird. Matching a birder's amazing skill in visual identification can seem nearly impossible until you know what to look for.

Taking a break from my indoor chores one cool, damp, spring morning, I stepped out onto the porch for a moment to stretch my legs and brain. Greeted by a chorus of sound, I needed only a moment to realize what captivated me about birding. I closed my eyes to listen to the life bustling around me and was thrilled to hear the season's first worm-eating warbler in the trees. A crow yapped away high above, and the white-throated sparrows' song of "Poor Sam Peabody Peabody Peabody" rang out from the field below. Off beyond the ridge, another warbler sang, and a cardinal's "cheer, cheer, cheer" echoed from the opposite direction.

The birdsong surrounding me instantly brought my life into perspective. I realized how easily I could let the details of daily problems throw my thoughts off kilter, causing me to temporarily forget what was truly important to me. Standing on the porch, listening, I remembered that I was just a small part of the whole—a player in an uncountable variety of life on earth. This flurry of birdsong helped me focus and gave me the ability to put my daily problems into their proper place. For here, on my front porch, on one small road, in one of many communities, it seemed as though the heart of the entire world existed and flourished with the melodies of the coming of spring.

The activities in this section break down birding into smaller chunks that make learning easier. A pair of binoculars and a good field guide will be helpful tools in the activities. Like a puzzle, the methods used by birders to identify species in the wild will come together to paint a beautiful picture of a world that surrounds us every day of our lives.

Silhouettes and Flight Patterns

Field guides present images of birds seen under optimum conditions. The brightness of light, direction of light, time of day, distance, and weather conditions all affect your ability to identify what you see. In unfavorable light, a bird might look devoid of color. At times, nothing more than a flash of movement will catch your eye. A turkey vulture sailing overhead on currents of air may provide only a glimpse of the shaded underside of its body. In other situations, you may see only the dark silhouette of a bird as it sits on a distant fence.

Many birds can be identified by knowing just what to look for, so don't give up if you cannot see the fine details noted in the field guides. Getting nose to nose with a bird is usually not possible. The following few hints explain field marks and habits to look for if the bird you are watching just doesn't know how to pose properly! *Do keep in mind that these are preliminary ideas to get your mind thinking like a birder.* More details will become apparent with experience.

Always make note of the size of the bird. Its silhouette or the manner in which it flies will sometimes be the only glance available before it moves on to another location. If it is in flight, notice the length and shape of its tail and wings. Are the wings held flat or in a V shape? Is the head extended? Do the legs trail behind? Is the bird flying in a relatively straight line, or does its flight undulate? Finding safety in numbers, certain birds leave a clue to their identity by flying in groups comprised of the same species.

The field guides to birds discuss in detail the silhouettes and flight patterns of different species. The information mentioned in them will help you come a little closer to correct identification of birds seen in the field.

Seasonal Versus Permanent Residents

Field guides and local bird clubs can provide both new and experienced birders with information about what species commonly inhabit an area during each season. (Of course, you will always find exceptions—some birds refuse to read the books!) Knowing that a certain species resides in a particular area during a specific season will help you include or eliminate a possible choice as you work on identification.

Habitats Through the Seasons

Most birds have places where you can *expect* to see them at specific times of the year. Knowledge of the habitats of each species will make it easier to narrow down a bird's identification.

For example, some birds breed at higher elevations and migrate altitudinally during the winter to a lower elevation. If you know the saw-whet owl is common over 5,000 feet in the spruce/fir or beech forests during breeding season, you would not expect to see it at the 1,000-foot elevation in a field behind the local mall in the summertime.

Eastern bluebirds usually show up in early summer in open areas around the edges of fields, where abundant insects provide food, so finding one in a hardwood forest would be odd. The American robin is also associated with fields, yards, and open areas. Once again, a robin found deep in the woods would be out of place.

Music to Your Ears

You can easily view birds in the high canopies of trees in fall and winter after the leaves have dropped, but observation becomes more difficult during the summer. With visibility diminished, vocal recognition is most rewarding. Sharpening your listening skills will help you hear the differences in the songs of birds.

Amazingly, each bird has its own distinct song or call that varies in pitch, rhythm, speed, length, and quality of tone—just like any song we sing. When we learn a new melody, we often put lyrics to it, or attach the pitches (do-re-mi) of the eight-note scale to a series of sounds we wish to remember. We easily remember melodies that we find interesting, especially if we hear them over and over again.

Attaching words, phrases, or sounds to a bird's song will help you relate that vocalization to something you are more familiar with. Authors of field guides and audio recordings suggest word patterns to help remember the song of a particular species. While learning, use their recommended phonetic phrases. If you later feel you do not perceive or hear the songs according to the commonly used phrases, then attach whatever patterns are more helpful to you. Listed below are a few vocalizations and the most typical ways in which they have been described.

Birds that say or suggest their name:	
Common flicker	"flicka flicka flicka"
Eastern peewee	"peeee-a-weeee" (slurring up) followed by "peeee-ur" (slurring down)
Gray catbird	mews like a cat
Whippoorwill	"whip–poor–weel" (repeated)

Birds of field and forest:	
Tufted titmouse	"peter peter peter"
Carolina wren	"tea ket´tle tea ket´tle" (accent on the middle syllable)
Eastern meadowlark	"spring is here" (quavering last note)
Northern cardinal	"cheer cheer cheer"
Wood thrush	"ee–ooh–lay" (quavering last note)
Rufous-sided towhee	"drink your tea" (quavering last note)

A few warblers:	
Yellow warbler	"sweet, sweet, sweet, I'm so sweet" (rapid, cheery, going up on last pitch)
Common yellowthroat	"whichity, whichity, whichity, which" (bouncy)
Ovenbird	"teach teach teach teach" (becoming progressively louder and stronger)

A couple of nighttime visitors:	
Screech owl	mournful, trembling wail
Barred owl	"who cooks for you, who cooks for you´all" (last note drops off)

Members of bird clubs or groups devoted to nature study will be invaluable to you when you are out in the field. They can take what might seem overwhelming at first and help you learn it in an enjoyable fashion. If you have trouble finding a local club, someone affiliated with the biology department of a nearby university or college should be able to put you in touch with the appropriate person.

The activities that follow will help you learn to identify specific birds, a few at a time. As you add to your list, take delight not only in the fact that you can recognize some birds by their song, but also in your ability to hear the differences. Notice the variations in pitch and rhythm. And when the opportunity arises, look for the subtle details of coloration and pattern.

ACTIVITY Musical Bird Chairs

- *A recording of bird songs (see sources at end of this section)*
- *Blank CD or cassette tape*
- *CD/tape player*
- *Chairs (one fewer than the total number of players)*

Repetition is the key to remembering, and playing Musical Bird Chairs is a painless and fun way to begin recalling songs for the activity following this one. From a recording of identified birdcalls, choose ten songs that reflect the learning level of the group, and rerecord them on a cassette tape or other medium. Copy the vocalization of each species about ten times before recording the next one.

Gather your group together and spend some time learning the songs. Discuss the vocalization patterns as you identify each species. Then set up the playing area by arranging the chairs in a circle facing outward in the same fashion as the age-old game of musical chairs. Remember to have one less chair than the total number of players.

Younger players might enjoy decorating the chairs before beginning the game. Ideas include drawing birds on large paper bags and slipping them over the backs of the chairs, buying feathers at a craft shop and putting them on the chair backs, stringing bird images together to drape over the playing area, or cutting pictures of birds out of magazines and gluing them to the chair backs. (Be careful not to damage the chairs!)

Choose one person to start and stop the recording, while the rest of the group walks around the circle of chairs. When the recording stops, everyone must try to find a chair. The person still standing is out of the game, a chair is removed, and the play continues until one person remains and is declared the winner.

Using a familiar game, such as musical chairs, enables participants to focus on what they hear, rather than trying to remember a new set of complicated game rules. After playing Musical Bird Chairs a few times, move on to the next activity, which will test the players' memories.

Multiple-Choice Birding

- *Recording made for Musical Bird Chairs*
- *Recording of bird songs (see sources at end of this section)*
- *Blank CD or cassette tape*
- *CD/tape player*
- *Paper and pen or pencil for each participant*

The purpose of this activity is to see how many vocal patterns the players can remember from the previous game. You will create a multiple-choice test of sorts, which will include a number of birdcalls. The preparation will take a little time and thought, but the challenges the game presents will encourage the participants as they add to their birding skills.

Record the sound of a new species (not on the musical chairs tape) at the beginning of the blank tape, followed by a recording of a species previously learned, and then add a third birdsong for good measure! If, for instance, you want the group to identify the chickadee's "chick–a–dee–dee–dee–dee," first record the song from another bird, maybe a cardinal's "cheer–cheer–cheer." Follow with the recording of the chickadee, and then record another species after it. Record nine more sets of birdcalls, sometimes with the song already learned first, sometimes second, and sometimes third. Do not record the songs in the same order they appeared on the Musical Bird Chairs tape.

Start the game by playing and studying the songs recorded for the musical chairs game. When everyone feels comfortable recognizing the birdcalls, give each person a piece of paper and a pen or pencil. Explain that they will hear three bird songs and must write down the number of the one you name.

After working through the entire tape, go back to the beginning and play each set again. Pick out the correct answers as a group. This process of review and repetition will further enhance each birder's feeling of success as he adds more and more birdsongs to his list of identifiable species.

BACKYARD BIRD FEEDING

ACTIVITY Attracting Hummingbirds

- *Hummingbird feeder*
- *Water and sugar for feeder mix*
- *Plants of your choice for garden*

Though they have a typical life span of four years, the "oldest" hummingbird on record lived for 25 years. Flying at an average speed of about 25 miles per hour and moving its wings approximately 55 times per second, the hummingbird has earned the reputation as one of the most delightful and intriguing birds to attract to your garden or home place. The ruby-throated hummingbird is the only known breeding species in the Southeast.

Hummingbirds begin their fall migratory route when the days become shorter and they have put on sufficient fat to sustain their trip to the tropics. Supplemental feeding has generally been a summer pastime, but individuals and organizations interested in hummingbird research have maintained heated feeders beyond the traditional time of taking down summer feeders, well into the migratory and winter seasons. As a result, rufous, Anna's, calliope, and black-chinned hummingbirds, among other species, have enjoyed nectaring on winter feeders throughout the Southern Appalachian range and farther east.

Keeping a feeder hanging during the late summer and fall will not discourage a hummingbird from migrating. If a bird remains behind, it is not due to your feeder, but to its inability to survive the long migratory trek. Most ruby-throats stay gone between October 15 and mid to late March of the following calendar year.

If you are curious as to whether any hummingbird species are present between October and March, consider leaving a feeder out in the daytime and bringing it in at night. Some folks have devised interesting ways to keep their feeders warm by hanging heat lamps above them or by using automatic thermostatically controlled heat tape. If you choose to use a heat tape, follow the manufacturer's directions carefully, as improper application can cause a fire. Exposure to rain or snow will cause the heat tape to short out, so hang your feeder in a place where it will remain completely dry.

Hummingbirds also eat small insects for protein, and they nectar on garden flowers. They have virtually no sense of smell, so to enhance your chances of attracting hummingbirds, choose plants that they will be drawn to by color and nectar production. Avoid using pesticides on your garden, as the hummingbirds will also ingest the poison, possibly killing the bird in addition to the bugs you hope to destroy.

A few perennials that you might plant include—but are not limited to—bee balm or horsemint (*Monarda*), bleeding heart, butterfly weed, cardinal flower, columbine, day lily, delphinium, four o'clock, foxglove, gladiola, hollyhock, hosta, lily, and lupine. Annuals include fuchsia, impatiens, jewelweed, lobelia, petunia, and snapdragon. Among the trees and shrubs, hummingbirds like azalea, butterfly bush, flowering maple, lilac, rhododendron, and weigela.

As you plan your garden, consider the blooming time of each plant, trying to insure a complete spring, summer, and fall growing season of continual and varying bloom. Keep in mind that you will not only be providing nectaring plants for hummingbirds, but will also heighten the numbers and species of butterflies visiting your garden.

Feeders can be found in many places, including hardware and home improvement stores, large bargain centers, and local shops. When buying a feeder, consider how easy or difficult it will be to clean. If it has too many tiny parts that will trap mold, look for something else.

You can make your own nectar by boiling water for several minutes and then measuring out four parts of the water to one part white cane sugar. Stir well and allow it to stand until it has cooled to room temperature. Ornithologists recommend that you do not add red food coloring. A mixture of sugar and water provides the same average sucrose content (about 21%) of the flowers the hummingbirds nectar upon.

Change the sugar water in your feeder every two to three days. Keep your eyes peeled for cloudy water, and change it immediately if it clouds and spoils. The solution will break down quicker in hotter, sunnier weather. Spoiled sugar water and moldy feeder parts can kill hummingbirds, so clean your feeder well every time you change it. A bottle brush helps remove all the black, moldy sections. After cleaning, soak the feeder for an hour in a solution of ¼ cup of bleach to 1 gallon of water. Rinse it well before refilling.

If you have problems with wasps or bees, consider removing the yellow part or the flower on the feeder. You can also move the feeder to another location. The flying insects are not as likely to find it, but the hummingbirds will not have any problem. Ants can also be pesky, as they love the sucrose as much as hummingbirds do. Some feeders have little moats that you fill with water and hang above the feeder. Birds may drink the water, but the ants will not make it through.

Now sit back and wait for your first nectaring birds. The joy of observing hummingbirds from your front porch or yard will far outweigh the preparation involved readying your home for their arrival.

ACTIVITY Homemade Feeders

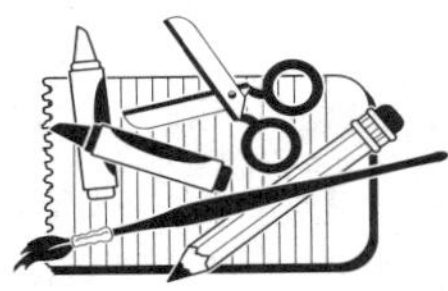

- *Suet (either pre-purchased in cakes, or made from high-quality animal fat)*
- *Bird seed (preferably black-oil sunflower seed and millet)*
- *Pinecones*
- *Peanut butter*
- *Stale bread*
- *Orange or onion bag*
- *Ingredients listed below for feeding*

Attracting songbirds to feeders allows you to study your field marks at a closer range and will help familiarize you with what you need to look for. Identification of bird species at the home feeder gives biologists additional data as to which species—and in what numbers—overwinter in particular areas. One such popular program, Operation Feeder Watch, encourages home birders to send their listings of birds and their numbers to the Feeder Watch database.

The birds you attract will depend on what feed you use. A bird that eats seeds, berries, nuts, crops, and fruit when not eating at the feeder will logically be attracted to feeders providing a diet of seed. On the other hand, a bird that dines on insects or worms in the field will prefer suet at the feeder.

Suet feeders attract brown creepers, downy woodpeckers, hairy woodpeckers, red-bellied woodpeckers, black-capped chickadees, and white-breasted and red-breasted nuthatches. Suet is a high-quality animal fat—preferably beef kidney fat—that you can purchase at the meat department in the grocery store or buy in preformed suet cakes from the bird feeding section of many local stores. Formulated to withstand summer's high temperatures, suet cakes may be a good choice for you, depending on how much time you wish to invest in experimenting with rendering your own suet. Homemade suet will go rancid once the temperature passes approximately 70 degrees Fahrenheit.

Birds will swallow small, hard materials, such as sand and ground shells, to help them "chew" their food in their gizzards, so some recipes list sand as an ingredient. Feed and pet stores usually offer grit for sale, but you can make your own with eggshells, which also provide a good source of calcium. Eggshells offered to birds must be baked for 20 minutes at 250 degrees to kill any Salmonella bacteria present. After cooling, crush them into pieces smaller than a dime and offer them in tray feeders placed next to your seed feeders.

If you would like to try your hand at preparing your own suet, experiment with one or all of the recipes that follow. Try mixing a few of the recipes for a new concoction all your own. If you do not use a commercial cage to hang your suet, save onion and orange bags and hang the suet from trees in them.

To render your own suet, grind beef fat with a meat grinder, or chop it up to a fine consistency. Heat at a low temperature until it liquefies. (Watch the temperature carefully because overheated fat can catch fire.) Strain it through a piece of cheesecloth and allow it to harden. Repeat the process a second time, or the suet will not cake properly. Store in a covered container in the freezer until you use it.

Recipe #1
½ cup of chopped rendered suet
½ cup of peanut butter (with or without nuts)
2½ cups of cornmeal
1 cup of mixed birdseed
Combine all ingredients and press into a jelly-roll pan. Freeze until firm and then crumble into large bowl and offer to birds with added foods, such as peanuts, chopped apples, raisins, bran, or uncooked oatmeal.

Recipe #2
1 cup crunchy peanut butter
1 cup chopped rendered suet
2 cups quick-cook oats
2 cups cornmeal
1 cup flour
⅓ cup sugar
Mix all ingredients and pour into jelly-roll or foil-loaf pan and refrigerate until firm. Serve on feeder tray.

Recipe #3
½ cup chopped rendered suet
1½ cups wild bird seed
1 cup unseasoned bread crumbs
1 cup graham crackers
½ tsp sand
Mix all ingredients and pour into jelly-roll or foil-loaf pan and refrigerate until firm. Serve on feeder tray.

Recipe #4 *Soft Suet Mix*
4½ cups of chopped rendered suet
½ cup black-oil sunflower seeds
¾ cup dried and finely ground whole wheat crackers
¼ cup millet
¼ cup dried and chopped raisins or berries
Combine ingredients to make a mixture that can be worked into the cracks of a pinecone or spread into the crevices of a tree.

To attract seed-eating birds to your yard, choose the meaty black-oil sunflower seed. It contains a good bit of nutrition, and the seed coat is not too hard, so birds with smaller beaks can break it to obtain the nourishing center. White proso millet, along with the sunflower seed, attracts chickadees, titmice, goldfinches, pine siskins, evening grosbeaks, cardinals, purple and house finches, and nuthatches. A thistle feeder will attract redpolls, finches, and siskins.

The multitude of feeders on the market can make choosing one difficult. You should consider the type of seed you will use and the species you wish to attract. If you make or buy a platform feeder, make sure it has ⅛" holes in the floor to allow for water drainage. Some feeders are made with a coated wire cage surrounding the perching area with the goal of (hopefully) keeping squirrels, raccoons, and other critters out of the feed. The addition of baffles, inverted cone-like objects that hang above and below the feeder, may deter unwanted visitors. But small mammals will often beat the system, finding creative approaches to obtain a free meal.

Hang your feeder, with cage and baffle, in an area without "launching pads" close by. If a squirrel can simply jump into the feeder from nearby vegetation, it will—and it would probably laugh at our human contraptions if it could! Provide some cover for the feeder birds so they will have places to conceal themselves as they fly to and from your feeder. Shrubbery, small trees, or even an old Christmas tree will create areas to protect songbirds from the elements and predators.

If you have a continual varmint problem, be creative and try thinking like the animal you want to keep out. Watch and see how it gets past your barriers, then try devising another method. Of course, you always have the option of giving in to nature's ways and simply enjoying all of your feeder visitors!

Keeping your feeder clean is important. If you allow it to become moldy and damp, you will create a lethal situation for your feeding birds. Take a few moments to clean the hulls off daily. Shake and remove any wet or compacted seed. Be sure to wash your hands after cleaning or filling your feeder. You will also need to periodically clean it with two gallons of water mixed with two ounces of bleach; rinse and dry well before refilling.

ACTIVITY Making a Pinecone Feeder

- *Pinecone (dry, so the bracts are open!)*
- *Peanut butter (creamy or crunchy)*
- *Sunflower seeds*
- *String or yarn*
- *Spoon*

This quick and easy feeder is fun to make for all ages. Take a dry pinecone (larger ones work better) and tie a long piece of string or yarn to the big end. Spoon peanut butter over the pinecone, stuffing it in the bracts. Next, roll the pinecone in the sunflower seeds, striving to coat it entirely. The seed will stick to the peanut butter that protrudes beyond the bracts, ensuring a successful feeder.

Now hang the feeder outside, providing a nutritious meal for many species of songbirds! Put it in a location that can be easily viewed from an indoor window. You might enjoy hanging several of these feeders in the same tree or area, creating a festive seasonal tree decorated for the birds.

More Feeding Projects

- Cut stale bread into fun shapes with cookie cutters. Spread peanut butter on them and roll in seed, as you did with the pinecones. Tie strings through them and hang in trees around your yard.
- Choose a tree and make it a decorative feeder tree. In addition to the ideas already mentioned, hang pretzels, donuts, or stringed popped popcorn. Fill scooped out orange halves with suet, and place in the crooks of the tree's branches.
- Other projects include setting out the heads of sunflowers, oatmeal, or pieces of fruit such as oranges, grapes, or soaked raisins.

Water for the Birds

Water will help attract birds to your new and old feeding stations. Many stores sell birdbaths, but shallow dishes and pans work just as well. Adding a small pond to your landscape will provide a more elaborate watering area. Change the water regularly and elevate it at least three feet off the ground, unless you are using a recycling pond.

Rocks and other objects that poke out a little above the surface act as islands that unwary bugs can use to escape from a drowning death. These islands, in addition to the edges of the container, also make good landing pads for the birds. A layer of sand in the bottom will keep the rocks from sliding.

Maintaining a water source in the winter is especially important and will require some extra work if you plan to refill the pan throughout the day. Never add antifreeze to the water, as it is poisonous to all animals. Birdbath heaters will keep the water from freezing without getting it too hot.

Saved from the Glass

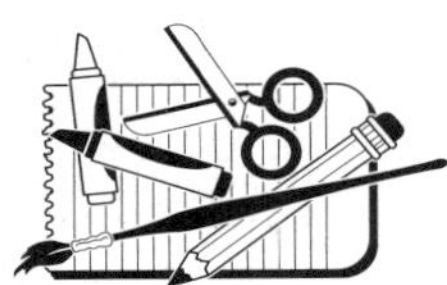

- *Black construction paper*
- *Scissors*
- *Tape*

If you have ever experienced a bird flying directly into your window, you will find this activity particularly helpful. Transparent glass reflects trees and sky, deceiving the bird into thinking it is flying into open outdoor space through a gap in a wall.

Take the black construction paper and create a soaring silhouette of a bird predator, such as a hawk, with a wingspan of 12 inches from tip to tip. Stick the silhouette on the window—outside if possible, to make it more easily seen—to deter birds from flying into the glass. The dark shape breaks up the transparency of the glass, reducing the illusion of flying into space.

BIRD CONSERVATION

One fall morning in 2002, I had an hour to spare and made an immediate dash to Carvers Gap at the Tennessee/North Carolina state line on Roan Mountain. The sun had just begun to crest the tops of the highest mountains, letting light filter into the lower valleys. Bright yellows and reds blanketed the sunlit mountain peaks, and blue wisps of smoke and fog rose slowly from the valleys. The definition of each ridgeline was as precise as a line made with a sharp pencil.

As I continued to the gap, I struggled to keep my eyes trained to two places: the road and the beautiful scenes around me. When I stopped in the parking area on top, I noticed a flurry of bird activity. I hopped out of the car, enjoying the cool, crisp air on my face, and grabbed my trusty binoculars to check out the action.

Surprise and delight filled me when I realized I was observing large flocks of American robins moving from Tennessee into North Carolina. I counted 50 to 70 at a time bouncing above my head. Some would light in the tops of the Fraser fir trees, while others just kept on moving. As the sun moved above Round Bald, its light shone perfectly on the garnet-like bellies of the robins above my head. They glistened brightly in the newly emerging sunlight. I stayed and observed them for about 25 minutes, counting over 500 birds in that short period of time. What an incredible and unexpected display!

To ensure the continuance of such experiences, all of us must to do our part in protecting birds worldwide. In October 2002, the National Audubon Society published "WatchList 2002." The publication placed birds in the United States into groups suggesting whether they were in danger of being extirpated from this continent or were at risk of decreasing significantly in numbers. The list of 201 threatened species amounted to over ¼ of the bird species in North America.

Habitat loss, both in the United States and globally, is one of the primary reasons for the declining number of songbirds. Some North American birds spend their entire life on the continent, while others migrate in the fall to other landmasses. Thus, our concern for and our actions toward preserving wildlife habitats should reach beyond our homelands. If migrating birds return to their wintering grounds to find them destroyed, the change will surely affect their populations and will become noticeable to us when their numbers continue to decrease here in America.

Domestic pets, especially cats, killing birds poses another serious problem. The Pet Food Institute, as of 2004, estimates that 75 million pet cats live in the United States, and only half of them stay indoors. This number does not include the strays and feral cats! Just imagine, based on that estimate, if an outdoor cat killed only one bird per year, that would amount to 37.5 million birds killed by pet cats alone!

The introduction of nonnative bird species presents a different problem for survival of native species. Introduced species, such as starlings and house sparrows, compete with native species for food, habitat, and nesting sites. These exotic species often out-compete the native birds, resulting in a declined population of the native species and an abnormal number of nonnative species.

Pollution and pesticides are blamed for affecting bird populations. The carcinogenic chemical DDT wiped out the peregrine falcon and the bald eagle where they formerly ranged. Fortunately, public awareness (greatly resulting from Rachel Carson's book *Silent Spring*) and government action helped to end the widespread use of DDT and related pesticides, and scientists successfully reintroduced these species to their native habitats.

Other factors also affect native bird populations: the collecting of eggs from nests, the ingestion of lead shot from hunting, the shooting of protected species such as hawks, the selling of bird parts, and disease (West Nile virus is a present concern).

With so many issues affecting bird populations, it seems almost impossible for individual citizens to make a difference. But by implementing positive conservation practices in our own lives, we can take action on small and large scales, knowing we are helping to ensure that our native birds have a healthy home in the future.

DAYTIME FLYERS

Dragonflies and Damselflies

As I sat beside a small pond one sunny, warm summer day, the air moved gently, much like the cooling breezes you feel while lying in the hot sun on the beach. This one small spot on earth teemed with small insects whizzing up and down, left and right. I tried to focus on just one flash of movement, but the many zips and dashes made the task impossible. The huge numbers of dragonflies and damselflies rapidly moving by caught my eye. They often landed on thin blades of grass; as they hung on in the breeze, I finally got my binoculars locked in on one to get a closer look. Bright blue and finer than the grass upon which it sat, the graceful insect lay in wait for its next victim, possibly a smaller insect that might venture a little too close.

Science groups dragonflies and damselflies in the order Odonata, which means "toothy ones." Suborders further group our subjects—damselflies in the suborder Zygoptera, and dragonflies in Anisoptera. Even though their name might sound a bit alarming, the toothy ones do not chew on or sting humans. The carnivorous odonates sit extremely still, waiting for the opportune moment to strike, using their larger lower lip to capture unsuspecting prey.

Odonates possess a number of the typical anatomical structures found in other insects—an abdomen, a head with two antennae, a thorax, six legs, and four wings—but their outer skeleton and jointed legs comprise characteristics particular to this order. The dragonfly differs from the damselfly in several ways, but I will mention only the ones most obvious to the beginner's eye. At rest, the damselfly holds its wings together over its back, with the exception of a few species, while the dragonfly holds its wings out to the side. In addition, dragonflies have large eyes that rest closely together, and small, bristly antennae. The damselflies' eyes are smaller and farther apart, and their bodies are slender and delicate.

Dragonflies have existed for a long time. Fossil records indicate that the forefathers of today's odonates flew across the landscape 300 million years ago! These amazing insects inhabit a myriad of wet environments, including ponds, seeps, small springs, and streams. Look around plants, across moving and still water, along the banks, and near prominent perching spots. They hide deep within the vegetation on rainy, cloudy days, making it more difficult to find them, but they are active during sunny days with a temperature of at least 65 degrees Fahrenheit.

ACTIVITY Providing a Habitat for Odonates

If you wish to encourage dragonflies and damselflies to visit your backyard, you will need wet areas. If your property has springs, seeps, or small streams, you may already have dragonflies breeding and feeding nearby. I have seen successful projects that involved partially blocking a small stream, enabling it to ooze out and create a wetter, bog-like area.

An available natural source of water comes in handy if you decide to build a pond, but you can also use water from the home. Local garden centers can provide information on recirculating pumps to help create a pond without a stream or spring on your property. Most can also provide the necessary products.

A few key elements will help ensure the success of a newly installed artificial pond or wetland habitat. Aim for a depth of two feet or more in a sunny area, and do not introduce fish or large frogs, which would feed on the breeding insects in your pond. Provide sufficient vegetation and sticks to perch on; a mowed bank will discourage, rather than encourage dragonflies and damselflies.

As wetlands decline worldwide, suitable habitats and certain species of odonates are disappearing. By providing environments for dragonflies and damselflies to reproduce and flourish, you can do your part to help preserve these interesting insects, which have survived on Earth for an impressive span of time.

ACTIVITY Creative Dragonflies

- *Popsicle stick*
- *Paint or markers*
- *Glue*
- *Beads, sequins, or small buttons*
- *Clear tape, approximately 1" wide*
- *Black or dark thread*

Before beginning the project, look at some pictures of dragonflies, noticing their venation (arrangement of veins in the wings) and body segment colors. Paint the Popsicle stick to match the body of the dragonfly. While it dries, you can work on your wings.

Decide how long you would like each wing—the two hind wings usually are a little bit smaller than the forewings—and lay four pieces of transparent tape, sticky side up, on your work surface. Then arrange the thread in an oblong shape on the tape to form the edge of each wing. Fill in the inside of this area with additional thread to create the appearance of veins. Put another piece of tape over the thread, sticky side down, to seal it inside. Your result will be a smooth wing on the outside, with thread in the center, creating a veinlike look. Next, cut out each wing along its thread border.

By now, your Popsicle stick should have dried. Choose two beads, sequins, or buttons to make the eyes. Glue them on the end of the stick that does not represent the abdomen.

Next glue your wings to the stick, two on each side (the larger in front near the eyes, the smaller behind), and allow to dry. Consider making several and transforming them into a mobile. You can create different species to hang, or prepare a mobile comprised of the same kind of dragonfly.

ACTIVITY Dragonfly Race

You can play this game with ten or more people, divided into two groups. One group will represent the dragonflies, and the other will portray small insects that the dragonfly might eat. Do not make the groups equal in number; you should have more insects than dragonflies. Each dragonfly should try to catch the most insects, while the insects strive to avoid becoming food.

Before starting the play, each person portraying a dragonfly will write his name on several small pieces of paper that he will give to each insect he catches. For a creative alternative, each dragonfly can have pieces of colored fabric or ribbon (a separate color for each dragonfly), copies of pictures of the dragonfly species he portrays, or any other safe item that will match the insect to the dragonfly who caught it.

The dragonflies must learn three movements. Normal flying consists of walking at a regular pace, with arms (wings) extended; hovering means to stand still and observe; and the propelling mode allows the dragonfly to run. The insects walk around when the dragonflies hover (stand still) or fly normally (walking), taking heed to avoid the dragonflies, or else they may get eaten! But when the dragonflies go into the propelling mode, the insects may also run to avoid capture.

As the person overseeing the game, you will determine what the dragonflies and insects do. You need three signals so everyone will know when to change from one mode to another. For instance, you could blow a whistle to indicate that the dragonflies should fly normally and walk, while the small insects also walk. Prior to propelling at a higher rate of speed, the dragonfly must hover to locate its prey. A second sound, possibly a ringing bell, could communicate to the dragonflies that they must hover. They would remain in hovering position, locating an insect, until the third sound (possibly yelling "go" or clapping—just make sure to use a distinctively different signal from the first two to avoid confusion).

While the dragonflies are in the propelling mode, they run after the insects. Do not allow the chase to go on for too long. After 30-45 seconds, make the sound that takes them back to the walking or hovering mode.

Before the game begins, determine how long the play will continue. The dragonflies will line up, shoulder to shoulder, at the starting line, and the insects will scatter across the field or playing area. Separated the two groups by at least 20 feet.

At each sound signal, the groups will walk, be still, or run. If a dragonfly catches an insect, remove that insect from the game, tagging him so he knows which dragonfly caught him. At the end of the allotted time, the dragonfly who has caught the most insects wins. (The surviving insects are also winners!) Repeat the game a few times so everyone has a chance to portray both a dragonfly and an insect.

Color in Flight: Butterflies

Placed in the Lepidoptera order, the butterfly can brag on having approximately 20,000 species worldwide, according to the North American Butterfly Association, with the center of its diversity in the tropical rainforests. Their beauty, gracefulness, and coloration make them well worth observation and continued study.

The word *butterfly* comes from *butterfloege,* the Anglo-Saxon name for a common European species, the yellow brimstone. Their intriguing name also has folkloric interpretations. Colonists in eighteenth-century America believed that witches would turn themselves into winged creatures that stole butter, hence the name butterfly. Ancient Greeks, who believed that our souls go to heaven as butterflies when we die, called them *psyche,* meaning soul.

"Butterflying," or watching butterflies, is an increasingly popular recreational pastime. Butterflies are no longer caught with nets, examined, and pinned to

A hitchhiking butterfly

frames; instead, observation through binoculars has become the method of choice.

An appropriate habitat provides butterflies with breeding sites, protection from the environment, and host and foraging plants. Unfortunately, worldwide deforestation and habitat destruction have caused their populations to decline rapidly. The butterfly collecting trade has also taken its toll on their numbers and diversity of species.

A new business, butterfly farming, offsets the pressures put on populations from the over-collection of wild specimens. Butterfly farms grow food and host plants—plants that a certain species of butterfly prefers to nectar on or lay its eggs on—of a particular species in hopes of attracting the female butterfly to these areas, where she will lay eggs. When the caterpillar hatches, the vegetation is kept in a healthy state to nourish and satisfy the small creature's voracious appetite.

You can determine which species you might find in a region or at a particular time of the year based on when the host plant grows and blooms. For instance, pearl crescent caterpillars prefer asters; pipe-vine swallowtails like the Dutchman's-pipe; sassafras and spicebush bring in spicebush swallowtails; and snapdragons attract the common buckeye.

School groups and clubs around the United States extensively study the monarch, a well-known migrating butterfly. By knowing that milkweed hosts the monarch, you can observe populations in your home area as you watch for egg-laying activity, feeding caterpillars, or adults nectaring in the late summer. Monarch Watch, a popular program with an interactive Web site (http://www.monarchwatch.org/) hosted by the University of Kansas Entomology Program, allows you to learn a great deal about this butterfly species. If you wish to follow their migration, visit Journey North (http://www.learner.org/jnorth), an excellent site where you can report and track the movement of monarchs and other migrating species.

ACTIVITY Brilliant Butterflies

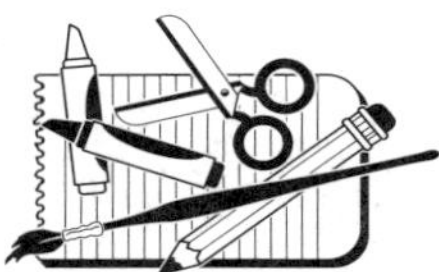

- *Stockings (in colors if you'd like; knee highs work well)*
- *Flexible, wrapped florist wire*
- *Scissors and wire cutter*
- *Glitter and craft glue*
- *Pipe cleaners (various colors)*
- *Paint pens (optional)*

Twist two pieces of florist wire to form two identical wings, or use four pieces of wire to create a butterfly with four separate wing sections, two on each side. You can cut the wire to make a small wing, or use an entire 10" piece to make a larger one. Longer pieces will be easier to manipulate, especially for younger folks. Keep in mind that the ends of the wire can be a little sharp, so bend carefully. Be creative, experimenting with different types of wing shapes. If you don't like your result, you can start over with the same piece. When your wings are finished, attach them in the center with the leftover ends or with an additional small piece of wire, again manipulating the final shape as you work with your creation.

Cut a piece of stocking—but don't use the toe or top—large enough to cover the entire butterfly. Place the wings inside so the head and "tail" are at the open ends of the stocking piece. Tightly stretch the stocking and twist the ends. When you have pulled and stretched it so that the stocking is sheer, tie the ends. Take a pipe cleaner and wrap it the length of the body, separating the left wings from the right. Push the tied ends of the stocking to the bottom of the butterfly, and twist the pipe cleaner to hide the knots.

Dress up your butterfly by adding pipe-cleaner antennae and decorating the wings. You could pattern the wings after a real species of butterfly, or create a wing pattern of your own. Use glitter and glue to make your butterfly sparkle!

If you glue a magnet to the back of the butterfly, you can use it on your refrigerator. Or you may attach a pin to the back and wear it on your shirt. If you make several butterflies, you might combine them to produce a beautiful mobile to hang in your home to spin in a breezy window.

Further Reading

Audubon Society Field Guides:

The Audubon Society Field Guide to North American Butterflies by Robert Michael Pyle
The Audubon Society Guide to Attracting Birds by Stephen W. Kress
The Audubon Society Master Guide to Birding by John Farrand, Editor
National Audubon Society: The Bird Garden by Stephen W. Kress
National Audubon Society Field Guide to North American Birds: Eastern Region by John Bull

Peterson Field Guides:

A Field Guide to Hummingbirds of North America by Sheri Williamson
A Field Guide to the Birds: A Completely New Guide to All the Birds of Eastern and Central North America by Roger Tory Peterson
A Field Guide to the Butterflies of North America, East of the Great Plains by Alexander B. Klots

Stokes Field Guides:

Stokes Beginner's Guide to Bird Feeding by Donald W. Stokes and Lillian Q. Stokes
Stokes Beginner's Guide to Dragonflies by Flair Nikula, Donald Stokes, Jackie Sones, and Lillian Q. Stokes
Stokes Beginner's Guide to Hummingbirds by Donald W. Stokes
Stokes Guide to Bird Behavior (3 Volumes) by Donald W. Stokes and Lillian Q. Stokes

Others:

Butterflies through Binoculars: The East by Jeffrey Glassberg
Dragonflies through Binoculars by Sidney W. Dunkle
A Field Guide to Advanced Birding: Birding Challenges and How to Approach Them by Kenn Kaufman
An Instant Guide to Butterflies by Pamela Forey and Cecilia Fitzsimons
National Geographic Field Guide to the Birds of North America by the National Geographic Society
Sibley's Birding Basics by David Sibley

Spineless Wonders: Strange Tales from the Invertebrate World by Richard Conniff

Audio:

Birding by Ear: Eastern and Central North America (Peterson Field Guides) by Richard K. Walton and Robert W. Lawson

A Field Guide to Bird Songs of Eastern and Central North America (Peterson Field Guides) by the Cornell Laboratory of Ornithology

More Birding by Ear: Eastern and Central North America—A Guide to Bird-song Identification (Peterson Field Guides) by Richard K. Walton and Robert W. Lawson

Stokes Field Guide to Bird Songs: Eastern Region (Audio) by Donald Stokes

Ground Dwellers

With so much to observe outside, you might find it hard to decide whether to look up or look down. Wildlife can appear and disappear rapidly from any direction, either soaring overhead or breaking the brush while trying to escape from possible harm. In other instances, only the more subtle signs might exist: a broken branch, a small path through the woods, or a single track near a creek bank or the edge of a pond.

In areas where animals reportedly abound, folks do not notice many of them for two primary reasons: some creatures lie low by day and hunt by night, and wildlife is just, well, wild. Wild critters have no interest in messing around with us. If they see people hiking along a trail, they will either run or become very still, with the intention of blending with their surroundings. Survival is all-encompassing in the natural environment; the animal focuses on finding food and shelter and not becoming something else's meal.

I have often led hikes along trails in the mountains with young people from area schools. Working with a small group allows greater opportunity to share ideas on a one-on-one basis. Sometimes, however, this close-up interaction is not possible, making it imperative to have some creative approaches ready for the larger groups of hikers.

One particular hike has always stood out in my mind, for the group size was way beyond the normal range. As I stood in front of over 100 fourth and fifth graders at the trailhead, I wondered how to make the trip meaningful for them. Before we got started, we talked about wildlife and their habits, discussed what the students might see, and spent some time playing sense-awakening games.

Knowing that I couldn't address the entire group once we got on the trail, I suggested a game of "pass it back," similar to the age-old game of "gossip." When I saw something interesting, I would share it with those near the front, hoping the message would remain the same when it reached the end of the line. The game would also teach the lesson that stories can change as they get told and retold. In this case, I hoped that when the story made it to the end of the long, long line of hikers, the last person would share in the same experience as the first.

Above all, I encouraged everyone to walk quietly, pay attention, and carefully look and listen to everything around them. They knew they probably wouldn't see an animal, a bird, or a snake unless they walked peacefully through the woods—something easier said than done with a large group of children.

Off we went on our two-mile trek, everyone eager and anticipating what might await around each bend in the trail. Occasional wails would come from behind, as boys shook wet tree branches on the girls following them. Spider webs in the trail and the occasional creepy crawly all added to the thrill of the adventure.

After a mile or so of walking—as I reminded everyone to remain aware of the life around them—we rounded a corner and started down the crest of a hill. I looked to my left and saw a small doe standing completely frozen, just three feet from the edge of the trail. Camouflaged beautifully with the vegetation around her, she remained as still as a tree, obviously not wanting to tangle with a crowd our size.

Hoping that the group would spot her on their own, I decided to walk slowly past her, signaling to those near me to walk quietly and keep their eyes open. After the first third of the group had passed this majestic, living statue, the doe apparently had had enough. She bounded through the line and crashed into the brush, heading toward the river below. Everyone screamed and jumped, never expecting an animal to be that close to them!

When those near the front realized they had passed just a few feet from the doe, they were amazed, knowing they never saw a thing until she moved. That single doe, caught in the forest between a hundred people and the river, left a lasting impression in the minds of the students. They quickly learned a great deal about camouflage and survival in the wild.

This chapter will help you learn more about the organisms that travel closer to the ground, as well as those seldom-seen critters that leave clues to their passage and presence. Delve into the activities with open eyes, ready to discover the less obvious signs of life in the forests.

TELLTALE SIGNS

Many wildlife signs are obvious, such as a deep track in the mud by a creek; other more obscure signs might not be seen unless you take the time to look. Often, the critters that inhabit or pass through a particular area leave only subtle markings as clues to their presence.

The study of animal droppings, called *scatology*, can be intriguing. In addition to identifying a species by its scat, you can also gather information on what the animal has eaten. You might find evidence that a wild animal (a bear, for instance) has raided a trashcan and eaten "people food" rather than its natural diet.

Bear and deer, among other mammals, mark trees. Deer will rub their antlers on a tree, frequently leaving behind traces of the velvet cover of a newly forming antler. A bear will stand up on its back legs and pull its front claws down the bark of a tree, tearing it and leaving a territorial sign—one that will definitely get your attention!

I had the opportunity to share a memorable mountain bike ride with a good friend one fall. We rode several miles on old Forest Service roads to a series of beautiful ponds, seemingly in the middle of nowhere. A highlight of the ride occurred when we found a tree marked extensively by a bear that must have also relished the wet environment within the mountain forest. Though we didn't see the bear anywhere, we remained wary in case he decided to return to the tree.

Keep your eyes peeled for broken-down vegetation, trails made by repeated use, and flattened areas used for bedding. Bones, feathers, fur, nut husks, and other plant matter lying in a small pile can indicate feeding areas.

Some small mammals leave a mark by creating tunnels and burrows; others drag their tails behind, leaving a track in the dirt. Listen for vocalizations of animals and birds, and look on the ground and in the trees for bird nests. Spiders will construct unique and attractive webs, and other creatures will build and conceal shelters, ranging from hornet nests to beaver dams.

Looking for animal tracks is a commonly used method of noting which critters have traversed a particular area. Following the path made by a set of tracks can lead you on many adventures and help you learn about what a particular species is doing at any given time. The best time to explore for tracks is right after a rain or snowfall, as the footprints are vivid and easily spotted. The chart on the next page describes some typical track patterns.

HOW MANY TOES?	BELONGS TO:
Two toes	deer
Four toes on the front and hind feet	bobcat or house cat (retract their claws), fox, wolf, coyote, or domestic dog, eastern cottontail or snowshoe hare
Four toes on the front; five on the hind feet	rodents: mice, chipmunks, and squirrels
Five toes on the front and hind feet	raccoon, weasel, mink, skunk, bear, beaver, opossum, otter

TRACK PATTERNS	BELONGS TO:
Wandering tracks	foragers: deer
Small triangular marks in front (claw marks)	raccoons, skunks, coyotes, foxes, and dogs
Walks on toes, indicating speed	deer and cats
Walks with toes and heels touching	skunks and bears
Two hind prints side-by-side, often landing ahead of, or beside, smaller front feet	jumpers: squirrels and rabbits

ACTIVITY Tracking—Follow That Print!

- *Paper and pencil or pen*

On the next page is a drawing of the forest floor in the wintertime, when the vegetation has died down and snow covers the ground, making animal tracks more noticeable. Carefully study the illustration and count how many sets of tracks blend into this environment. Choose one and see if you can identify the animal, then visually follow its path and look for clues as to what it might be up to.

Repeat with each of the other tracks in the drawing. Record your observations on your paper, then answer the following questions. Do any animals live here? If so, where are they? What do they do? (You can find an explanation at the end of the chapter, on page 140)

Since many animals lead nocturnal lives, your ability to identify and follow tracks is an invaluable tool in helping understand the comings and goings of a particular critter. Now that you have practiced on paper to unravel a day in the life of some common forest animals, take your skills to the woods, fields, and creek banks, and see if you can identify and track a living creature in its native habitat!

ACTIVITY Making Track Casts

- *Plaster wall patch*
- *Water and large spoon*
- *Container to mix plaster*
- *Animal tracks*

This easy project will reproduce tracks with plaster, so you can hold them in your hand and observe them at home or in the classroom. As you find and make casts of animal tracks, you will develop an interesting collection that will allow further study of the prints.

Begin by searching for tracks in a natural environment. Making plaster casts will not work in the snow, so plan the activity for a day when the ground is clear. The best track casts will be made in the dirt or mud.

If the tracks are dry, carefully moisten them. Mix the plaster according to the directions provided with it, and spoon it gently into each track. Allow the plaster to dry until hard—drying for a day produces better results. When the plaster hardens, it will lift out easily, and you will have created a great replica of an animal's track.

Walking Like an Animal

- *Music of your choice for interpretive dance*
- *Slips of paper with animal names written on them*
- *Box to hold slips of paper*

The purpose of this charade-like activity is to create a situation in which participants can appreciate how animals move as they adapt to their environment. Prepare slips of paper with the names of animals written on them. Choose animals with obviously different methods of getting around. Deer, bear, opossum, skunk, and bobcat all move on four feet but have distinct gaits and rhythms to their movement. Birds, snakes, and fish present a totally different challenge.

Each player will draw a slip of paper from the box to see which animal he will portray. Have a practice session where each person, one at a time, demonstrates to the group how he thinks his animal moves. After each demonstration, discuss that particular animal, and have the group share their input on how they perceive that critter's movement.

When everyone has finished, turn on a slow piece of music and ask them to interpret and imitate their animal's movement through dance. Each person will dance as an individual, even though they will perform at the same time. Ask them to envision a woodland scene in which they are engaging in a hunting activity and stalking their prey. Turn the music back on, and they will continue the "dance" as they stalk their prospective meal.

Next, convert the slow and thoughtful dance into something a little more active. Spread the group out along one end of a field or gym. Identify the finish line, and on the call of "go," they will race to the finish as they move like their animal. Players who revert to "human" running must go back to the beginning and start over.

At the end of the race, sit the group down and discuss how a snake could never win a distance race with a bobcat, or a mouse with a soaring hawk. Ask each person to reflect on how his animal would hunt and hide in its environment. Does it rely on speed or something else? After a few thoughtful moments, give everyone the opportunity to share how they interpreted the movements of their animal.

ACTIVITY Dinnertime

• *An open area to run and hide in*

Begin this group activity by dividing into pairs; one person will act as the predator and the other the prey. Each pair will decide which creatures they wish to portray, or the leader can assign roles. As the players assume their new identities, they should simulate the behavior of their chosen animals. The predators must try to find a meal, or else they may not survive the coming cold winter days, while those who represent prey animals will try to escape.

Denote areas in the playing field where prey animals are safe from the waiting predators. When they are at the shelter, the predators cannot harm them.

As the game begins, the predators will find a place to hide and camouflage themselves. While they hide, the prey must close their eyes or go to a separate area. When the hunt begins, the predators will remain still, hidden from the prey. Imagine you are a snake (the predator), lying in wait for an unsuspecting mouse (the prey) to happen by. If the mouse saw you, it would make haste and get away as quickly as possible. Thus, the snake must remain stationary and blend well so he can successfully catch his meal.

When all of the predators have hidden, have the prey wander through the area of play. (Remember the safe areas of shelter where the prey can find haven.) They must be aware of danger as they live their day, looking for food and water, and soaking up the warm sunshine. A predator can tag only its partner; all other critters are safe from its grasp! A prey will eventually pass near his predator, who can then jump up and attempt to tag him. When the prey runs, the predator may begin the chase; if the chase appears to be unsuccessful, the predator may slip away and hide again while the prey is not looking. Continue the game until everyone gets caught or a specified amount of time has passed.

ACTIVITY Who Will Survive?

- *Index cards*
- *Permanent marker*

Animal populations peak and plummet as their access to food changes. With ample food available to a particular species, their numbers will increase; failure of a food crop might result in a considerable drop in numbers for several years.

This game illustrates this concept of food supply by making a specific amount obtainable to a set number of animals. To adequately show how food affects populations, conduct the activity twice. The first time, everybody will have plenty, and all or most will live and thrive. The second time will cause a little stress for some, as there will not be enough nourishment for all of the living things in your habitat. Those who cannot find food will have sealed their fate; they will not make it through the winter months.

Begin by identifying two groups of animals—for instance, bears and bobcats—and what they eat. For the purpose of this game, the bears will eat berries and roots, and the bobcats will hunt for rabbits and mice. Prepare food cards by writing either *berries, roots, rabbits,* or *mice* on each one. Make more than two cards per person, which will give everyone a reasonable opportunity to find some food.

In order for one bear to survive the winter, it must find a minimum of two cards that represent its food (two berries, two roots, or one of each). Each player needs only two to survive, but he can gather as many as he wishes. One bear may easily pick up half the cards before the others find any!

Scatter the food cards (faceup or facedown or a combination) around the playing area, either outdoors or inside in an open, safe place. Hide them or leave them in obvious locations, depending on the age of your group. For the first round, distribute all of the cards with the goal that each animal will find at least two cards and survive the winter. They will emerge from this activity feeling confident, assuming that it is easy to find ample food in a natural environment.

For the second round, spread your cards in the playing area again, but do not put out enough for everybody. Remind the players that sufficient food is not always available. Drought, flood, disease, and other factors might cause an

A buck blends in with this woodland setting

unexpected die-off of the very things needed for survival. Participants will have a harder time finding something to eat, and ultimately, a few will not find anything.

It may seem a hard lesson to share, for no one wishes to see another suffer. Yet nature must have a way to prevent overpopulation, ensuring that the strongest survive to produce young, with the goal of maintaining a healthier population in the wild.

After playing the game two times, sit down and discuss how you have seen the concept of food supply in action in the real world. You might remember years when huge herds of white-tailed deer passed through the fields near your home; other years, you may have seen less than half the number. Recall seasons in which the nut crops have failed in the forests. Wildlife may suddenly become more visible, as they move into more populated areas, searching for something to eat. Often we notice the actions of wildlife, not always realizing what has prompted our observations. By sharing what you have seen, you can help everyone understand the patterns of nature.

WILDLIFE IN WINTER: WHERE DO THEY GO?

One of the most intriguing mysteries of wildlife is how they survive in the coldest months of the year. As we retreat into our homes, turn up the thermostats, and snuggle beneath cozy blankets, wild creatures remain in harsh conditions. Fortunately, they have a plan to get them through the winter.

Their plan gets under way at the beginning of the growing season, in early spring. With no guaranteed meals, all birds, insects, mammals, reptiles, and the like spend each day or night in search of nutrition. The nocturnal ones live almost entirely at night, hunting under the cover and protection of darkness, while the diurnal ones search for food during the day. Making it through any 24-hour period involves a struggle for nourishment, water, avoidance of predators, successful reproduction, and shelter from adverse conditions.

As the days pass, each creature packs in nutrition. With the approach of fall and winter, as the days progressively grow shorter and colder, the animal puts on as much fat as possible to compensate for the lack of food during the winter. Deposited around the animal's organs and across its back and shoulders, the added fat, called brown fat, provides quick energy to the animal when it comes out of hibernation.

Some Southern Appalachian mammals, such as bats and ground squirrels, are true hibernators. They will find shelter and go into a deep sleep, dropping their body temperature and their heart rate, though they sometimes venture out during warm spells to eat a little before the weather turns cold again. Skunks, raccoons, bears, and opossums are not true hibernators. Their body temperature lowers slightly while sleeping, and their breathing slows, but not to the degree of the true hibernator. Sometimes called light sleepers, they are easily stirred from their winter naps and forage between snows.

Cold-blooded animals, such as snakes, turtles, and frogs, cannot warm themselves, so they must find adequate shelter during the winter. Turtles and frogs will bury themselves in the mud below the frost line and get their oxygen from the mud. Snakes will gather in underground and above-ground shelters, such as rotten logs. Insects that die off will leave egg cases, larvae, or pupae to overwinter. Some birds remain, while others migrate south to warmer temperatures. Adaptations of living things are many and often complex, but all are geared to survival and continued reproduction of their species in the coming season.

ACTIVITY One Cold Day

This group activity provides individuals with an opportunity to learn about the specific needs of one particular creature, then share the information through an interview. Ask everyone to choose an animal they find interesting or wish to know more about. Keep their choices secret from the rest of the group. Provide books, magazines, videos, or library access to participants and give them ample time to research their animals, paying close attention to winter survival strategies.

Next have them prepare a set of interview questions they would ask as a reporter who hopes to learn more about animal life in winter. (If time is short, you could provide them with a list.) Sample questions might include:

"Was the snow deep where you live?"

"Did you disturb any other creatures?"

"What did you hear?"

"Did you search for food on warm days, or did you sleep all winter?"

"What types of food did you find?"

"Can you climb trees?"

Working in pairs, one person will represent an animal, and the other will interview him, trying to acquire clues as to the animal's identity and habitat. After five minutes, have the partners switch roles, so the interviewer becomes the interviewee. At the end of the second round of questioning, each interviewer has three guesses to correctly identify the animal chosen by his partner. Keep the identity a secret and have everyone change partners. You may switch as often as time allows.

Finally, allow everyone a few minutes to share with the entire group the animal they chose and three interesting facts they learned about their animal in winter. If time permits, all of the researchers can prepare more in-depth reports on their animals, complete with posters and illustrations.

> Explanation of diagram on page 133: Deer enters from right, stops at edge of creek, jumps over creek, continues on to left. Chipmunk enters from left foreground, encounters bobcat, struggle ensues, chipmunk escapes down hole, bobcat continues on. Beaver exits creek (dragging tail), stops to gnaw on tree, then reenters creek. Bear enters from right, strolls along, stops at tree, plants both rear feet and scrapes trunk with claws, then continues on.

Further Reading

The Audubon Society Field Guide to North American Mammals by John O. Whitaker, Jr.

A Field Guide to Animal Tracks (Peterson Field Guides) by Olaus J. Murie and Roger Tory Peterson

A Field Guide to Mammals: North America North of Mexico (Peterson Field Guides) by William H. Burt and Richard Philip Grossenheider

Field Guide to Tracking Animals in Snow by Louise Richardson Forrest and Denise Casey

Mammal Tracks & Sign: A Guide to North American Species by Mark Elbroch

Skulls and Bones: A Guide to the Skeletal Structures and Behavior of North American Mammals by Glenn Searfoss

Southern Appalachian Wildlife: An Introduction to Familiar Species of Birds, Mammals, Reptiles, Amphibians, Fish and Insects by James Kavanagh

Stokes Nature Guide to Animal Tracking and Behavior by Donald W. Stokes and Lillian Stokes

Moon Walks: Watching Nature After Dark

At one time, I thought I was pretty much in tune with the mountains during the nighttime hours. My senses were keen, and I used an artificial light only if I absolutely needed it.

One particular night during a routine check of a population of wood frogs, my flashlight went out, and I wound up wandering around the woods in total darkness. I suddenly learned that, until then, I had never been totally immersed in the spirit of the evening.

The wood frog of the Appalachians begins to call and lay eggs in February. At this time of year, nightfall comes early and quickly. I started walking, with my trusty flashlight, to a reliable breeding pool. I had to approach the site slowly and quietly, for any noise would hush the chorus of singing frogs. I heard nothing in the cool, still night—that is, until I closed in on their annual spot. Their call penetrated the winter silence with a sound so vibrant that I knew I had arrived at a peak time in their reproductive cycle.

I spent at least thirty minutes listening and trying to determine the number of frogs present, and then I took a moment to shine my flashlight in the pool to see if eggs had yet been laid. Remembering a vernal pool on up into the cove, I decided to venture a little farther to see if their population had spread. Using my flashlight to ensure safe travel, I wandered deeper and deeper into the forest, stopping occasionally to listen for any sounds of life.

Spending too much time listening and searching, and not enough paying attention to where I walked, I soon realized that I had traveled a little farther than I had planned. Since I hadn't heard anything and could find no sign of any amphibians, I turned around and started back. I had wandered off the trail, slowing my return trip. Rocks, logs, and slippery holes all made the walk treacherous.

I still had a long way to go, when in an instant, my light went out! The sudden onset of darkness gave new meaning to the phrase "Now you see it, now you don't." Standing there for a moment, I wondered how to stumble back out to the trail. Though I knew where I was, I didn't have a clue as to what hazards awaited if I started walking. Crawling on hands and knees didn't seem like an option, so I cautiously started feeling my way, one step at a time.

Going very, very slowly, I slid here and there, tripped over logs, stumbled into holes, and stepped awkwardly off small embankments. A small sliver of a crescent moon shone beyond the canopy of the trees. In a sense, it gave me a tiny feeling of security and immediately brought to mind how much we depend on our sense of sight. Fortunately, I quickly became comfortable with my new situation and began to thrive on the unexpected experience.

The sounds of the forest became more pronounced; each rustle, breath of wind, and trickle of water echoed musically inside my head. Previously unnoticed odors whiffed past my nose, sharing their warm, woodsy smells. I detected an old, familiar scent of an animal lingering to my right, much like that of a musky wet dog.

Continuing onward, I soon found myself back on a flatter trail, one that I recognized. Though I still had difficulty seeing, after a few more steps, I knew I had reached the field that would take me back to my starting point. The wisp of the breezes around me and the sounds of civilization became evident. Now feeling a little overconfident, I walked along at a comfortable pace.

Hungry raccoons feast on sunflower seeds at a bird feeder.

My dreamlike state was quickly interrupted by a sudden, loud snort, followed by the sounds of many hooves running and crashing through the brush. I nearly jumped out of my skin, unaware of the fact that I was a mere five to ten feet away from several white-tailed deer. My heart pounding out of my chest, I became more alert as I finished my walk back to where I had parked my car.

Though my adventure could have turned out more hazardous than it did, I would never trade it. Fortunately, I didn't break any bones or turn an ankle. Due to my lack of preparation, knowing I should have carried extra batteries and a bulb, I put myself in a situation that forced me to open up my mind and senses to our world in the night.

We do not have the acute eyesight of many night-hunting animals, so we sometimes feel uncomfortable and threatened in darkness. When I've led night hikes with groups of families and children, the flashlight often became a big obstacle to total enjoyment of the walk. Almost always, some folks will flash their lights on to help them find comfort in their new, dark surroundings. But since our eyes need to adjust to the dark, a flash of bright light will impede that adjustment, forcing our eyes to start over and over again to let in what natural light exists in the night environment.

This chapter will explore ways to become immersed in the mountain life that thrives during the hours when most people usually sleep. Of course, the purpose of the following activities is to produce the same results, without the hazards of my unplanned night hike, as you gain awareness of the life that carries on at night.

NIGHT SIGNS—OBSERVING LIFE AROUND YOU

ACTIVITY Signs in the Night

The night can seem strange and somewhat eerie if you are not accustomed to the natural world after dark. To compensate for your inability to see at night, other senses grow sharper—you become immersed in the nighttime environment and begin to smell subtle scents, feel the wind and dampness on your face, and hear strange and unusual sounds you may not have noticed before.

Many folks head out with tunnel vision, anticipating the approach of a large animal, only to miss the odors and breezes around them. Below I have listed a few of the sensations and experiences that may be unusual or new to those just beginning nighttime adventures. Try to match the sensations on the left with the correct letter from the column on the right. The answers are mixed up, but the key follows. You can quiz yourself, or present the activity to a group, to begin thinking about what you might experience. Add your own observations to the list as you become more in tune with the world of the night. You can also apply these signs to other activities in this chapter.

SIGNS OF MOTION	
1. Tree branches waving	a. owl
2. Flash of white tails moving high off of the ground	b. bats, moths
3. Flash of white tails moving low to the ground	c. mice, shrews
4. Darting, zigzag movements in the air	d. whippoorwills
5. Darting movements in the grass	e. rabbits
6. Ghostlike wings bearing heavily feathered bodies	f. possible approaching storm
7. Circling, fluttering movements of small bodies on the ground	g. white-tailed deer
8. Black-and-white streaks moving about 6-12" above the ground	h. skunks

EYESHINE AND NIGHT LIGHTS	
1. Gleaming points of light in pairs	a. bullfrog
2. Golden, orange-red eyeshine, often seen on tree trunks	b. eyes
3. Eyeshine of many tiny specks in beam of flashlight	c. flying squirrel
4. Green eyeshine that glows like opals	d. raccoon
5. Flashes of light in the air	e. jack-o'-lantern mushroom
6. Bright yellow eyeshine	f. fireflies
7. Tiny rows of light on the ground	g. foxfire
8. Bits of glowing light in rotten logs	h. glow worms
9. Pale greenish glow from the ground or on a stump	i. beetle grubs
10. Greenish, glowing gills on a mushroom	j. moths
11. Reddish-orange eyeshine	k. trap-door and wolf spiders and some others (their eight eyes create the effect)

SOUNDS	
1. Cooing whistle followed by a purr	a. male striped skunk
2. Deep boom like a heartbeat	b. foxes

3. Loud hiss	c. flying squirrels
4. Soft bleating	d. wounded rabbit
5. Deep loud moan, growl, or grunt	e. bullfrog
6. Honking from sky or pond	f. female deer calling young
7. Croaking at night from trees	g. wild boar
8. Bass, bellowing sound from pool	h. turtle falling in pool
9. Guttural grunts	i. Canada geese
10. Shrill screams	j. black bear
11. Whistling snort	k. crows, ravens
12. Yaps and yelps together	l. ruffed grouse
13. Solid plunk like large rock hitting water and sinking	m. alarmed white-tailed deer
14. High, whistling preep, preep, preep in cadence	n. spring peeper
15. Chuck-chuck sounds or musical chirping notes from nests; sounds like birds chirping at night	o. opossum; barn or barred owl

ODORS	
1. Strong and faintly sweet	a. fox, dog, or bear
2. Aromatic and spicy	b. ground after a warm rain
3. Tangy and piney	c. honeysuckle
4. Musty	d. fir
5. Rich and earthy	e. decaying leaves, mushrooms
6. Faintly musky and doggy	f. spicebush
7. Unpleasantly strong to nauseating	g. shrew
8. Strongly musky, from dead leaves	h. skunk

Key to Night Signs:

Signs of Motion

1-f 2-g 3-e 4-b 5-c 6-a 7-d 8-h

Eyeshine and Night Lights

1-b 2-j 3-k 4-a 5-f 6-d 7-h 8-i 9-g 10-e 11-c

Sounds

1-a 2-l 3-o 4-f 5-j 6-i 7-k 8-e 9-g 10-d 11-m 12-b 13-h 14-n 15-c

Odors

1-c 2-f 3-d 4-e 5-b 6-a 7-h 8-g

ACTIVITY By Day and By Night

- *Flashlight with red cellophane or thin red fabric over the lens*
- *Insect bait (brown sugar or molasses, yeast, overripe banana, and absorbent cloth)*

Think of an area where you have seen wildlife nearby—preferably a place providing cover and protection, open feeding areas, and water—and find a good spot where you can sit quietly without being detected. Your blind (the objects that conceal you from wildlife) might be within several shrubs or behind a tree.

Since some animals are active in the day and others at night, begin in the light of day and see what might frequent the area. Take your journal along and record behavior patterns you see and any interactions that might take place between critters. Don't limit yourself to looking only for mammals; check out the less obvious also. Watch for ants building and carrying, birds moving in and out, or insects flying through. Look for signs such as tracks, scat, trails, and rubbings, as discussed on page 131.

A little before dusk, return to the same spot and notice the subtle changes as the scurry of the day gives way to the mystery of the night. Stay alert to anything and everything that might come your way. Flying squirrels, white-tailed deer, raccoons, opossums, and small rodents, such as mice and shrews, are but a few of the animals that might happen by. Note that the cover of darkness aids many creatures as they search for their evening meal. Your journal will be indispensable as you record all of the new experiences the night has to offer.

A flashlight with a red lens will come in handy when observing wildlife after dark. Since a number animals cannot detect red light, it will help you see a little more without alarming your viewing subject. Some camping and hiking stores sell flashlights with a built-in red lens, but you can easily make one by covering your light with red cellophane or thin red fabric, secured by a rubber band.

Insect bait will encourage a host of interesting nectar-feeding moths and insects to visit your area. Make a batch of bait in the morning prior to the night you will go out: mash up a banana and add ½ packet of dry yeast and approximately ½ cup of brown sugar or molasses, then allow it to ferment throughout the day. Late in the afternoon, find a place along the edge of the field and either paint your mixture onto the trunk of a tree, or soak an absorbent piece of cloth with the mixture and hang it in an obvious area. When you return at dusk, check your bait to see what it has attracted. Later, before you leave for the night, check again and see what has come to the insect bait after dark.

Many insects and some animals are attracted to blue or white light. On a different night, try hanging a white sheet from a clothesline or from a tree branch and then carefully place a flashlight with the white beam shining behind it. Watch and see what comes to the white light in comparison to your sweet insect bait!

ACTIVITY Hunters of the Night

This predator/prey game, designed for group play under the cover of darkness, creates a scenario that mimics the conditions under which nocturnal critters spend their active time. The mysterious setting will seem challenging, for our eyesight does not work well in the darkness.

During daylight, delineate the boundaries of the playing area and inspect it for safety. Check for all possible hazards, looking for places someone could trip and fall (like logs or holes in the ground), poisonous plants (such as poison ivy), nests of bees (on the ground or hanging), or anything else that could make the scene unsafe. When the game begins, make sure everyone knows they cannot leave the designated playing area for any reason, because of unknown dangers if they wander farther off into the dark.

Discuss the predator/prey relationship with the group. Some might find the concept cruel, so remind them that everything must eat. In order for a carnivore (meat eater) to obtain adequate nourishment, it must catch and ingest another creature. In addition, all ecosystems have a carrying capacity (the maximum population of a species an area can support), so if some animals were not sacrificed for the benefit of others, they would eventually die out anyway, due to lack of sufficient habitat and food.

For the game, divide the group into a few different predators (such as coyote, fox, bobcat, weasel, mink, owl, or bat) and several prey animals (like mice, shrews, voles, lemmings, flying squirrels, rabbits, deer, raccoons, flying insects, or opossums). If twenty participate, for instance, you might have four predators and four each of four prey critters, for a total of sixteen.

Show the predators—perhaps a bat, an owl, a fox, and a coyote—how to move in a specific way to make their identities known to their prey. A bat darts and hunts quickly on the wing, so the person portraying it could flap his hands quickly as he moves; the owl could walk slowly with arms outspread but not flapping to imitate its ability to fly silently; the fox could hold his hands behind his head with two fingers up on each hand, inferring attentive listening; and the coyote could walk and use his arms in strong, forward, circular motions to indicate its long stride and stalking ability. Allow the predators to practice their motions, improvising if they wish, but agree on a slow, thoughtful movement to help the prey identify the predators.

The predators will hunt their particular prey animals. For instance, the bat will search for flying insects, the owl for mice, the fox for rabbits, and the coyote for young fawns. Assign the prey a sound to make if a predator discovers them while they are hiding, so after the game begins, the predator will know if he has found the correct prey. Insects could make a short "tee" sound, repeated over and over (tee-tee-tee-tee-tee-tee-tee); mice could make a squeaking sound; the rabbit can have a little scream, "eeiiii"; and the fawn might "baa" like a sheep. The identity of the prey must be kept secret from the predator, so practice the vocalizations with each group of prey in a place where the predators can hear but not see them.

After everyone knows the movements of the predators and the sounds of the prey, instruct the predators to cover their eyes while the prey hide. Once hidden, they cannot move or run elsewhere when they see their predator coming. Their goal is to remain still and quiet, and attempt to camouflage themselves by getting down low in the grass or hiding behind something, so the predator cannot easily find them. *Do not allow them to cover themselves and become buried beneath anything.*

The predators begin by standing quietly and listening for any sounds of a possible meal. (The predators will know which animal and sound they are listening for, but they will not know who represents their prey.) When they think they hear something, or wish to begin hunting, they should move slowly and stealthily through the area. They should stop, listen, smell, and be alert to anything that might give them a clue to the location of their prey.

When they find one of the hiding critters, they should hover above it. The hovering motion tells the prey that it has been found and should identify itself by *quietly* making its sound. If the vocalization does not match his prey, then the predator must continue his search, while the prey remains hidden and becomes quiet again. Once a prey has made his sound, however, he has given his predator a hint as to his approximate location. An alert predator will pick up the signal, so the prey should be prepared!

If the sound matches the predator's specific quarry, the critter has been caught and must stand up. Each predator needs to mentally keep count and, after finding his fourth dinner item, gather them on the side of the playing area, while the remaining players continue the hunt. The game ends when all of the preys have been found.

Follow up with a visit to an active nighttime habitat. The water's edge is one of the best places to find creatures hunting and interacting at night. Mammals come looking for food and water, and you can see aquatic creatures such as frogs and fish. Sounds fill the air, from the croaking of frogs to the splashing sounds of fish and other creatures. You might encounter tracks on the muddy banks or hear the call of an owl overhead. Sit quietly in a camouflaged spot, absorbing the actions of the life around you.

ACTIVITY Rope Walks

- *Rope (long enough—or enough sections—to run the course)*

During daylight hours, find a path or area that you would like to guide your group along at night. If possible, find a place that passes from field to forest to water. The greater the variety in sounds and sensory experiences you can access, the more inspiring and educational the trip will be. As with the previous activity, make sure no hazards mark the course!

In order to keep everyone on the same safe path, string a rope or cord from point to point—tree to tree, post to tree, post to post, etc. Since many hands will run along the rope, choose one that is not rough to the touch. As you tie the rope along the trail, notice what everyone will walk on or through. Be sure the path will keep everyone's feet and legs out of harm's way and on a sure footing.

When you have completed the course, put your hand on the rope and walk the path with your eyes open, checking for possible problems. Once you feel that the course is safe and well located, walk it again with your eyes closed, to give you an idea of how the terrain feels underfoot in the dark. Be careful as you wind your way along the path for the first time without the use of your sight. As evening falls, take another look just prior to bringing the group to the trail, to make sure nothing has fallen or gotten in the way since you laid it out.

Before presenting this activity, share information about life at night—who is out there and what they are doing. Discuss the group's awareness and perceptions of the night environment. Using the rope to guide them, instead of flashlights, allows their eyes to adjust to the darkness, which will heighten their abilities to smell, touch, and hear.

Ask the hikers to walk quietly and silently, with eyes open, using all of their senses in the night world, while maintaining a safe distance between each person. Stress safety at all times, especially if working with young people. Do not try to take large numbers of people along the trail at a time. I have found fifteen or fewer to be a good number.

At the end of the walk, gather as a group and share experiences and perceptions with all involved. Encourage everyone to write their feelings and observations in their journal.

ACTIVITY Owl Prowls

- *Portable cassette or CD player*
- *Recording of the species of owl you wish to attract*

You can do this activity for your own personal pleasure, or you can enjoy it with a group. The preparation can take a little time, but you will be more than pleased with the experience of trying to call in a native owl near your home or vacation spot. Owls typically found in the Southern Appalachians include the Eastern screech owl, the barred owl, the great horned owl, occasionally a barn owl, and Northern saw-whet owls at higher elevations.

While the screech owl and barred owl are found closer to communities, the more secretive great horned is uncommon around developed areas. The numbers of barn owls have decreased over time, as they have been hunted until their populations have suffered throughout their range. An unwarranted fear that they would catch small livestock such as chickens has added to their sad fate.

Fortunately, this problem is slowly reversing; an occasional nest is found each breeding season. The Northern saw-whet owl exists in isolated populations on the highest mountains, then moves to the lower elevations during the winter, and is sometimes, but not reliably, seen or heard in and around communities. For your first owl prowl, I suggest trying to attract the Eastern screech owl, as you will have a greater chance of getting a response.

Begin with a commercial CD or cassette of birdsongs, such as those found on page 128 at the end of the "Life on the Wing" chapter. Prepare a recording that repeats the call of the same species, with quiet spaces between. I recommend you record the call, allow 15 seconds of silence, record the call again, allow 30 seconds of silence, record the call once more, allow a minute of silence, record, and follow with 15 seconds of silence. Continue with a scattering of breaks, which produces a more natural calling pattern and provides time to listen for a response. You may also pause the tape to lengthen your listening time. Be patient, listen, and look to the sky for any signs. If you think you hear a bird responding, control your calls so that you play the tape as an answer to the calling bird.

Remember that there is no guarantee. You may have luck, you may not. Getting a return call depends on whether an owl is within reasonable distance. Not knowing what might happen actually adds to the mystery and suspense of the prowl.

One of the first times I ever tried to call in a barred owl, some friends and I had climbed about ½ mile up a gated road, away from traffic and the lights of homes. We played a cassette tape of a barred owl for over an hour, staying quiet and taking the appropriate breaks between calls to listen and wait. We knew that nature moved in its own time and didn't care about our busy schedules and lives, but after about an hour and a half, we were getting tired and decided that we just weren't going to have any luck at all. Breaking our spell of silence, we began talking and laughing as we got ready to leave.

We almost jumped out of our skin when a sudden "who cooks for you, whooo cooks for YOU all" vocalization emerged just a few feet above our heads! Our shock quickly turned into excitement as we realized that a barred owl had responded to our efforts. Later, as we walked back down to the cars, we wondered how long the bird had hung out in the trees above us, checking us out, because we knew it hadn't been there when we arrived. We learned quite a lesson as we reflected on just how *silently* an owl flies.

Experiment with other methods of calling in owls. With practice, many folks become skillful at imitating owls themselves, without the use of electronic devices. Listen to your recordings and see if you can mimic the songs and calls of your favorite owls. Catalogs and stores that sell hunting supplies sometimes carry "owl hooters" that beautifully imitate the call of the barred owl.

However you choose to learn more about the native owls of your area, approach this activity with open eyes. Owls may swoop in your direction, though it happens rarely. In my experience, most birds, once they realize you are not food or an invader, move on to other things. Enjoy your experiences and encounters with these mysterious and dynamic birds of the night.

ACTIVITY High-Elevation Adventure—A Full-Moon Walk

- *Emergency hiking equipment (flashlight, first aid kit)*

The night has a mysterious and intriguing air to it; we know life thrives all around us, yet we see very little. Several of the previous activities involved total immersion in the darkness, but a walk during a full moon will allow you to use your sense of sight more fully. The light from a full moon enables you to see obstacles more easily, so you become a part of the night world in a much more relaxed sense.

To ensure a successful and inspirational walk, find an area with clear fields, such as grass balds found only on the highest mountains in the Southern Appalachians. Open areas at lower elevations will work equally well, as long as you remain outside of the dark cover of the forest.

My favorite location for a full-moon walk is a section of the Appalachian Trail on the highlands of Roan Mountain on the Tennessee/North Carolina border. Every stone beneath your feet is visible under the blanketing light of a full moon, and tree silhouettes melt into the backdrop of the night sky. Ridges upon ridges of surrounding mountains blend and wave around you like the flowing colors of a watercolor painting. The sounds of the wind rustling the leaves of trees along the bald's edges, and the distant hoot of an owl, all add to the overwhelmingly spiritual experience of becoming one with the night. The setting gives the potential for an adventure unlike any other. It is a time of reflection, thought, and personal examination, drawing from the quiet of the night.

The full moon shining over Carvers Gap

Several years ago, I led a memorable group on a full-moon walk across the Roan Mountain balds. The sky foretold a beautiful, clear, full moon, yet just an hour before sunset, a thunderstorm rolled into the valleys around us. As the storm passed and night began to fall, the fog started to rise; pretty soon the mountain summit was completely out of sight. I certainly had a hard time deciding what to do with 50 people who wanted to go to the highest peaks (possibly in the fog!) and enjoy the wonders of the full moon.

I gathered everyone together, and the group decided unanimously to take the chance and drive up to Carvers Gap. So off we went, through thick fog, convinced we'd never see the moon that night. Then the mountain performed its magic, and we drove right out of the clouds to find nearly indescribable views under a crystal clear sky. Below us were layers of clouds so thick, they looked like we could walk on them. At the farthest edge of the clouds, the end of the sun's descent left shades of red, yellow, and orange reflecting on the higher layers. The color show, as spectacular as a summer rainbow, rendered everyone speechless; no one had expected such a surprise after leaving the fog and rain at the lower elevation.

Yet this fantastic show was only the beginning. After this unexpected treat, we walked up Round Bald with a clear sky above. As we arrived, we were greeted by the rising of the fullest orange moon I had ever seen.

We continued to Jane Bald, across the top of mountains so open and treeless we could see for miles in every direction. The bright moonlight rendered the highest ridges of the surrounding mountains as clear to the eye as on a bright sunlit day.

When we reached Grassy Ridge, the quiet aura that overcame the group told the story. Venturing into the night had proven to be a new and fulfilling way to study nature, truly capturing everyone's hearts and minds.

Moon Walk Activity Extensions

Migratory Shadows

During the fall season of migration, plan a full-moon walk on a high, open mountain and take along a spotting scope, telescope, or binoculars. Set your scope on the moon to watch for silhouettes of migrating birds as they pass in front of the full moon.

Reflections

If you are traveling with a group, class, or club, take the time to discuss the life of the night: Who is out there? What are they doing? Let your imaginations merge with the life around you as you reflect on the possibility that an owl might be hunting nearby for an evening meal as the birds of the daytime are perching or sitting on their nests.

GETTING BUGGY

If you think it's hard to find your friends in the dark, just imagine how difficult it could be for two tiny insects! Fortunately, nature has provided them with special adaptations to find their own kind. As darkness falls, the sounds of many insects begin to emerge.

Crickets hang low in the bushes, rubbing a scraper on one wing against the ridges of the other. This action produces the call we hear when they hope to attract a mate, warn other crickets of danger, or claim their territory. Up higher in the trees, the late summer sound of the katydid begins to ring out. Folks in the mountains say their call signals the start of a six-week period until the first frost.

Many more insect sounds rise and fall through the spring, summer, and fall months. Here we focus on a few to see just how our insect friends find a mate.

Cricket Songs—Calculating Temperature

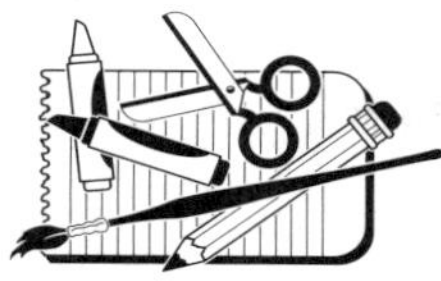

- *Stopwatch or wristwatch with second hand*
- *Outdoor thermometer*
- *Pencil and paper*

This fun activity for late summer or early fall will help you calculate the outside temperature while enjoying the nighttime chirping of crickets. You may hear other insects at night, which might confuse you, but listen for the call of the field cricket, which produces low, musical chirps. Each chirp is brief and distinct and repeats with a steady beat. Other species of crickets sound more trill-like. If you can hum along with the call or mimic the pitch, then it is *not* a field cricket. The grasshopper, which has a mechanical vocalization, cannot be hummed along with either.

Once you have identified the field cricket, concentrate on its call. Check your watch and count the number of chirps in 15 seconds. Add 40 to this number, and you will have a close estimate of the temperature in degrees Fahrenheit. Compare this number to the reading on your thermometer and see how close the crickets have predicted the temperature.

Try this activity on different nights and at various times on the same night, and you will discover that the period of silence between chirps will change. If you present this activity to a group of people, ask them if they can figure out what makes the cricket chirp faster or slower. By referring to the data gathered from several observations, they will find that when it is cooler outside, crickets chirp much slower, and they speed up in warmer temperatures.

If you are familiar with the call of the snowy tree cricket, you may use it with a slight change to the formula. Instead of 40, add 37 to the number of chirps in 15 seconds to get the approximate temperature. To convert to Celsius, subtract 32 from the degrees Fahrenheit, multiply the result by 5, and divide that answer by 9.

ACTIVITY Cricket Chirps—Attracting with Sounds

- *Subtle noisemakers such as combs, pencils, and bottles*

Though crickets are quite small, their loud calls compensate for their tiny size. Of course, they do not produce their chorus of sound for the purpose of calculating the outside air temperature; their chirps are patterned in a repetitious format so the same species can find each other and attract mates.

This group activity focuses on learning to distinguish one particular sound among the many existing simultaneously in the environment. Begin by dividing the group in half and separating the teams from each other. Choose team leaders and give them both a collection of the same set of sound makers. For instance, if you have ten people with five on each team, you need two each of five sounds.

Have the leaders pass out the sound-making objects to team members. Give everyone time to practice their sounds, helping them when needed. When everyone is comfortable creating their sounds, ask them to scatter throughout the playing area in a random fashion. Instruct everyone to continually make their sound while trying to find their partner, or mate, amidst the other sounds of the entire group. As each pair finds one another, they should discontinue making the sound, until everyone finds their mate. Play the game again, but continue making the sound until all mates have found each other.

The sound made by running your thumb over the teeth of a comb closely mimics the call of a cricket. You can use different sizes of combs to produce a variety of pitches, teaching the group to listen intently for the tiniest nuance in sound. Someone cannot just say, "My mate sounds like the teeth on a comb." The question becomes, "Yes, but *which* comb?"

Using only combs might prove a little too complex for younger ages, so experiment with sounds produced by everyday household objects. Clack together two pencils or two candles or two sticks; all will make distinct sounds. Knock a pencil gently against a bottle or cup, or rub two objects together repetitively. Strive to create sounds that will remain the same when repeated over and over again.

ACTIVITY Moth-ing Around—Attracting by Scent

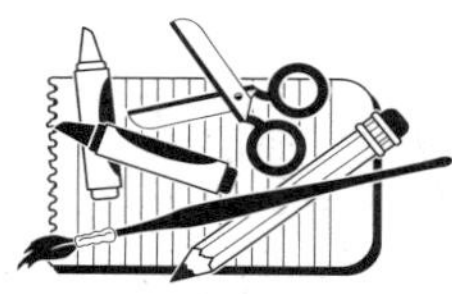

- *Several different scents—cooking extracts, perfumes with distinctive odors, or body spritzes with fruity scents—preferably one scent for each pair of players*
- *Cotton balls*

Moths are interesting, night-active insects that feed and search for mates under the cover of night. All of us can probably remember a time when we ventured out in the morning to find a wide variety of moths, boasting many colors, sizes, and shapes, resting around the outdoor lights that burn throughout the night around our homes.

Most moths seen circling lights and campfires during the night belong to the *Noctuidae* family. Coming from the Latin word *noctua*, their name means "night owl." Noctuid moths navigate by keeping their wings at a constant angle in relation to the moon, so bright lights confuse them and draw them in. They use their antennae, which are sensitive to odors, to locate nectar and help them to find a mate. The scent emitted by a female moth can draw in a male from as far as six miles away!

Moths are not the only ones out at night looking for nourishment; they can also become the meal of something preying upon them. Creatures such as the long-eared bat use echolocation to detect a moth's whereabouts. But in an attempt to outsmart the bat, some moth species produce ultrasonic clicks to confuse the bat's reception. The bat counters this challenge by relying solely on the sound of the moth's wing beat and not using echolocation when approaching a moth.

This group activity demonstrates a moth's ability to locate a mate through its olfactory system. Participants will have to depend on their noses to recognize the scents, though, since humans do not have antennae! Divide the group in two, so half the players portray males, and the other half females.

Separate the males from the females. Take a cotton ball and apply an ample amount of a different scent to the back of each female's left hand. When all the scents are applied, ask the females to scatter out across the playing area.

Gather all the males and give each of them a cotton ball used to apply a scent to one of the females. Allow them to smell the scent until they feel familiar with it. When they are confident they can "sniff out" the correct partner, send them out in search of their mates. Instruct them to sniff the back of the left hand of the females and, when they think they have found a prospective mate, stop and stay with her.

At the end, check to see if they did find their correct partner. More than likely, they will, making this activity an excellent exercise in learning to depend on a sense other than sight. If time permits, wash the scent off the hands of the females and switch roles so everyone has a chance to use their sense of smell.

ACTIVITY Firefly Flashes—Attracting by Sight and Light

- *Flashlights (1 for each person)*
- *Index cards and pens or pencils*

As evening falls in the summertime, we are enchanted to see the growing number of firefly flashes against the dark backdrop of the night sky and woodland edge. Very little can compare to the childhood delight of carefully catching and observing the flashing firefly before allowing it to go free again. Maybe our human need for the security of light makes the tiny flash intriguing, but for whatever reason, the firefly captures the imaginations of us all.

The firefly—actually a beetle and not a fly at all—creates light in its abdomen without heat through a process called bioluminescence. The reaction begins when luciferin, a light-emitting pigment, and luciferase, an enzyme, combine with oxygen to produce what we observe as the firefly's flash.

At twilight, crepuscular fireflies—those that are active at dusk—emit a yellow light. Fireflies in the family Lampyridae—beetles that emerge later at night—give off a green light. Other species appear at different times of the year and in varied habitats. A glow-worm in the ground could be either an immature firefly, which has not grown wings, or a wingless adult female from the genus Phengodes, which flashes from the ground to attract a flying male.

Fireflies emit light not only to attract mates, but also as a defensive signal or to show aggression. Each species produces its own pattern of flashes. The length of the flash and the amount of time between flashes create a pattern similar to Morse code.

For this group activity, participants will portray fireflies and search for their mates by using flashlights to repeat a series of short and long flashes. Split the group in two, and choose someone to act as leader of the female fireflies and someone as leader of the males.

Ask the leaders to create unique flash patterns and record them on individual index cards. Copy each pattern on another card, so both members of a firefly pair have one to refer to. Try to keep it relatively easy, especially when working with children. Complex patterns make it hard to accurately repeat the flashes over and over again and can lead to confusion.

Some ideas for patterns include:

3 short flashes

1 short flash – 1 long – 1 short

3 long flashes

1 short flash – 1 short – pause (count to 2 slowly) – 1 long – 1 long

While the leaders prepare flash patterns, conduct a practice session with everyone else working in unison to produce shorts, longs, and pauses with their flashlights. When they all have the hang of it and the leaders have rejoined the group, separate the male fireflies from the females.

Ask the leaders to give all the participants an index card with a pattern written on it. Each firefly should have a partner in the other group who holds a matching card. Let everyone practice their flashing pattern, helping when necessary.

When everyone is prepared, line up the male fireflies in front of the females, approximately 15 feet apart. Leave sufficient space—at least an arm's length—between each person. Everyone needs to see all of the flashes of every member on the opposite side, so you may need to make adjustments for a larger group.

So everyone can have the opportunity to focus on the flash patterns before everyone starts flashing at the same time, I recommend a gradual approach. Ask the males to flash their patterns one time on the call of "flash." Pause for a moment, and call "flash" again, and have them repeat the pattern. While they are flashing, the females should closely watch the patterns to try to identify the one that matches theirs. Then ask the females to flash their lights two separate times, just as the males did.

Next, instruct both groups to reproduce their flash patterns one time, at the same time, on the call of "flash." Continue calling "flash," allowing a few moments between each call. The goal is for each group member to find his mate and stand beside him. When everyone has paired up, check their cards to see if they are correct.

Challenge participants to find their mates under more natural, yet difficult circumstances, since fireflies don't take turns in a normal situation. Give everyone a new card and make sure they can accurately reproduce the flash pattern. Ask them to scatter randomly across the playing area. On the call of "flash," have everyone begin flashing as they wander around trying to find their mate, who may be right next to them, or clear across the field!

THE NIGHT SKY

Gazing into the depths of the night sky can be humbling, for it doesn't take long to feel lost in the enormity of the universe. Throughout time, different cultures have interpreted the stars and the sky in a multitude of ways, all in an attempt to understand themselves and what lies beyond. Folk legends have emerged, and scientific facts have been added to our knowledge base.

Many of us do not spend much time gazing at the stars; other folks cannot even see them because they live in and around cities with much background light. The following activities are suggested as a way to introduce you to the night sky and encourage you to find places to view the stars, the galaxies, the planets, and all of the other miracles of the universe.

ACTIVITY Star Relay

- *Books or illustrations of constellations*
- *Paper cut-out stars (enough for each constellation learned)*

Before playing the game, spend a little time learning three to nine constellations, depending on the number of participants, their ages, and how easily they can remember the patterns associated with the names. (Use an odd number to avoid having a tie.) Try to choose a view of the night sky that matches the season, so you can compare to the real stars above you.

Divide the group in two, and give each team a field guide or illustrations of the constellations, marking the ones they need to know. Their goal is to reproduce each formation, using their bodies as the stars that form the points of the constellation. You may work with them, or if they are older, let them study within their group.

If you have enough room available, encourage them to spread out. I often describe the space they need to use by telling them that if an airplane flew over, the pilot should be able to recognize the constellation from the air. If everyone bunches together, they will look like just that—a bunch of people, not a shape.

Begin the relay with both teams standing on opposite sides of the playing area. Tell the participants that after you call out the name of a constellation, they should move to the appropriate positions to create the shape. Instruct them to call out "ready" when their team is in place. While you check to see if the first team has correctly formed the constellation, the second team should hold its position. If the stars are not in their proper place, continue until one team is a winner. Each time a team wins a round, give them a paper star. At the end of all of the rounds of play, the team with the most stars wins.

To finish out the session, bring the teams back together and divide everyone into small groups to form all of the constellations they have learned (or as many as possible). Give them a chance to review where in the sky the constellations rest in relation to each other. Tell them that they will create a view of a portion of the night sky, therefore they must not only form a constellation, but they need to figure out its location.

Assign each group a constellation, reminding them to spread out and think about where their group needs to be on the playing area in relation to the others. Instruct them to extend their arms to the side (parallel to the ground) when their constellation group is in position.

Work your way through the playing area, scanning the re-created view of the night sky. If a group is in the right place and has properly formed the constellation, ask them to wiggle their fingers (like twinkling stars). The ones who are wrong must try to figure out where they belong in your "cosmos."

When everyone is in the correct place, have them spin slowly, arms and fingers extended, acting like sparkling stars gracing the night sky. If possible, follow up with a nighttime star observation party to find the real stars twinkling above.

ACTIVITY Imaginary Worlds

- *Paper to write on and pencils or pens*
- *Paper to draw on and any desired art medium (pencils, crayons, paint, etc.)*

This activity works well with any number of people and gives the opportunity to let imaginations work overtime. Since we know so little about what exists in the universe, participants can take a few liberties to create a few fictitious worlds beyond our own.

Give each person a piece of paper and a pen or pencil. Ask them to write a description of a make-believe planet, telling its temperature, climate, what grows there (if anything), water availability, strange phenomena, and any other detail that makes their "new" world unique. Their goal is to paint as elaborate a picture as possible, as in the following example.

> *The planet Bergynan never goes over 10 degrees Fahrenheit during the day, but at night it soars to 44! Trees are everywhere, but they grow no taller than 8 inches. Daily windstorms are common, but the short trees have adapted so they are not affected by the high winds. The ground appears dry and dusty with signs of underground tunnels, much like mole tunnels on Earth. There is little vegetation, with the exception of the many trees. The leaves of the tiny trees form droplets of water around the edges early in the morning, but the planet's surface shows no sign of running water. The daylight lasts only a short time, 4 to 5 hours at the most. When darkness falls, the temperature rises and remains this way for 30 hours or more at a time.*

After everyone has finished writing their descriptions, fold them and drop them in a box or container. Ask everyone to draw one back out of the box, making sure they do not have their own. Have them read the description and draw a life-form that might live in such an environment.

Share the descriptions and drawings at the end of the activity. It will be fun to see what a person has come up with to live in the world you have described, in addition to all of the other creative descriptions and inhabitants!

Further Reading

The Constellations: Stars and Stories by Chris Sasaki and Jo Boddy
Find the Constellations by H. A. Rey
A Guide to Night Sounds (Audio) by Lang Elliott
Keepers of the Night: Native American Stories and Nocturnal Activities for Children by Michael J. Caduto
Nature's Living Lights: Fireflies and Other Bioluminescent Creatures by Virginia B. Silverstein, Alvin Silverstein, Pamela Carroll, and Walter Carroll
Turn Left at Orion: A Hundred Night Sky Objects to See in a Small Telescope—and How to Find Them by Guy Consolmagno
A Walk through the Southern Sky: A Guide to Stars and Constellations and Their Legends by Milton D. Heifetz and Wil Tirion

Living Together

The pages of this book have focused on many things, including the seasons, plants, insects, animals, the environment, the sky, and more. As you move toward the end of the book, think about how everything fits together on Earth.

Countless life-forms exist on Earth, all-striving to grow and survive in a system that works well if not tampered with in a negative way. Numerous things, many involving human interference, can throw the natural world off balance. Pollution of the air, land, and water, coupled with destruction of wildlife habitat or the introduction of nonnative species, all play a role in destroying plants and animals.

As we strive to ensure a healthy planet, everyone should know and understand the word *biodiversity*. Within this word are two parts with individual meaning: *bio*, referring to biology or life, followed by *diversity*, meaning the condition of being different. A healthy environment boasts a large variety of species of plants and animals, a concept that applies to both local habitats or the world as a whole.

An accurate determination of the health and diversity of a habitat cannot be assessed without the ability to name, describe, and group living things. Scientists and biologists use taxonomy to classify forms of life according to similar characteristics, ultimately giving each living thing a species name to indicate its distinction in some fashion from others in its group.

Scientists have named approximately 350,000 species of beetles—⅕ of all known forms of life and ¼ of all animals—and they believe there are millions of beetles yet to discover within the canopies of the world's rain forests. Biologists disagree on the number of undescribed species of plants and animals that exist, but one thing they do agree on: the number is high. Scientists have classified only a small portion—a mere 1.75 million species.

Why would ten little beetles, all of which look basically the same, fall into totally different scientific categories? The determination of a species can be complex, and scientists can have slightly different interpretations. Biologists refer to a "biological species concept," which defines a species as a set of actually or potentially interbreeding organisms. The gene pool—the set of genes contained in an interbreeding population—helps delineate the makeup of a particular species. Typically, the morphology, or the form and structure, of an organism determines whether or not it gets classified as a distinct species.

The bottom line is that our planet provides a home to an enormous variety of life! The numbers are staggering and nearly impossible to comprehend, considering that we have so much left to learn. As a culture and society, we attempt to make life more rewarding and comfortable. Plants and chemical components found within the natural world can cure certain diseases or aid in their management. In most cases, however, we do not know what benefits and attributes particular organisms may possess, so destroying what we do not truly understand seems illogical. Should we haphazardly, without thought and consideration, wipe out and pollute parts of the world before considering the final outcome? Realizing how little we know makes the concepts of pollution, habitat loss, and, ultimately, extinction frightening. Therefore we must use great care and knowledge when making decisions regarding Earth.

The activities in the previous chapters helped awaken your senses, while you discovered the smallest forms of life and the vastness of the universe. Keep your senses keen as you participate in the games, crafts, and activities that follow.

GAMES FOR NATURE LOVERS

ACTIVITY Leaf-Passing Relay

- *Several leaves in different sizes, some that feel sturdy, and others that feel as though they might easily tear*

Every part of the natural world, no matter how strong it appears, can be very fragile and easily altered or damaged if treated unwisely. If we as caretakers of this land do not think before we act, the results of our actions can sometimes be irreparable.

The trees and shrubs in the Southern Appalachians boast a great variety of shapes, colors, and forms of their leaves; some are thick and fleshy, while others are light and delicate. The canopy formed by the layers of leaves acts as a home and a shelter to inhabitants of the forest. The Leaf-Passing Relay emphasizes the importance of doing our part to protect trees.

Begin by forming teams with at least four people on each team, but no more than ten. Give all teams a similar leaf. The object of the game is to successfully pass a leaf from the front of the line to the end without damaging the leaf. When the leaf reaches the end of the line, the last person will run with it to the front of the line and start over the process of passing the leaf from front to back. Continue until all team members have run from the back to the front, and the original starting person returns to the first position.

The real challenge of these games is to finish with an undamaged leaf, while completing the relay as quickly as possible. If a team finishes first, but the leaf has become torn or crumpled, that team will not win. If it is too close to call, declare both of the teams winners. Though more difficult for younger children, the activity vividly illustrates how delicate our environment is and the need to be careful with our actions at all times.

To make the game more exciting, conduct several relays with different passing techniques.

- Relay #1—Pass the leaf in an over-and-under pattern. Everyone faces the front, and the first person passes the leaf between his legs, the second passes over his head, the third between his legs, and so on down the line.
- Relay #2—Pass the leaf from chin to chin. The first person holds the leaf under his chin and passes it to the next person, who must keep it under his chin, and so on. No hands allowed! If the leaf falls to the ground, pick it up and start over at the front of the line.
- Relay #3—Pass the leaf from shoe to shoe. Place the leaf on top of the first person's shoe, and pass it back by sliding it on top of the shoe of the next person in line. Once again, no hands allowed!
- Relay #4—Pass the leaf between fingers. The first person holds the leaf between his ring and middle fingers. The person behind him will take it in the same fashion. Use only one hand to pass it to the end of the line.
- Relay #5—Carry the leaf across the field. For this relay, create two

teams, then split each team into two lines facing each other on opposite sides of a playing field, so you end up with four lines. Give a leaf to the first person in each line on one side of the playing field. On the call of "go," they will both run across the field, lay the leaf down at the feet of the first person in the facing line, and go to the back of the line. The next runner will carefully pick up the leaf and run across the field to the person waiting at the front of the line on the other side. Continue until everyone has passed the leaf, and the first people to start the lines are back in the front on the opposite side of the field.

ACTIVITY Crawdad Tag

There are other ways to be mobile besides the upright method people are accustomed to. In the natural world, the way animals move and defend themselves plays a major role in determining who lives. Sometimes we take for granted the challenges some creatures must meet to survive on a daily basis.

Introduce this game with a discussion—presented by a leader or as a group sharing ideas—of different animals and how they move through their environment. Consider those who travel on four legs with feet; those with claws, fins, or wings; and snakes, which use their muscles and scales.

This game will give the players a chance to experience a more difficult type of movement and appreciate some of the unusual ways other creatures get around. The crayfish—sometimes called crawfish or crawdad—lives in an ever-flowing river or creek and must constantly battle the force of the water to eat and exist. As it lumbers along the streambed in a less than graceful fashion, it must endeavor to hang on, lest the water sweeps it downstream.

Divide into two teams—this game works better with 10 or fewer team members—both portraying crawdads that will move with a slight upside-down waddle around the field. Give everyone a little practice time walking on all fours, with their backs to the ground and their bellies to the sky.

Delineate boundaries so the play area is not too large, and line the teams up, in crawdad position, on opposite ends of the field. Instruct the players to move toward the middle on the call of "go," in an attempt to tag each other. Those tagged join the team that tagged them and move to the other side of the field.

Once someone has switched teams, his original teammates can tag him so he can return to his old team. The game ends when all team members except one have been tagged and have joined the other team. The one remaining crawdad is the surviving team "elder" and will have first pick when choosing a new team for the next round of play.

For a variation on the game, divide the players into teams portraying crawdads and snakes. (Queen snakes love to dine on young crawdads.) The object of the game is for the snakes to travel on their hands and knees and tag the crawdads, who move in the same upside-down fashion as before. (Though snakes have no hands and knees, attempting to play while lying on the ground with your hands and feet tied together presents too much of a challenge! Our bodies and muscles just do not possess the strength needed to crawl on the ground like a snake.)

ACTIVITY Turtle Run

- *A large box, piece of cardboard, or piece of paper*
- *Poster paints and brushes (if you decorate the box)*

Portraying a turtle in this game takes a cooperative effort, as two people try to become one beneath a homemade shell. A box big enough to cover both individuals makes the easiest and most effective prop for the shell, but if you don't have a big enough box, a large piece of cardboard or sheet of paper will work. To make an interesting turtle shell, paint the outside of the box to give it a realistic look. You can make as many turtles as you wish, or make only one and allow everyone a turn playing the turtle.

As you create the shell, keep in mind that the two players will be on their feet in an upright position. At the front of the box, near the top, cut a hole big enough for the first person to stick his head in and out without bumping it too much. His feet represent the turtle's front feet, while his hands are above his head, holding up the box. The second player, standing behind the first and unable to see where he is going, will also use his hands to hold up the box. His feet represent the turtle's back feet.

Assign each turtle one specific predator, who does not need a shell like the turtle but must travel on all fours. Begin with the turtles on a starting line, underneath their shells, not looking while the predators hide around the perimeter of the playing area. Not knowing where the predator is coming from will make it necessary for the turtle to be aware of what might appear from any direction.

Give the turtles a short head start before releasing the predators. Each turtle duo must exist as one unit, for it would fall to pieces if a front foot tried to go to the right while a back one went off to the left. Communication is imperative underneath the shell, and the person playing the back of the turtle must depend on his partner to navigate.

Each turtle must travel to the designated finish line in order to survive the advances of the predator and win the game. The person at the front of the turtle may stick out his head to look around at any time. If he sees the predator coming, he and his partner can duck inside the shell, pulling in all their toes and lowering the box. If nothing is sticking out, and the box rests flat on the ground, the turtle is safe, but the turtle eventually will need to rise up and travel to the safety of the finish line.

A predator, in order to win the game, must tag one of the turtle's four feet. Or when the turtle is up and moving, the predator can tag its shell. Of course, the predator cannot pull the shell off of the turtle; he must be patient and wait for the turtle to get up and move. The predator must be sly and try to trick the turtle; in turn, the turtle must also outwit his enemy. If the predator remains nearby, the turtle will probably stay inside and refuse to come out! If the predator slips away, the turtle will feel safe and come out of his shell, trying to move a little closer to the finish line.

The game ends when either the turtle makes it to the finish line or the predator tags the turtle during his journey. Switch places and play again, with a new predator and different people inside the turtle's shell.

Dinnertime—Food Chains

- *Large ball of string or twine*
- *Name tags, index cards, or pieces of paper to hang from or attach to each player*

Many people become alarmed when thinking that a beautiful, soaring hawk might swoop down to a bird feeder to scoop up an unsuspecting songbird for its dinner. But in order to survive, everything in the natural world must eat. Some creatures are purely vegetarians and do not eat meat, but carnivores obtain nourishment from eating other animals. The predator/prey relationship provides a system of checks and balances, guaranteeing that one species does not become dominant and overpopulate an area. The strong survive to produce young to ensure the continuance of their species in a particular habitat.

The carnivorous animals may feast on other carnivores, or they may eat herbivores, creatures that eat only plants eaters. Plants, which must survive, grow, and flourish to provide food for the plant eaters, depend heavily on a healthy climate—just enough rain, sunlight, and nourishment.

Every factor that leads to the success of a food chain can be altered or destroyed. A natural disaster, human interference, or a sudden change in the reproductive capacity of a certain population can all aid in throwing the odds in favor of one species or the other. A bad season with not enough food for a particular species can quickly cause its population to drop for one or more years. The decrease, in turn, may affect another animal that depends heavily on that species for food.

This group activity is designed to help you visualize the complex interactions of living things and the many factors that can affect them. Life on Earth is fragile and easily altered, thus it is important for humankind to not interfere in a negative way. Hold a discussion on our food and where it comes from. To help get the players' minds on track, and to put the natural world into perspective, have them consider our own lives and what we do to survive. You might pose the following questions:

"How do you eat?"

"How did your dinner grow?"

"What do you eat?"

"Where does your food come from?"

Answers might include vegetables, which grow by soil nutrients, water, and the light and energy of the sun. Discuss how water comes from the water table, rain, creeks, and streams. Talk about how decomposition returns nutrients to the soil. As the deliberation continues, you will have established a verbal food chain, but visualizing the food chain will leave a more lasting impression.

Create a human illustration of a food chain using between 5 to 30 players who will each portray a plant, animal, or natural element. Before the activity begins, cut up small pieces of paper, or use name tags, and write an element, plant, or animal on each tag or paper, then place them in a box. Include everything necessary to produce a good illustration of the food chain. You will need a variety of animals, plants, soil, rain, clouds, sun, insects, and decomposers, such as mushrooms.

Assemble the players in a circle and choose someone to draw a paper out of the box. Announce to the group what it says, and attach the tag to the person. When everyone has chosen, your circle will have representatives of the components of an ecosystem, in no particular order.

Next, connect the food chain with the ball of string. Pick any player at random to start the string and ask, "Who in this group could you eat, could enable your survival, or would help you grow?" When he responds, ask him to toss the ball of string to that person while holding on to the end of the string. Pose the same question to that person, who, in turn, holds on to the string and tosses the ball to the person chosen as his food or survival tool. As the game continues, the web becomes more and more entangled and complex with each toss.

Each person will have several choices within the circle, so you can continue tossing the string after everyone has had at least one chance. For example, every plant could choose the mushroom, a decomposer that returns nutrients to the soil to help all plants grow. All living things need the sun, clean air, and water; therefore, the health and survival of certain components of the ecosystem are crucial to their existence.

When everyone has tossed the string, an intricate food "web" will have been constructed in the center, illustrating the complex interactions within our natural world. Take some time to discuss how each creature depends not just on one thing, but on the entire system. Then ask, "What would happen if something injured a part of our web?"

To illustrate the answer, clip the string at one person, trying to pick a spot important to most of the others. For instance, clip the string at the person playing the part of the air. Ask how people harm the air and if it is important to our survival. When you clip the string, the web will collapse, creating a memorable illustration of the fragility of nature and the interdependence of all living things.

ACTIVITY Rainbow Scavenger Hunt

- *A piece of paper and a pen or pencil*

Rainbows form during or just after a gentle rain, as the sun shines through the glistening drops of water. What could be more delightful than observing the colors of the spectrum arching across the daytime sky? I have never met a person who has not indicated excitement in seeing a rainbow.

In this scavenger hunt, participants search throughout Mother Nature's domain for all the colors of the rainbow. Give everyone a piece of paper and ask them to make seven columns and write the colors of the rainbow—red, orange, yellow, green, blue, indigo, and violet—at the top of each column. Designate an area for the "hunters" to explore, trying to spot as many rainbow colors as they can, listing them in the appropriate columns. Tell them to look closely for the subtle shades of color that any one object might possess. For instance, are trees all one shade of green, or do numerous greens, browns, grays, and blacks make up what they see?

At the end of the hunt have each person share what he has found. Consider having a special certificate or award for the best observer.

ACTIVITY The Spider and the Fly

- *A large ball of string*
- *Blindfold*

The purpose of this game is to encourage the players to concentrate on their senses in a most acute fashion. Often in the natural world, a creature's ability to focus in on his prey, or to be still and camouflage himself to avoid being the prey, is an ultimate survival skill. This activity will enable participants to practice both of these skills, as they portray a spider trying to find a fly.

Before the game begins, construct a string web at about waist level, so the spider may follow it by running his hand along the string while standing upright. Since the spider will wear a blindfold, be cautious in your planning, and make sure the play area has no holes to fall in or objects to trip on. The web can be any shape and size, tied across an open area from tree to post, stake to tree, or to whatever you can find to create your structure. Although the fiber of real webs typically crosses a number of times, you should try *not* to cross your string, because it may inadvertently create areas the spider cannot access.

First, blindfold the spider, then instruct the fly to find a place to wait silently somewhere in the web. He cannot move from there and must concentrate on staying quiet. The poor fly has become stuck in the spider's web and cannot get away!

Give the spider a set amount of time to find the fly, depending on the size of the web and the age of the players. Rather than moving through the web haphazardly and without a plan, the spider should stop and listen carefully for any sounds that might direct the him to the fly. Spectators must remain silent so their sounds will not distract the spider.

If the spider finds the fly at the end of the allotted time, the fly has become his dinner, and they both choose a new spider and fly for the next round of play. If the spider has not found the fly, he becomes the next fly, and the old fly may choose a new spider.

ACTIVITY The Fox and the Bird

- *A small rock*

This game works best with 10-25 players. Choose one to play the fox and another to play the bird. The remaining participants will play trees; instruct them to form a circle and keep their hands behind their backs. The fox stands inside the circle, where he cannot see the hands of the trees, and the bird stays outside, holding a small rock.

The rock symbolizes an egg, which the bird wants to hide and protect from the fox, who in turn is quite hungry! Begin the game with the bird circling the trees and reciting, "I have an egg within my nest. Where can I hide it from the sly fox's quest?"

As the bird walks around the circle, she pretends to drop the rock in each player's hand. The bird should try to bluff the fox so he cannot tell which tree has the egg. After the bird has left the egg somewhere, she should continue on as if she still has the egg and then stop at a random point in the circle. The fox must then guess which tree holds the egg.

The fox gets only one guess; if he answers correctly, he becomes the bird, the bird becomes a tree, and the tree holding the egg becomes the fox. If the fox guesses incorrectly, he trades places with the tree holding the egg, and the bird gets to hide her egg again. After the bird has stumped three foxes, she becomes a tree and chooses a new bird as a replacement.

ACTIVITY Camouflage Hide and Seek

Have you ever experienced the thrill of a small mammal, or possibly a deer, approaching you closely while you sit quietly in a forest or field? The excitement is nearly indescribable, as it seems improbable for a wild animal to approach a human. Sometimes, by remaining completely still and unthreatening, you increase the chances that an animal will move a little closer than you might have expected.

In this activity, the players will practice hiding and blending in with their environment so quietly and without movement, that the seeker will find it difficult to discover them. Any number of players can participate in the game, with one person seeking and the rest hiding. If several join in, you might consider using two seekers.

Designate the boundaries for the game, and send the hiders off first to find their spots, while the seeker hides his eyes and waits a predetermined amount of time before heading out. The seeker's job is to find all of the hidden inhabitants of this environment by alert observation, listening for the slightest rustle or breath.

Those hiding need to become an integral part of their surroundings by getting their imaginations and personalities into the game. They might pretend to be a moth on the side of a tree, a small mouse behind a rock, or a tiny snake curled up under a bush, remembering all the while to stay absolutely still, trying to become a part of the environment.

After a hider has been found, he will wait in the center of the playing area until the seeker has found everyone. The last person found becomes the seeker for the next round.

Trivia Maze

- *10-20 questions and answers written on paper*
- *Index cards*
- *Paper and pen or pencil for each team*

Teams with no more that five members each try to find their way to the end of the trail in this game of questions and answers. With smaller groups, individuals can compete against each other. It's fun to play and can be quite a creative endeavor for the organizer, who lays out the trail and writes the questions.

Compose a series of 10 to 20 multiple-choice questions—make sure each question is appropriate for the group playing—and post them at station numbers corresponding to the question number. The stations can be outdoors, posted on trees, rocks, fences, and so on, or around the inside of a home or school. Provide two answers, one correct and one incorrect, to each question. After each answer, whether right or wrong, also tell participants which station to proceed to next. For example, Question 1, next to a red oak tree at Station 1, might ask, "Which of the following birds would you most likely see swooping from the sky to catch a mouse in a field? A) Bluebird—proceed to Station 6. B) Hawk—proceed to Station 4." For the last question, add a note to return to the leader to have answers checked.

To begin the game, gather all the teams in an area where they cannot see Station 1. Send one team to the first station, where they will write down the answer they think is correct and advance to the station designated by their answer. When they arrive at the next station, they will see another multiple-choice question arranged in the same manner as the above example. After a few minutes, send another team, until all have had a chance to answer the question at Station 1.

After answering the last question, the team must take their answer sheet to the organizer of the game, who will check it for accuracy. If all of the questions were answered correctly, that team becomes one of the winners. Keep in mind that all of the teams may win, or only a few. If they missed one or more of the questions, they must go back to the beginning and start over.

The easiest way to set the game up is to arrange your stations for the winning combination of answers first. For instance, you may want Station 1 to be followed by Station 5, then Station 8, then back to Station 2, etc. Then go back to the beginning, answer Question 1 incorrectly, and assign the next station (different from the station for the correct answer). Go to the station that the players would go to if they answered Question 1 wrong, and continue assigning stations for incorrect answers.

As you work through preparing the maze, you will notice that a team could answer one or more questions wrong, but may eventually end up at the last station. Therefore, it is important to check everyone's answers at the end, so the players will endeavor to complete the maze with correct choices for each station.

Another, but complicated, way to set up the maze involves a layout insuring that a team making a wrong choice at any point in the course could never reach the final station. In either case, consider awarding prizes, ribbons, or some type of recognition for those who successfully complete the maze without error. Trivia Maze challenges both the players and the individual setting up the course, with endless possibilities for questions or themes related to specific units of study.

ACTIVITY No-Touch Scavenger Hunt

Scavenger hunts allow groups of all sizes to share the discoveries they make during an outdoor adventure. The no-touch scavenger hunt has one very important and special rule: Do not collect, pick, or bring back anything from the habitat or environment you explore.

Before the scavenger hunt, prepare a sheet listing what everyone needs to look for, leaving adequate room to sketch beside each entry. Tell the hunters that when they find something on the list, they should not gather it and bring it back, but instead draw the item on their paper and name it, if they can.

This activity can help enhance each participant's ability to observe sounds, textures, and other sensory experiences. For instance, your list might ask the players to find something soft and damp. There are many different things that hunters may sketch on their sheets, with all of them being correct. By adding these types of items to your list, everyone will have to use senses other than sight to participate in the scavenger hunt. A possible listing might include:

PLANTS		
A leaf with veins shaped like a hand	A leaf with branched veins	A plant not more than 1" tall
A plant not less than 6' tall	A plant in bloom	A plant with seeds
A plant that doesn't die in winter	A mushroom	A plant growing on a tree
The best hugging tree	A "patch" of something	

CRITTERS		
Tracks	A critter that lives in a tree	A snail
A toad or frog	A spider	Something that buzzes

MISCELLANEOUS		
Something smooth and wet	Something rough	Something furry
A sweet odor	A sour odor	Something unnatural to the forest
Something you think would taste good (don't try it!!)	Something that would make a good seat	Your favorite spot (why did you choose it?)

Continue the hunt until everyone has had the opportunity to explore the designated area, sketching the objects they have found. When everyone finishes, gather in a group and go through the list, letting each person share what they found. Everyone will likely be surprised to discover that several different choices were made that might fit each description. The game has no winners or losers; instead, participants should come away as more enlightened individuals who look a little closer at their environment.

ACTIVITY Story Twists

• *Paper and pen or pencil for each participant*

Everyone has an imagination, though some need more coaxing than others to let it free! One way to inspire imagination with friends, family, and classmates is by playing this activity where everyone builds a nature story that will always be different.

Give each person a pen or pencil and a piece of paper and ask them to write down one to three lines of a nature story. It can be the introduction, middle, climax, or ending of the story. They might write a line that says, "Before long, I saw the fox dashing across the field," or "The poor, tired bird fell six feet out of the tree when we shook it from the bottom!" The lines can be silly, serious, exciting, or short and sweet. Writing, "Aaaaahhhhhhhhh, I can't believe this," and similar lines requiring emotion will encourage readers to speak with enthusiasm when sharing the story.

When everyone finishes, fold up all of the sentences and place them in a container. Choose one person at a time to draw out a paper and read the line or lines on the sheet. As the game proceeds, the readers will develop a usually funny and nonsensical nature story written by everyone in the group.

Another approach to Story Twists does not require writing the lines first. If you have a group that feels comfortable thinking on their feet, then you can create a more logical story. Allow each person to draw a number, indicating who goes first, second, and so on. Use a timer to give everyone a chance to participate. This approach lets each storyteller add on in a more logical fashion to what the person before him said. The finished story may or may not be as whimsical, but will be exciting and interesting and, above all, one written by many authors.

ACTIVITY Closing In

- *Sheet of 8½ x 11" paper*
- *Scissors*

As you continue your explorations into the natural world, you may become overwhelmed by the number of discoveries you make! Living things grow, change, and ultimately die at an amazing rate, and the numerous choices awaiting you can make it difficult to decide just what you want to learn about and explore. By closing in, you can zoom in for a close-up of your favorite places, bringing out the details that may have gone unnoticed. You might choose to close in on the bark of a tree, the insects in a small section of grass, or the larva found on a rock in a nearby river or creek.

Make an aid to help you focus on one small area and take away the distraction of something larger or more visually obvious. Fold a piece of 8½ x 11" paper in half and cut out the center, leaving a 1" frame around the edge. You will have created a small window to observe a tiny area of the environment through.

As you travel with your personal window, concentrate only on what you see within it, blocking your mind to the areas outside its borders. When you find the perfect view or scene, lay your window down and closely study the details of the object you have discovered. Have a pencil and paper or your journal handy so you can record and sketch your observations.

To become further involved, you may enjoy making a series of smaller windows to carry with you. You will then be prepared to get closer and closer as your discover the beautiful details of many living things.

NATURAL ARTS AND CRAFTS

ACTIVITY Forest Finger Puppets

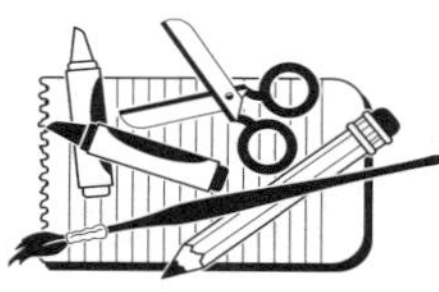

- *Inexpensive gloves*
- *Construction paper in various colors*
- *Felt-tip markers*
- *Glue*
- *Scissors*
- *Yarn scraps*
- *Wiggly eyes (or use cloth, yarn, or other materials)*

A finger puppet can represent virtually anything your heart desires, from a tree to a bear, or even the sun! You can create lots of totally unrelated critters, or if you are working with a group, you can make the components necessary to put on a play after you finish.

Cut the fingers from the gloves to make the base of your puppet. Decorate it with construction paper, yarn scraps, and felt-tip markers to create the image you desire on the front. Add wiggly eyes for a whimsical touch. Let your imagination go as you make a fancy character to wear on your finger.

ACTIVITY A Natural Remembrance

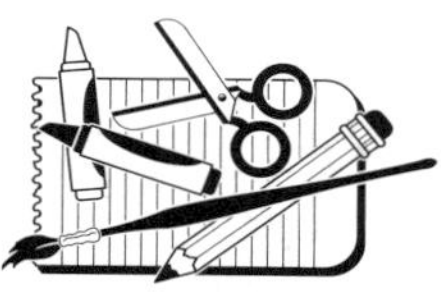

- *Natural objects from the forest floor, such as pinecones, acorns, hickory nuts, pine needles, sticks, tiny pebbles, and dried seed pods (sweet gum balls, maple seeds, elm seeds, etc.)*
- *Glue*
- *Scissors*
- *Construction paper scraps, pipe cleaners, yarn, pom poms*

Everyone probably has a favorite animal, insect, bird, or living thing, either in person, in a book, or possibly on television. An outdoor excursion can tempt you to bring home that little salamander for a pet, or make you wish you could catch that chipmunk, which probably would bite you if you caught it! Yet we all realize that any wild creature would be much happier in its natural setting. Bringing it into our homes to live in cages and aquariums would be unnatural and unkind.

This craft project is designed to create a replica of a creature—an insect, animal, or bird would all work well—while leaving the real thing in its home. Collect fallen natural objects and spread them out. Choose one of the larger items to use as a body for your creature.

Glue the smaller things you have gathered, such as seeds and pine needles, to the body for arms and legs, antennae, whiskers, or tails. If natural materials are not available, use manmade products such as yarn, pipe cleaners, etc. Remember to be patient! You will need to hold each piece on for several minutes until it dries enough to hold fast. As you continue working, be gentle, as it takes several hours for the glue to dry completely. Your finished product will give you a nice model of a wild animal or creature that you admire!

Fancy Mobiles

- *Fallen sticks from the forest floor, or small strips of wood from a craft store (Skewers work well, but watch the sharp ends.)*
- *Natural objects found out of doors (Do not pick up anything you are unsure of.)*
- *String, thread, or fishing line*
- *Scissors*

Begin this project with a little trek out into the woods, field, or your own backyard to see what has fallen to the ground. Different seasons of the year will yield totally different items. The number of unusual shapes and objects you can find beneath your feet might surprise you. Among your discoveries, you may spot pinecones, leaves, feathers, and sticks of interesting forms.

Find enough natural materials to make a good mobile, making sure not to pick up anything still alive. You will also need some straight sticks of varying lengths from which to hang your objects. Try to choose items that will balance the weight when you put it together; if you have a pinecone hanging from one side, the other side will need something of a similar weight or maybe two objects to equal the weight of the cone. Otherwise, everything will tip off to the heavy side and your mobile will not hang and spin.

When you have gathered your materials, lay the straight sticks on a flat surface in the pattern you would like your mobile to hang. From the center of the top stick, tie a piece of string or fishing line from which you will hang the entire finished project.

From each stick end, either tie one of the objects you have found, or counterbalance one end by tying on another stick to hang more natural artifacts. Once everything gets tied together, look at it closely and decide if it looks basically balanced in weight. If it appears balanced, hang it up to see if you have any conflicts in weight. You will probably have to do some shifting and sliding of strings to get your mobile to hang properly. Once you have finished, you will have a wonderful, natural mobile to hang in your room, window, or in a favorite place in your home or classroom.

ACTIVITY A Nature Collage

- *Natural objects found on the forest floor that will lay well on a piece of paper (fallen leaves, crumbled soil, small sticks, bark, fallen seeds)*
- *Sheet of paper*
- *Poster board or cardboard*
- *Glue*

Making a collage out of natural objects is fun and a great opportunity to let your imagination flow free. Begin with a nature ramble through the woods and fields, keeping your eyes peeled to the ground. Look for unusual items and odd shapes in a variety of colors that will make your collage appealing. Pick up things as you notice them, so when the ramble ends, you will have all you need to begin your creation.

Find a flat surface to work on, such as a table or a level section of ground. Since your collage may contain some heavy objects, glue the piece of paper to poster board to give it support. Use colored poster board if you wish, and cut it a little larger, which will give the appearance of a border.

Next, spread out the items you gathered. Study them for a moment, noticing the more unusual shapes, the different hues and tones, the textures, and possibly a theme. Place part or all of your collection on the paper in a pleasing arrangement. You may want to develop a story that relates your ramble through the woods, or you may prefer a visual perspective—how appealing is it as a shape and color composition?

Your first arrangement doesn't have to be the final one. Move things around until the placement satisfies you, then glue your objects to the paper so they will not fall off. When you finish, you will have made a beautiful and fragile remembrance of a trip into the natural world.

Rain Brush Paintings

- *Paper (any color), preferably a thicker grade or poster board*
- *Paint that does not dry quickly; tubes of acrylic or powdered tempera work well*
- *A tray to catch the splattering colors and help lift the paper when it gets wet*
- *An old vinyl or plastic tablecloth*

Perfect for a rainy day, rain brush paintings are easy to make and a lot of fun, for you never really know just how your creation will turn out. Just imagine each tiny raindrop acting as a small precision brush, blending the colors of your painting.

Begin by choosing three to five colors. With acrylic paint, squirt tiny blobs where you want them on your paper, then spread the color slightly, leaving it a little thick. If you use premixed tempera, apply the paint loosely, not thinning it out too much. Or sprinkle powdered tempera paints on your paper and let the rain melt it down and mix the colors, creating an interesting effect.

Once you start applying paint to the paper, you need to work quickly, for if the paint becomes dry, the rain's tiny "brushes" will not blend your colors. You don't have to rush with powdered tempera, though, as the powder will not be dampened until the rain hits it.

If the rain is falling hard, wait until the shower is a little gentler. Spread out the tablecloth to catch any flying drops of color, then place the tray in the center. Put the painting in the tray and let it stay in the rain just long enough to wet the paper and blend and swirl the colors. Leaving it out too long will make the paper become so waterlogged, it will fall to pieces. If your paper has areas too thick in paint that will not blend well, take a brush and help the color along.

When you are happy with the finished product, put your picture somewhere to dry and do not handle it too much. After it dries, you will have a lovely rain splatter painting created by your hands combined with the actions of a warm shower.

Shapes and Shadows

- *The bottom of a shoe box or cigar box*
- *Cardboard strips cut to fit inside the box*
- *Nonliving natural objects (pinecones, rocks, sticks, etc.)*
- *Pencil and paper*
- *Tempera or poster paint and brush*
- *Scissors*
- *Glue*

In this activity, you will create an aesthetic, viewable collection of your favorite and most memorable natural objects. The box will serve as a frame for you to display items from exciting hikes, walks, or field trips.

Take a piece of paper and create a template of the inside bottom, back, and sides of the box. Paint the outside of your box your choice of color, and paint the inside black. While the box dries, use the template to measure and cut cardboard strips that will act as shelves and partitions for the inside of your shadow box.

By first arranging and rearranging your objects on the template, you can find the best way to place them. Consider their shape and size to create a visually pleasing display. If something is particularly tall or heavier than the rest, decide where it will go first. If an item is tall enough to stretch from the bottom to the top, you might place it on one side, and then construct your partitions off to the other side. Heavier pieces work better on the bottom of the box.

Imagine the shelves and partitions as the floors and walls of a house. Add ½–1" of overlap so you can glue the cardboard to the inside of the box. After cutting, hold each shelf in front of the box and make a light pencil mark where the shelf meets the edge of the box. Fold the cardboard at the mark, then glue it inside the box. Insert upright partitions the same way. To avoid a square effect, try offsetting the partitions so they are not directly above and below each other.

Once the glue dries, place your natural objects in your display box and exhibit your new creation in an area that is well illuminated.

Cloud Lakes

When venturing to the highest mountains in the Southern Appalachians, you are usually greeted by incredible views of the hills and valleys below. However, certain atmospheric conditions can sometimes create a phenomenon known as cloud lakes, a mirage where the clouds billow so thick and smooth, they look like water across the horizon.

Many years ago, I led a group of hikers across the highlands of Roan Mountain, along a trail that culminated at Roan High Bluff, an impressive rock cliff and overlook. The first portion of the trail was enveloped in rhododendron and Fraser fir, thus we had no views of the surrounding valleys. Upon rounding a curve, we encountered an outstanding view of cloud lakes.

A gentleman in the group suddenly and emphatically commented, "Wow, I'm coming back up here with my fishing pole after this hike!" The group looked out for a moment, then started laughing. Within moments he joined in the laughter as he realized what he had said and perceived.

If you have never seen cloud lakes forming below you from the highest Appalachian Mountains, I definitely recommend a trip in hopes of catching a view of this amazing natural occurrence. Even though the hiking group laughed at the comment about fishing, they realized that his misconception was warranted. Anyone not familiar with the area could easily assume, at a glance, that below them lay an unbelievable expanse of water.

As the breezes blow, the clouds continually change in shape and size, and I'm sure you have, at some time, turned your head to the sky and found a familiar shape in the clouds above. Whether above or below, clouds offer you the opportunity for your imagination to work overtime.

Cotton-Ball Clouds

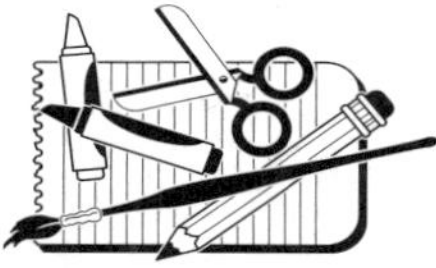

- *Cotton balls (about ¼ bag per participant) in several colors, including white*
- *Glue*
- *Colored construction paper*
- *Markers or crayons*
- *Pencil*

Conduct this activity outside to have an opportunity to become totally absorbed in the changing shapes of clouds. If heading outdoors is not possible, reflect on the times you have gazed up and thought about how unusual or beautiful the clouds looked. When you recall an image particularly pleasing to you, lock it into your mind so you can recreate it.

On a sheet of construction paper, lightly sketch the cloud shapes you wish to create. If you plan to include a landscape across the bottom, sketch that in also, so your cloud placement will leave adequate room for the background. Next, arrange your cotton balls across the skyline. You can stretch and pull them apart to create wispy clouds, or you can keep them thicker to resemble specific shapes. Once you are happy with your placement, glue the cotton balls to the paper. Do not use too much glue, for it will take the light, airy appearance away from your clouds and make them seem heavy and soggy. While the glue dries, use markers or crayons to complete the landscape portion of your creation.

Make Your Mark!

Life is miraculous, full of variety, and packed with constant change. Environmental changes can be for the better or the worse. Each of us, individually or in groups, can effect that change for the benefit of Earth and ourselves.

Countless environmental issues face society, sometimes making us feel overwhelmed and insignificant. If all people did their part, we would not have such vast problems; however, this cooperation does not happen. Small things can add up to big results, and you can set positive examples for others by sharing your commitment for protecting the environment.

We can all help by putting litter in its proper place and not polluting our own communities. Reduce the demand for natural resources by reusing and recycling; instead of using a throwaway paper cup, take the time to wash a glass. Support businesses that do not overpackage their products; excess packaging creates an enormous amount of waste.

When considering a new vehicle, check out the latest gas/electric hybrids available. They get better gas mileage, emit less waste, and don't use as much fuel. With each passing day, new, environmentally sound vehicles and fuels come on the market. Do some research to find the best option for you. Consider driving less by carpooling, using public transportation, or walking. In addition to conserving oil, gas, and other fossil fuels, you will be doing your part to help lessen the problems associated with environmental issues. Plastics and synthetic clothing also depend on oil for their production, so decreasing your use of these products will also help conserve limited resources.

In your home, make a family plan to use less electricity. Turn off lights in unoccupied rooms, turn off televisions when no one is watching them, and cut back on your use of air conditioning and heat. Carry this ethic with you in the work and community environment.

Not often do you find a tree this large!

Before you shop, educate yourself as to where your goods are produced, and do not support companies that destroy habitats of endangered species to make their products. Wildlife habitat is not as easily "rebuilt" as a manmade structure; once the integrity of the land is destroyed, it can rarely go back to what it once was. Technology can do much for us, but it is not as perfect or complex as nature's creations.

Be aware of issues near and around your home. Is there the potential for development that might affect an important habitat? Look for a point of compromise, where saving wildlife habitats can occur while also meeting our needs. By doing so, you will have acted to save a piece of Earth.

Buildings, shopping centers, and parking lots come and go in our modern society at a rapid rate; they are bulldozed down almost as quickly as they are built. We live in a disposable world, where it is easier and cheaper to discard items and purchase new ones, rather than to repair and keep what we have. I am forever complaining about all the things in my garage that I cannot afford to fix because it is more economical to throw them away and buy new a new and better piece of equipment. I am not referring to small items; I am talking about computer printers, computers, audio equipment, televisions, and the like—items that, years ago, I would've had repaired and continued to use for many more years.

The concept of responsible environmental stewardship helps promote personal lifestyle changes that will positively affect our planet. Your actions can begin a lifelong commitment to keeping the world healthy and diverse. As you read on, consider other ways you can stay involved in environmental protection and the education of others. You will discover limitless possibilities as you strive to find the niche that interests you.

PERCEPTIONS: WHAT WAS, WHAT IS, AND WHAT WILL BE

Remember how you perceived the world when you were young? Did you consider that life would ever be any different than what it was then? In my world, in the suburbs, I had special places where I enjoyed hanging out with friends. Our favorite spots were not in shopping centers, but in fields or by a lake or in the woods. I can still close my eyes and see the big abandoned field that I loved to walk through on the way to the store. I could have followed the sidewalks and the streets, but the field was much more appealing.

In the field, something different was always happening. Birds would fly up, or a grasshopper or two might appear. The nonpoisonous resident snake was always good for a few screams and giggles. At the time, I never dreamed the field would change. But now, some 30 plus years later, the field has become home to a shopping center. One of my favorite small pieces of earth has changed—dramatically.

As the days, months, and years pass, we become witnesses to rapid changes in every facet of our lives, our world, and society. Those innocent and protected days of youth eventually give way to the reality of adulthood and an ever-changing society.

Not only can we learn from our own experiences, but we can also draw on the experiences of others. Finding out about past environmental actions and issues, whether positive or negative, can help us become more critical and educated thinkers as we consider the proper action to take in any given situation. As a result, we will become wiser caretakers of Earth, prepared to make a difference in the future of the planet.

The following activities will help you look deeply into what you see on a daily basis in your community—the people, places, and things that make up a part of your present life. Though it is hard to imagine that the natural attributes of your home environment could have ever been different, you may find that massive change has occurred in a relatively short span of time. The changes may have been positive or negative—that will be for you to determine. The goal is to evaluate the environmental health of your community through understanding what natural features exist today, what has disappeared through time, and what is necessary for its future healthy survival.

ACTIVITY With Open Mind

What you see does not always represent the entire picture. To help you develop a strategy to learn more about the history of your home, this activity represents the "what was" of the environmental story. When I first came to Roan Mountain, Tennessee, I could see a community on the verge of change. With the development of a state park, tourism grew. Multitudes of people visited and sometimes settled permanently in the area.

Behind this obvious human action, I could sense a fascinating and remarkable history within what was once a quiet mountain community. Fifteen years of talking to folks, collecting photographs, and digging through old library collections culminated in my writing a book *(Roan Mountain: A Passage of Time)* on Roan Mountain's natural and cultural history. More importantly, I gathered an incredible amount of information about the Roan's biological past and how people had interacted and affected change to its environment.

Historical information and individual memories can be rapidly lost if someone is not there to capture and document the past. To find information on the area you wish to discover more about, interview those who have lived through changes and can remember the past, or those who can recall stories told to them by their elders.

When you plan an interview, call and request a visit in advance. Prepare specific questions before you arrive, so you can keep the conversation on track and gather the information you search for. Document your interview by recording the date, time, location, and name of interviewee. If the person does not mind, make an audio or video recording of the interview for accuracy.

When you have finished, evaluate what the person said. Take note of what information is valid and what might be completely incorrect. If you are gathering first-time information, you may not be able to verify its accuracy. If you have previous, correct documentation of something that invalidates someone else's recollection, then you will need to interpret the information appropriately.

Each situation is totally unique, and what you hope to learn will differ from place to place. Reflect on what makes your area special. What is its story? Jot down your thoughts and begin developing a line of questioning from those ideas. If you have trouble getting started, an interview might help.

Speak with someone who can tell you about environmental changes during their lifetime, changes in the population of an area (numbers, where people have settled, cultures), important historical events and their effects on the community, historical structures that may or may not still exist, industrial areas and shopping centers that were once farmland, and specific and memorable trees that are now gone. Also ask about discoveries in science, technology, and transportation that have changed the area, and how any of the changes have affected the water, animals, soil, and people of the community.

After the interview, consider the issues involved in restoring a developed area. Aside from the manual labor involved, think about the following questions and issues: Is it possible to restore an area to exactly what it was before its destruction? Do you need to consider the financial and business interests of others? Who would be affected by changing the area back to its previous condition? How would members of the community accept this action? Do people use the area in a positive manner?

You will discover that the issues are incredibly complex. Sometimes areas are changed for the better of the community, and sometimes the changes are frivolous. Once an area has been destroyed or changed, going back can be difficult, if not impossible. Therefore, it is important for communities and their leaders to enter into careful, educated thought before making a change they might lament in the future. A host of pros and cons, legal issues, and ethical issues will need consideration.

You may sympathize with the regret you sometimes hear in the voices of those you interview. Many adults have told me that our society went through a period of rapid and unchecked growth after World War II. The desire for the conveniences of a quickly growing modern society gave way to common-sense thinking. Special areas were altered or destroyed unnecessarily for a variety of reasons. In retrospect, those who were teens and adults during that time often grieve for those places that are gone forever.

ACTIVITY Everyday Life—Land Use in Your Community

For this activity, to help you discover the "what is" of your community, choose one specific area for deeper study. Pick a place that receives considerable use and incorporates natural settings with developed ones, such as a park, playground, recreation area, or school. Find a location with grassy areas, gardens, trees, and pathways, along with picnic tables, sports fields, and the like.

Observe the area and how people use it; make note of what works and what doesn't. As you identify specific management problems, make a determination of how to handle the issues. For instance, if you notice an area suffering from erosion, find the cause and design a plan to control it.

Another problem you might encounter could involve the interactions of wildlife and people. Concerns might include inhumane treatment, feeding the animals unhealthy "junk" food, and the possibility of disease carried from some wildlife to humans.

You may notice issues involving assaults on the land, ranging from picking plants and flowers to building campfires in unauthorized places. Identify unsafe areas that present hazards to people playing or visiting.

When you have completed your study and feel you have developed some good ideas, consider presenting it to the organization that manages the area. If possible, offer your help in developing and implementing a plan to enhance the property.

ACTIVITY Issues, Issues, Issues

Many factors come into play when the preservation of a natural area interferes with development, when pollution issues affect business and industry, and the findings of science are in conflict with a business need or desire. Complicated problems may arise, resulting in heated debate and controversy.

In the previous two activities, you looked at the past and the present and identified places near your home whose environments have changed. In this activity, you will look at the impact of future decisions. The "what will be" is strongly affected by individual beliefs, education, and background.

First, choose a national environmental issue to analyze and study. Preferably, choose an issue frequently debated in newspapers and magazines or on radio and television. Study the facts and decide how you feel that people's attitudes and interests affect the outcome of these and similar situations. In some instances, you will find that people and their communities worked well together and compromised to find solutions to their problems; other issues and actions might appear to be spiraling out of control.

Next, choose a local issue and look for differences and similarities in the handlings and outcomes of these issues in contrast to the national situation. Do you feel that logical, environmentally correct decisions have been made? Are these issues handled in a manner conducive to both environmental and human interests? Do you see balance in the debates over how to handle land use and preservation? Do people consider, or even care about, the consequences of permanently losing a natural area?

In conclusion, make a list of conservation organizations in your home area and on a national level. Choose one—or more if you wish—and gather as much information as possible about the organization. What is their purpose? What do they do? Do they have an active membership? What are their successes and failures?

As you search out your place and your role on our planet, reflect on the "what was, what is, and what will be" of the natural world. Endeavor to develop opinions or act on decisions that are derived from gaining accurate information, blended with a common-sense understanding of the permanence of environmental destruction. Question whether the human need that warrants the destruction of a natural area is necessary or frivolous, or if it can be accomplished in a different location that will not impact a sensitive or unique natural area. In the end, ask yourself, "Can we go back if we have made a mistake?"

ACTIVITY Aesthetics and the Natural World

Throughout time, every culture has expressed the moods and feelings inspired by the beauty of the natural world. Nature comes into play in all facets of art and existence, aiding in spiritual and emotional growth. You can see this concept in action in a museum, an art gallery, or an art book that reviews the collection of a gallery or artist. How many works do you see that are built around a natural setting or that use nature as a primary theme? Make note of the natural resources that have inspired artists.

Visit a library and find books written on environmental themes. Look for biographical and historical books that document natural history and the people involved. Find novels that build their stories around natural areas and spend a great amount of time developing the atmosphere of the place through vivid description.

Nature has also inspired musical creations. Notice the titles of songs and classical collections. Study the life of the composer to see if nature played a role in his style and his work. Listen to a selection of music that interprets the environment within its lyrics.

After learning about expressions of art and music in different cultures, plan a project of your own. Choose a theme that expresses your feelings or observations of an environmental area or issue, then write a poem or short story, or create a painting or drawing. You could also compose lyrics set to a well-known tune, or if you feel especially creative, write your own music.

ACTIVITY Watch the Water

Water, particularly clean water, is necessary for survival. To determine the

cleanliness of a waterway near your home, plan a project in which you or a group will monitor a section of a creek or a river for water quality. The results of this endeavor will be personally gratifying, and you will be a part of ensuring clean water for your community and Earth.

Begin by becoming completely familiar with the waterway you wish to monitor. Find out what is taking place above the area. Are there factories, does trash get dumped in the water, or do sewage systems drain there? Is the water source a series of pristine mountain springs coming together? Notice where the water flows and where it blends with another creek or river system. As discussed in the section titled "An Aquatic Expedition," which begins on page 58, the species present can tell whether or not the water is healthy, so do a little investigating into what lives in the area.

Various organizations have developed check sheets to guide you through the process of deciding the health of your waterway. The most common method involves turning over rocks or working with nets to gather insects and larva, then gently placing them in white trays filled with water. Count, identify, and record your data to determine the health of the water based on the presence or absence of certain organisms.

The Isaak Walton League has developed an educational program called "SOS: Save Our Streams," which involves the adoption and monitoring of a wetland or stream. They have created a data sheet that groups aquatic organisms based on their ability to survive in polluted versus clean water. For more information, go to www.iwla.org and click on "Conservation Programs."

One of the determining factors in survivability is the presence of dissolved oxygen. Generally, stoneflies, caddis flies, mayflies, water pennies, gilled snails, and dobsonflies require a high level of dissolved oxygen, which is not present in polluted water. Crayfish and the larvae of damselflies, dragonflies, and crane flies can live in water of fair quality. Creatures who can tolerate pollution include aquatic worms, black fly larvae, leeches, pouch snails, and pond snails.

Once you have established the health of the water system you have chosen to monitor, make a plan as to how and when you should reevaluate the area. If you work with a group, encourage members to look for changes that might affect the quality of the water, and plan monthly meetings at the site to look for any changes in aquatic fauna. The season of the year may affect what you find, so be sure to have several months of data available before coming to any conclusions.

ACTIVITY Clean It Up

Gather your neighbors and friends to participate in litter pick-ups. Discuss your community's trash problems to help prevent discouragement or the feeling that you are attacking an endless and thankless task of repeated cleanup behind those who do not care. Plan times to meet periodically to clean up an area that needs a little tender loving care. Not only will you feel personally satisfied, you will aid in promoting a healthier environment.

This mountain hillside didn't get the respect it deserves.

Educate others on the waste of excess packaging and how society generates a huge amount of trash. Challenge folks to recycle and use environmentally friendly products. Above all, if you can involve a good portion of your community in keeping their surroundings clean, you will have less and less of a problem.

AFFECTING CHANGE: BE A CATALYST!

If you would like to devote some time to share your desire to preserve a portion of the environment, consider the following suggestions. Stay open-minded at all times, realizing that everyone will not always agree with you. Individual backgrounds can create differences of opinion that could result in a negative interaction if you are not understanding of others' needs and thoughts. Your goal is not to antagonize, but to educate, inspire, and share. Realize that if people need jobs, your argument to preserve a habitat rather than invite industry to that area will fall on deaf ears unless you suggest a viable alternative. Try to find a point of balance as you suggest options that will protect special environments. Every situation will be different and will require your total understanding.

Gain support by educating and involving folks of all walks of life. As you successfully develop your project, organize groups for children and adults to continue your goal to educate, inspire, and share. Plan meetings and community-oriented activities that will involve members, and be inviting to nonmembers of your group.

If things do not go the way you wish, reevaluate your methods and the situation, and be willing to adopt a new approach if necessary. Value your work, and have respect for yourself and what you feel is right. Above all, make time in your life for continued personal growth and learning in an outdoor environment, sharing it with those around you.

"Nature never did betray the heart that loved her."
William Wordsworth
(1770-1850)
Written July 13, 1798, a few miles above Tintern Abbey, on revisiting the banks of the Wye.

Further Reading

Interpreting Our Heritage by Freeman Tilden

The Lorax by Dr. Seuss, Theodore Seuss Geisel

Nature and the American: Three Centuries of Changing Attitudes by Hans Huth

Silent Spring by Rachel Carson

Wilderness and the American Mind by Roderick Frazier Nash

Out of Print:

Nature in American Literature: Studies in the Modern View of Nature by Norman Foerster

Voices for the Wilderness William Schwartz, editor

Jennifer Bauer holds a B.S. in biology and art, an M.S. in science education, and an M.A. in teaching, all from East Tennessee State University. Since 1980, her career—including a 21-year stint as an interpretive specialist at Roan Mountain State Park and presently as the manager at Sycamore Shoals State Historic Area—has provided her the opportunity to enthusiastically share her love of the environment through tours, hikes, and interpretive programs with visitors of all ages and walks of life. A frequent contributor to *The Tennessee Conservationist,* she is also the author of *A Naturalist's Teaching Manual* and *Roan Mountain: A Passage of Time.* She makes her home in Roan Mountain, Tennessee.

Janet Brown, a native of Lake Charles, Louisiana, graduated summa cum laude in pre-medicine from McNeese State University and received a doctoral degree from Louisiana State University. In 1987 she moved to Johnson City, Tennessee, where she practices general ophthalmology and lives with her husband, Larry McDaniel, and children, Kevin and Heather. This book features her first published illustrations, though she is a lifelong student of nature and a compulsive sketcher.

Kenneth Murray, one of Appalachia's leading photographers, earned a B.S. degree in art and journalism from East Tennessee State University. Currently employed by the *Kingsport Times-News,* he has also freelanced for a number of nationally known publications, including *Time, Newsweek, U.S. News & World Report,* and the *New York Times.* In addition, he has taught photography and authored six books.

Dr. Jerry W. Nagel is emeritus professor of biological sciences at East Tennessee State University. His research efforts resulted in seventeen scientific publications dealing with vertebrate natural history in northeastern Tennessee. He has also been active in the spring and fall Roan Mountain Naturalist Rallies in a variety of capacities since the early 1970s, and he founded the Roan Mountain Fourth of July Butterfly Count. He currently serves as a member of the Board of Directors of the Friends of Roan Mountain and maintains their Web site.

Also by Jennifer Bauer

This second edition of *Roan Mountain: A Passage of Time* contains over thirty historical photographs not previously published. Added chapters tell of intriguing new biological discoveries, notable historical visitors, and the findings of the author's research conducted since publication of the first edition.

Hardcover • $27.95 • ISBN: 1-57072-147-5

Trade Paper • $17.95 • ISBN: 1-57072-100-9